TINY HOUSE IN THE TREES

Books by Celia Bonaduce

Tiny House Novels
Tiny House on the Hill
Tiny House on the Road
Tiny House in the Trees

Fat Chance, Texas Series
Welcome to Fat Chance, Texas
Slim Pickins' in Fat Chance, Texas
Livin' Large in Fat Chance, Texas

Venice Beach Romances
The Merchant of Venice Beach
A Comedy of Erinn
Much Ado About Mother

Published by Kensington Publishing Corporation

TINY HOUSE IN THE TREES
A Tiny House Novel

Celia Bonaduce

LYRICAL PRESS
Kensington Publishing Corp.
www.kensingtonbooks.com

Lyrical Press books are published by
Kensington Publishing Corp. 119 West 40th Street New York, NY 10018

Copyright © 2018 by Celia Bonaduce LLC

All rights reserved. No part of this book may be reproduced in any form or by any means without the prior written consent of the Publisher, excepting brief quotes used in reviews.

All Kensington titles, imprints, and distributed lines are available at special quantity discounts for bulk purchases for sales promotion, premiums, fundraising, and educational or institutional use.

To the extent that the image or images on the cover of this book depict a person or persons, such person or persons are merely models, and are not intended to portray any character or characters featured in the book.

Special book excerpts or customized printings can also be created to fit specific needs. For details, write or phone the office of the Kensington Special Sales Manager:
Kensington Publishing Corp.
119 West 40th Street
New York, NY 10018
Attn. Special Sales Department. Phone: 1-800-221-2647.

Kensington and the K logo Reg. U.S. Pat. & TM Off.
LYRICAL PRESS Reg. U.S. Pat. & TM Off.
Lyrical Press and the L logo are trademarks of Kensington Publishing Corp.

First Electronic Edition: November 2018
eISBN-13: 978-1-5161-0239-6
eISBN-10: 1-5161-0239-8

First Print Edition: November 2018
ISBN-13: 978-1-5161-0240-2
ISBN-10: 1-5161-0240-1

Printed in the United States of America

To Elle—my right-hand woman

And

Elliot—my wingman

Chapter 1

Joy
Focus
Graditude

Graditude?
That couldn't be right.
Molly stared down at her hand, where she was writing her words of affirmation. She'd meant to write "Gratitude." She let out a sigh, took a dab of antibacterial gel, and rubbed at the "d." All it did was smear. But Molly was determined to stay positive. She shook her wrist until the gel dried. She wrote in a "t" where the "d" had been—and frowned. It now read "Gra**T**itude." She was a perfectionist, and the aesthetics of the word bothered her. She caught sight of herself in the mirror and smiled encouragingly.
"Today," she said out loud to the image in the mirror, "I will let the little things go."
She mentally embraced the outsized "**T**."
Having to remind herself to see the good in life was new to Molly. When she was a kid, her brother, Russell, who the family called Curly due to his wild corkscrew hair, used to say she was upbeat to the point of annoyance. She'd taken her perky outlook with her to Cobb, Kentucky, where she was working as a waitress until she got her master's degree in civil engineering. The last few months had been tough. Her car needed work, but the money she was making at Crabby's Restaurant barely paid for food.
Let's not even mention rent.

She'd hoped to finish her thesis in time to graduate in June, but she'd accepted the impossibility of that. She had informed her family in Iowa that she now hoped to graduate in December. It was only eight months away, but it seemed like forever. Missing her June deadline also felt like a failure. But the biggest obstacle to a peaceful mental state was the fact that, even with the breathing room of eight more months, her master's thesis was not going well.

It was not going well at all.

Molly was working on a scale model of a tree house, complete with electricity, ramps, and plumbing. One member of her thesis committee, Professor Cambridge, a compact man with a perpetual frown, seemed skeptical.

"Civil engineers use their knowledge and expertise to make society a better place through infrastructure," Professor Cambridge said. "A tree house seems a bit…lighthearted…for a thesis."

Molly wanted to say she thought she was going to have to defend her thesis at the end of her master's program, not before, but she held her tongue.

"I realize that, sir," Molly said, wondering if the "sir" was laying it on a bit thick.

The frown lines in the professor's forehead neither tightened nor slackened, so she proceeded. She drummed up all the University-Speak she could remember.

"Civil engineering is also about design and beauty—a bridge that is aesthetically pleasing as well as a way of getting from point A to point B. And fountains, which usually have no reason for existence except to… cheer people up."

"Cheer people up?" Professor Cambridge sneered. "You are getting a degree to cheer people up?"

Molly was silent. She knew "yes" would be the wrong answer…but her answer *was* "yes."

Molly was passionate about her idea. She argued that she considered a tree house the perfect subject for a scale model. Tree house designs could be miniatures of traditional houses, so a tree house model was a scale of a scale.

Professor Cambridge said she might be better suited to a philosophy degree. But in the end, her thesis was approved. Immediately another problem arose. While Molly had lots of theories about how to build the structure, she found her knowledge was lacking when it came to a very fundamental element—the tree.

After her thesis was approved, Molly had visions of securing a job at the large Christmas tree farm just outside of Cobb, owned by the handsome-to-the-point-of-absurdity Quinn Casey. Quinn was a town legend. He piloted his own helicopter—a beat-up chopper he called Old Paint—harvesting the largest trees on his farm, carrying them through the air at top speed to the trucks that were waiting to take them across the southern United States for distribution.

Quinn's farm boomed with workers from October to December, but he kept a skeleton crew year-round who trimmed growing evergreens, uprooted felled trees, and planted saplings. She could learn firsthand what it took to live *with* evergreen trees, the first step in envisioning what it would take to live *in* one.

Molly was gregarious by nature and was loved by the locals who hung out at Crabby's. But she was shy around Quinn. Whenever Quinn was in the restaurant, which was often, given that he was Crabby's nephew, he was surrounded by people. She practiced her pitch for weeks. But before she got up her nerve to ask for a job, her research revealed a new snag.

It was possible to build a small tree house or decorative platform in a pine, spruce, yellow poplar, cedar, or redwood tree. However, she learned that the strength of the wood was a factor. So hardwood trees like oak, hickory, walnut, or cherry lent themselves more to her ambitious ideas. While this smashed her hopes of having an organic reason to work alongside Quinn, she'd magically picked the right state in which to do her homework. Kentucky was one of the most biologically diverse temperate zones in the world, with oak and walnut dominating the landscape. She spent much of her free time walking in the woods and studying trees.

She never did ask Quinn for the job.

Galileo, the cantankerous African Grey parrot her father had rescued twenty years ago who now lived with Molly, was the first to point out her obsession with Quinn.

"I love you," Molly said to Galileo one morning.

Waiting for his ubiquitous "Bite me" response, the bird startled her with: "I love you, Quinn."

"Whose side are you on?" Molly asked.

"I love you, Quinn."

She felt her cheeks redden just at the thought of Quinn hearing this. She realized that when she tried out new lipsticks, she'd kiss her hand and say, "I love you, Quinn."

The African Grey never missed anything!

"Let's stick to 'Bite me,' shall we?" she said.

Molly checked her cell phone for the time. The days of worrying about Quinn learning of her secret crush seemed years—instead of months—ago. Crabby's had been jumping and the tips plentiful. If she could keep her mind off Quinn, she could focus all her energy on her thesis.

But Crabby's wasn't very busy of late. With money worries always in her thoughts, the tree house languished. It sat on a table by her front door, the tree's limbs stretched out for attention. One evening, as she covered Galileo with a sheet—a standard practice among many parrot parents—she did the same to the tree house.

In the morning, she only uncovered the parrot.

Crabby Cranston was trying everything he could think of to resuscitate the business. He'd opened for breakfast, closed for breakfast, reopened for breakfast. He made the dining room more formal, then more casual, turned up the volume on the TVs in the bar, then taken the TVs down. But so far, nothing seemed to be working.

The words "Joy," "Focus," and "GraTitude" bounced up and down as she flicked on a coat of brown mascara. She thought her good thoughts.

There was Joy in going to work at a place she liked.

She refused to think:

Even though the place is tanking.

She would Focus on her thesis.

She stopped herself from adding:

…and not on my money problems.

She had GraTitude for her health, her family back home in Iowa, and the progress she was making toward her life goal of being a civil engineer.

By the time she had her lipstick on, she actually did feel better.

Grabbing her messenger bag, Molly opened a latch on Galileo's cage. The latch swung down, creating a ledge, so he could hang out during the day and not feel locked up. Her father had spent years teaching Galileo not to fly away when the cage was open.

"You're spoiling him," Molly's mother would say. "Maybe you could help with dinner instead of spending all your time talking to that bird."

"How would you like to spend your life in a cage?" her father would reply, when dinner was ready without his help once again.

At the time, Molly agreed with her mother. But now, she was grateful to have such an independent and well-trained companion.

"See ya," squawked Galileo, swaying manically on the ledge. "Wouldn't want to be ya."

You and me both, she almost said.

Instead, she held out her hand to Galileo.

"See this?" Molly pointed to "Joy," "Focus," and "GraTitude" one at a time. "This is the new order of things around here. Got it?"

"Bite me!"

Molly headed confidently out the door. She jumped into her old blue Buick Lucerne and started the ignition. Instead of the snort of the engine roaring to life, all she heard was a rapid *click click click*. She tried again, but the clicks just came faster. Then it stopped entirely. She dug through her purse, looking for her AAA card.

Please don't be the alternator.

The last time the AAA guy came by to jump-start her car, he looked apprehensive. He said it sounded like her alternator might be going. And if the alternator broke, it would stop charging the battery. She still didn't exactly know what an alternator was, but from the look on the man's face, it was expensive.

Molly found the card. It was expired. She slumped in her seat. She'd let her AAA membership lapse in a misguided attempt at economy. She stared accusingly at the positivity radiating from her hand. She closed her eyes, trying to come up with her next move. Her apartment building was on the main road. She could probably stand next to the car looking pathetic and hope some local person might give her a ride.

A knock startled her. She opened her eyes to see Bale Barrett smiling through the window. Bale was the owner of Bale's Tiny Dreams, a tiny house emporium that kept expanding as interest in minimalist living continued to sweep the country. Molly and Bale had gotten to know each other during Bale's visits to Crabby's Restaurant. She tried to roll down the window, but since everything in the car was electric, nothing happened. She opened the door.

Bale's dog, Thor, jumped in her lap and gave her an energetic kiss.

"Hey, Bale," Molly said. "Hey, Thor."

She knew her voice was shaking—a dead giveaway that tears were soon to follow. Trying to buy some time before the tears started, she gave Thor a quick human kiss on the red patch of fur that sprouted between his ears.

"Hey," Bale looked at her, concerned. "I was driving by and saw you sitting in your car. Everything okay?"

Molly turned away from him as hot rivulets of tears rolled down her cheeks. Joy, Focus, and GraTitude were deserting the ship. She put her head on Thor's and sobbed.

"Don't cry," Bale said. "Whatever it is, I'm sure we can fix it."

"I think it's the alternator!" Molly sobbed.

"See? No big deal. We can rebuild it."

"We?"

"Well, 'we' being me."

Molly laughed as Thor licked at her tears.

"Sorry. I'm just being stupid."

"You're not stupid. I mean, how many stupid people know their alternator is shot?"

She looked at him as he knelt on the open door frame. Bale was always so cheerful. Molly was disconcerted being eye to eye with Bale. He was a large man who usually towered above her. Although a decade or so older than she, Molly and Bale had bonded over their passion for miniature house solutions and ideas, sharing discoveries and failures whenever Bale stopped in at Crabby's.

Molly didn't want to admit she had no way to get the car to his lot, thanks to her less-than-brilliant decision to dump the AAA. Bale saved her from her confession.

"I've got my truck. I can drop you off at work, then come back and tow the car over to my place."

Molly was about to ask him how he knew she was on her way to work, but she remembered she was wearing Crabby's latest uniform—black pants with a stiff white shirt with the name "Crabby's" embroidered in cursive over the left breast pocket. Above the name was an unpleasant-looking cartoonish crab. It was the owner's latest attempt at energizing the place.

Where else would she be going? Her life revolved around work, Galileo, and her thesis.

"That's way too much trouble," she said. "Thank you, though."

"No trouble. Happy to help."

Molly thought she should protest a little more, just to be polite, but decided that was a waste of energy. And she really didn't have the money for Plan B—if she even had a Plan B. She grabbed her messenger bag and hopped into Bale's truck.

"How are things going at Crabby's?" Bale asked.

Molly knew this was just small talk, but she longed to talk to somebody about how dismally sparse the crowd had been lately. Even *thinking* the word "crowd" verged on hyperbole.

"We're hoping things will pick up," she said, looking down at her uniform.

"I've heard that trendy restaurants are in, then they're out, then in again," Bale said. "Popularity comes and goes."

"I've never really thought of Crabby's as trendy."

"Then you guys might be in trouble."

Molly looked at Bale. He shot her a wink. She wished she had just a touch of his *que será, será* attitude. In any language.

Bale's truck pulled into Crabby's parking lot. There were two cars belonging to locals and an overloaded pickup truck with out-of-state plates parked in front. Bale and Molly exchanged a look. A stuffed pickup truck not belonging to someone from Cobb usually meant a new tiny-house owner was heading to Bale's to pick up his or her (mostly "her," Molly noticed) new house on wheels.

"Expecting company?" Molly asked as she got out of the truck, nodding toward the pickup.

"As a matter of fact, yes," Bale said. "A lady is coming by to pick up one of the log cabins with the whiskey barrel shower."

Molly remembered how she and Bale sat in Crabby's late one night after she'd closed the place, perfecting the whiskey barrel shower. She planned on using one in her model tree house as well. She was surprised to feel a little pinch of jealousy at the mention of the "lady" who was the latest owner of one of Bale's tiny masterpieces.

Jealousy was a new sensation. Molly chastised herself. She'd met a least two dozen women who had stopped by Crabby's on their way to Bale's. Bale even brought a few of them to dinner before the women headed off on their new adventures. Molly had never felt anything but mild interest in why the women had chosen their new lifestyle. Was jealousy brought on because Bale was being kind to her and she was feeling alone and a little fragile?

Get over yourself.

"Thanks for everything, Bale," Molly said. She patted the dog. "You too, Thor."

"I'll text you later and update you on the car."

"Great. I'll bring you a cinnamon bun…. I'll bring you two."

"Deal," Bale said. "Oh, and if my hunch is right, the lady with the green truck and New York plates is named Cynthia. Tell her I'll meet her over at the lot in about an hour. That'll give me time to get your car."

Bale could be such a sweetheart. Her car was taking precedence over a New Yorker named Cynthia. A paying customer!

Molly looked down at her hand.

GraTitude.

Probably not what the self-help books had in mind…but it was a start.

Chapter 2

Molly rushed into the kitchen, relieved she'd beaten Crabby to the restaurant. With business being slow, he would be less-than-philosophical about broken-down cars.

She nodded to Manny, the short-order cook. From her days of being both waitress and cook, she recognized the orders on the grill…a ham-and-cheese omelet and two over-medium eggs with a side of bacon.

"Thanks for letting the customers in," Molly said as she washed her hands—careful to keep her affirmations intact. She raced toward the dining room. "I owe you."

"You owe the lady out there a bowl of oatmeal," Manny said, nodding toward the front counter.

"I'm on it," Molly said.

"Hi," Molly said to the woman who must be Cynthia. "Sorry to keep you waiting."

"That's okay," Cynthia said.

Molly placed a bowl of steaming oatmeal in front of her. "Can I get you anything else? Eggs? Toast? A pastry?"

"No thanks," Cynthia said. "Just oatmeal."

Molly suspected nerves might be the reason for Cynthia's lack of appetite. She had the slightly dazed look Molly had come to recognize in Bale's clients. It was as if they couldn't quite believe they'd pulled the plug on their past lives and were now moments away from embarking on the unknown. Cynthia appeared to be in her late fifties, a little older than most of the women who swung into Bale's, but by this time, Molly had seen everyone from very young women to retired couples stop in for a bite at Crabby's before picking up their tiny house over at the lot.

Manny flicked the service bell on the counter. Molly retrieved the omelet and bacon and eggs. She took them to Sammy and Fred, two locals sitting together at one of the tables.

"Hey, Jane," Sammy said, scooting back his chair to make room over his ample belly so Molly could put the omelet on the table. "How about more coffee?"

"Anything for you, Sammy," Molly said with a bright smile.

She refused to give him the satisfaction of reacting to her nickname, "Jane"—so given because word of her tree house model reminded the people of Cobb of Tarzan's house. Very few people had actually seen her work in progress, but that didn't stop the good-natured teasing.

When Molly returned from refilling the coffee cups, she noticed Cynthia had gone. Molly silently wished her well. With the work Molly was doing on her tree house model, she'd come to appreciate the details of living tiny—although she personally had no desire to haul her home around the country. Her tree house was taking shape—even in miniature—to be her dream home. Instead of wheels, she was looking for roots.

Sammy and Fred were next to leave. Molly had the sinking feeling the morning rush was over. She stopped filling the sugar containers and counted her tips. Three dollars—which she would split with Manny. Her stomach did a flip. Even if Bale could fix her alternator, the day her rent was due was coming at her like a bullet train. She felt her pulse quicken with anxiety.

Joy.
Focus.
GraTitude.
Joy.
Focus.
GraTitude.
Joy.
Focus.
GraTitude.

She felt herself calm. Maybe this affirmation thing would work! Molly returned to the sugar shakers. She heard the front door open and looked up. Her heart started to race again.

It was Quinn.

"Hey there, Jane," Quinn said, throwing a muscular leg over a stool at the counter.

When other people called her "Jane," it seemed as if they were making fun of her. But when Quinn said it—and now that she thought about it, it was Quinn who first dubbed her "Jane"—it seemed like an intimate nickname.

Color rose in Molly's cheeks. She was always flustered when Quinn came into Crabby's. Once, when the hot star of the recent superhero action movies was doing a national publicity tour, he and his entourage stopped in at Crabby's on their way to…somewhere else. Quinn was in the restaurant at the time. Molly wasn't the only one who noticed the striking resemblance between the two—the captivating eyes that always seem to be smirking, the perfect physique, the great hair. The publicity crew snapped cell phone shots of the superstar and his doppelganger. The actor seemed more impressed that Quinn was a helicopter pilot with his own Christmas tree farm than Quinn was with the actor's multiple star turns as a world-saving action hero. But that was Quinn. He radiated confidence.

Except this morning.

This morning he radiated hangover.

"Hey, Quinn," Molly said. "Want some coffee?"

"Do I ever," Quinn groaned.

"Rough night?" Molly asked, pouring coffee into a cup as Quinn rubbed his temples. She resisted the temptation to put out the cream she knew he used. She didn't want it to seem she'd memorized his preferences.

Although she had.

"Just a friendly game of poker gone wrong," Quinn said. "Lost a bundle."

Long before Molly came to Cobb, Quinn and several of the locals had been playing an organized poker game at least once a month. Crabby joined the game from time to time, but never let "the boys" use the restaurant after hours, even when he himself was playing.

For Crabby, work and play never mixed.

For Quinn, the transition from work to play was seamless.

Molly thought if she ever had a bundle of money, she'd hang on to it. But Quinn probably had it to lose.

"Anything else this morning?" she asked, although she knew the answer would be a glazed donut.

"A glazed donut," he said, still sounding miserable.

Molly pulled the glass top off the case of donuts. Her expert eye selected the most fragrant one and popped it on a plate. She saw Manny smirk on his way out; his shift was over. She was a little obvious, she knew. She slid the donut in front of Quinn. He was sipping his coffee with his eyes closed.

Molly took the opportunity to study his insanely long lashes.

"Okay, looks like I'll live another day," he said.

As Quinn slowly opened his eyes, Molly snapped out of her reverie, hoping he hadn't noticed her intense scrutiny. She started to stuff the napkin dispenser on the counter. It gave her something to do without moving out of sight. Quinn reached out and took her hand.

"What's going on here?" he asked, gently turning her wrist so he could see the words she'd written.

"I'm trying positive affirmation," Molly said, hoping she didn't sound too new agey for his taste. "So I'm putting out the energy I want to come back to me."

Chills ran up her spine as Quinn took his index finger and traced the words.

"I like your choices," he said.

"Really?" Molly said, sounding a little more eager than she knew she should.

"Yeah."

"What three words would you write?"

"I don't know...maybe 'Money,' 'Money,' and 'Money.'"

Molly was pretty sure that wasn't the way it worked, but she nodded. Who was she to dictate what the universe found acceptable?

"Thanks for the coffee," Quinn said, draining his cup. "Gotta go."

"But you didn't eat your donut!"

Quinn bestowed one of his killer smiles on her, wrapped the donut in a napkin, and shoved it in his jacket pocket.

"I'll take it to go," he said, as he gave the pocket a pat. "Thanks."

He slapped down a ten-dollar bill and started out the door.

"Let me get you some change," Molly said.

"Keep it."

Molly stared at the bill. He was leaving her a one hundred percent tip. His words were "Money, Money, Money"...and yet, thanks to Quinn, money had come to *her*.

Molly was still getting the hang of how the universe worked.

As she watched Quinn pull out of the parking lot at top speed, she hoped he was more careful when he was piloting his chopper. Molly called Crabby and told him she could work lunch and dinner as well as breakfast. Since she didn't have her car, she might as well make a little extra Money, Money, Money.

Lunch was as slow as breakfast. After the last customer left at two, Molly was putting out the white tablecloths they used at dinner when her cell phone buzzed. She looked at it. Bale was calling.

"Hey," she said.

"Hey yourself."

"Did Cynthia get to the lot okay?" Molly asked, feeling it would be rude to jump into questions about the alternator too quickly.

"Yep. Here and gone. She's on her way to Oklahoma to be closer to her grandkids. Those kids are going to go crazy when they see that log cabin."

Molly smiled. Bale had such enthusiasm for his work. He probably would never need to remind himself the world was a great place by writing on his hand.

"So what's up?" Molly asked.

She knew she sounded lame. She obviously wanted to know about her car. She would be cringing if she'd said this to Quinn. But good old Bale wouldn't care.

"Good news about your car," Bale said. "I can fix it."

"That *is* good news," Molly said, the tension of not-knowing draining out of her.

She had only about fifty dollars left on her credit card.

"I can have it ready by tomorrow," Bale said. "What time do you get off work? I can swing by and give you a lift home."

"Oh, that's okay," Molly said, wondering if she might be able to finagle a ride with Quinn. He sometimes stopped by for a drink after a long day at the farm. "Somebody here can give me a lift."

"Suit yourself," Bale said. "But call if you get in a jam."

"I will."

Half the town called Bale when they were in a jam. He really was one of the good guys. Molly wondered why Bale was still unattached. She'd seen so many women come into town to buy tiny houses. She knew he'd been interested in at least one of them, but he was still very, very single. Molly hoped he'd find someone. He deserved it.

Manny walked in the restaurant shortly before five.

"What are you doing here?" Molly asked.

Manny never worked the dinner shift.

"Crabby said I should come in," Manny said with a shrug.

That was weird.

Within a half hour, everyone who worked at Crabby's—at any time, on any shift, was in the restaurant.

Could there be a big event nobody knew about? Was a celebrity stopping by? Crabby was a huge fan of the restaurant renovation shows—maybe they'd been selected for a makeover? The staff was giddy with possibilities. The restaurant could use a boost.

Molly turned to say something to Donna, a bartender on the weekends, when she saw Crabby silently glide into the room through the kitchen. She studied his face, looking for clues.

But Crabby always looked...crabby.

He tapped his knuckles on the counter. Anyone who knew him—employee or patron—knew that meant he expected silence.

"Restaurant closes permanently in two weeks," he said.

It was impossible to work at Crabby's and not know closing shop was a possibility. But it didn't make it any easier to hear. Molly felt fear travel up from her toes—she couldn't survive without this job. She was already two months late on the rent. What would she do for this month's—or next month's?

Why did everything have to come down to money? It wasn't that she was asking the universe to make her a millionaire. Just enough so she wasn't paralyzed.

Murmuring voices swirled around her. She surreptitiously lifted her pinky finger to her eye to catch a little escapee of a tear when she caught sight of her affirmation words. They looked ridiculous.

She ran to the bathroom and scrubbed them off.

Chapter 3

Bravery
Gumption
Strength

Molly woke to the sound of herself crying.

"Shut up, Galileo," she said, rubbing her puffy eyes.

Galileo was a perfect mimic when it suited him, but the fact that he had perfected her crying over the last few months was as annoying as it was impressive. Molly didn't really think of herself as a crybaby. She really had to get it together.

"Sorry," she said to the parrot. "I love you."

"Bite me," he said.

Molly laughed. When her father first brought Galileo home, her mother had argued that the family had to stop saving every animal in Iowa that needed help. But she was as easy a mark as the rest of the family. While cats, dogs, rodents, and rabbits made their way in and out of the McGinnis household, Galileo stayed. And stayed. Galileo's species could live up to fifty years in captivity.

Molly's dad had spent hours teaching the African Grey sarcastic replies to the mundane things people usually said to birds.

"Hello, pretty bird," "Can you talk?" and "What's your name?" were all answered with:

"Bite me."

"You're so smart" and "Aren't you something?" were also fair game for Galileo's tart response.

Molly's mom didn't see the humor, but it annoyed Molly's father that humans didn't show Galileo the respect he deserved.

"Serves people right," her father used to say when Galileo would fluff his feathers and offer his signature retort.

When her father died almost ten years ago, Molly had begged her mother to let her take Galileo with her when she left for college. It meant getting an apartment rather than a dorm room, but Molly didn't care. She felt a little guilty, not telling her mother the real reason she wanted—needed—to take the African Grey with her. One night, about two months after her father's fatal heart attack, when everyone was asleep, Galileo started to sing in her father's sweet tenor. The bird usually sang "The Female Highwayman," a song about a young woman who dresses up like a man and robs a man as she falls in love with him.

"Why can't you just sing 'Danny Boy'?" her mother used to say to her father.

"'Danny Boy' has no spunk," her father said. "I want Molly to have spunk when she grows up."

He went back to crooning about the lady robber.

"You can be anything you want, Molly girl," her father would say as he tucked her in. Making a show of looking around for her mother, he'd whisper, "But if you become a highwayman, I'll deny I said it."

Molly smiled at the memory. As annoying as Galileo could be with his unpredictable outbursts, the fact that Mr. Detman, her landlord, had a pair of budgie parakeets helped get her a pass on the rent more than once. Mr. Detman was often at her door, asking advice. He had two male budgies, Lancelot and Romeo, he'd raised since they were little. The birds had bonded with each other instead of with him, much to his distress. Molly helped where she could, getting Lancelot and Romeo to spend time outside their cage and letting Mr. Detman cuddle them without fear of losing a finger, but there was only so much she could do. Budgies were not African Greys. They were never going to sing in any voices but their own.

Galileo only sang for Molly. She took it as a sign she was meant to be the keeper of the bird, so when she headed off to Cobb, she took the African Grey with her. Even with Galileo's company, her father's death left an emptiness that never went away. Especially now, when Molly's future looked so uncertain.

Molly sat on the bed with her eyes closed, envisioning the words she wanted to write on her hand today.

"I need to be brave," she thought.

Was bravery a positive emotion? Could you choose it? She thought she could. She wrote "Bravery" on her hand, followed by "Gumption"—a word her father always used—and "Strength."

If she could master these, she'd get through the day. She felt better already. Her phone buzzed.

"Hi, Bale," she said cheerfully.

"Hey there. Just checking in. Do you need a ride to work this morning?"

"No. Manny said he'll pick me up," she said.

"Oh? Oh. Okay."

Molly detected a hint of disappointment in Bale's voice.

That's weird. You'd think he'd be relieved he isn't stuck having to do another good deed.

"Aren't you doing enough fixing my car?"

My car.

She took a deep breath. "How's the car coming along?"

"I should have it done this afternoon," he said. "As promised."

Maybe things were turning around.

"That's great," she said. "Manny's outside—I'll see you after work."

"Call me if you need a lift."

Molly was still hoping for Quinn to stop in at the perfect time, but it was sweet of Bale to offer.

"Okay. Thanks!"

Molly texted Manny that she was on her way down, then hand-fed Galileo some broccoli.

"Bye, G," Molly said, stroking the bird's soft feathers through the bars of his enormous cage. "Will you miss me?"

"Bite me."

"Back at ya."

Molly grabbed her bag and headed out the door. She turned on the TV so Galileo could watch the Animal Galaxy network. The shows kept the social bird company and gave him all kinds of animal noises to mimic. To date, the bird could impersonate barnyard animals, endangered species, and sea life.

Molly didn't glance at the model of the tree house on the dining room table. The lack of progress was just too overwhelming.

"Good morning," Molly said as she got in Manny's truck.

"What's so good about it?" Manny asked.

Molly looked out the window. She had to remember she wasn't the only one at Crabby's losing a job. They rode the rest of the way in silence.

Manny and Molly exchanged a look as they pulled up to Crabby's.

"I guess word is getting around that Crabby's is closing," Manny said as they surveyed the small crowd waiting for the place to open.

The breakfast rush was appropriately named. Everyone in town seemed to be stopping by, offering their "end of an era" condolences, revisiting memories of the place over the years. Molly couldn't help but think if all these folks came in even once a week, none of them would be having these conversations now.

Quinn rolled in around 9:30, when things were slowing down. He sat in his usual place at the counter. Molly poured him some coffee. She was about to mention the closing, but realized, since he was Crabby's nephew, he must have heard—probably from Crabby himself. She decided against bringing it up.

As if reading her mind, Quinn said, "I heard the bad news."

"Yeah," Molly said, trying to muster her Gumption. "But maybe it's for the best."

She cringed, hoping Quinn would not pick up on such a lame statement.

"How so?"

Crap.

"I don't know. Maybe…maybe there's a better opportunity out there."

She worried that she sounded selfish.

"For Crabby, you know," she added.

"I guess," Quinn said, downing his drink in one gulp. "I'm sure the old goat will be fine. But what about you?"

"What about me?" Molly asked, her heart pounding.

"What are you going to do?"

"I'm not sure yet," Molly said, pouring more coffee.

"Want to come work for me?"

The pot of coffee clattered against Quinn's cup. She tried to steady her hand. Could this possibly be happening?

"Are you serious?"

"Sure. April is a busy month on a Christmas tree farm."

Molly looked up quickly. Was Quinn joking? The whole town appeared to be aware of her tree house project and considered her an expert on all things related to horticulture. There didn't seem to be any way to convince the townspeople that she knew more about how to fix the covered bridge that collapsed in the flood than how to keep chickweed at bay.

Probably best not to announce that she knew very little about evergreens.

"Seedlings and transplants go in this month," Quinn continued, saving her from having to say anything. "I can always use a few extra hands."

"That sounds good," Molly said. "I could start in two weeks. After Crabby's closes. If that's okay."

"That's fine," Quinn said.

Molly could not believe this was happening! She took a quick look at her watch. Her shift was over. She caught sight of her words of affirmation on her hand. Summoning all her Bravery, Gumption, and Strength, she asked "Hey, Quinn. I need to pick up my car at Bale's. Could you give me a lift?"

Quinn gave her a dazzling smile.

"Sorry, kiddo. Gotta get back to the farm."

She pulled her phone out of her pocket as she watched Quinn go. She dialed Bale—under "Favorites."

"Hey, Bale," she said when he answered. "Looks like I'll need to take you up on that offer to pick me up."

"No problem," he said. "See you in a few."

* * * *

"Wow," Bale said as he drove her back to the tiny house lot. "So Crabby's is kaput?"

"In two weeks," Molly said, absently scratching Thor's head. "I'm surprised you haven't heard. It's all over town."

"I don't really hear much gossip at the lot."

Molly blinked in surprise. She didn't think of the closing as gossip. She thought of it as news. She stole a look at Bale. Gossip or news, he did seem concerned for her, which was nice.

"Wow," Bale said again. "Sorry, I know I just said that."

"That's okay. It pretty much sums everything up."

Bale turned into Bale's Tiny Dreams. As soon as Molly opened the truck door, Thor raced over to her car. He studied the driver's side front tire from every angle before christening it. Even with his blank expression, Thor's body language suggested he and Bale had done something marvelous. He waited patiently for praise.

"Runs like a champ," Bale said as Molly stared at her car.

"Thanks so much for fixing it. I'm really grateful."

"Alternator brushes aren't brain surgery."

"Maybe not," Molly said as she ruffled Thor's red patch. She looked up at Bale. "But I didn't need brain surgery."

"How is the tree house going?" Bale asked.

Molly loved that Bale referred to her eighteen-inch model as "the tree house." It was as if he saw it as clearly as she did.

She didn't want to burden Bale with the truth: her money worries were paralyzing her. Her creativity was limited to trying to un-teach Galileo swear words her father had taught him.

"Slowly," Molly said. "But it's a process. You know?"

"I do know! Come see something I've been working on. I think you'll find it interesting."

Molly followed Bale and Thor to the Tiny Dreams workshop—a cavernous lumpen structure. Molly was always surprised that such gossamer designs were created within its hulking walls. She noticed that Bale's staid maturity disappeared whenever he walked inside the shop. He became like an excited boy, ready to show off his new toys.

"Check this out," he said, leading Molly to an elongated tiny house on a ten-foot-by-thirty-six-foot trailer bed.

She stared up at the modern green-and-glass house on wheels. Without going inside, from her endless discussions with Bale and her engineering research, she knew the house had a loft on each end. She could see the kitchen through a wide opening in the front. She studied the house. The opening seemed oddly large.

How could any door fit?

"Right?" Bale asked, grinning.

It was as if he were reading her mind.

"Watch," he said, climbing into the house by way of the makeshift stairs in front of the house. Thor started after him, but Bale gave him the signal to stay. Thor looked up at Molly. Even through Thor's blank expression, Molly felt accused.

Molly could hear Bale rummaging around, then he returned to the theatrical doorway, a remote of some kind in his hand. He dispensed with the stairs this time, leaping to the ground.

"Look at this!" he said, sounding like a kid.

With a rumble, a glass-and-steel garage door slid effortlessly down its tracks into place. The house was now sealed.

"I tried several different garage doors," Bale said. "The problem was getting one that would travel. Super sturdy, so it wouldn't twist out of shape on the road, but light enough to work with the weight restrictions."

Molly loved coming to Bale's Tiny Dreams. She could put her own problems behind her and immerse herself in the fantastical world of tiny houses. Bale's imagination was limitless. Molly studied the garage door with a practiced eye.

"I love that you can see through the door," she said. "It makes the place look open—like a dollhouse."

"I like that too," Bale said proudly. "I'm working on adding a technology that can turn the transparent glass opaque, but the cost is out there right now."

Molly sighed. Money always seemed to get in the way.

"May I go inside?" Molly asked.

"Sure."

She thought of him as a mad scientist, keeping his experiments under wraps until they were perfected. It was a huge compliment that Bale always let her check out his works in progress.

The house was amazing. A kitchen with full-sized appliances greeted her as soon as she stepped inside. Bale's artistry included interior as well as exterior design. The glass and steel of the garage door was mirrored in the cabinetry of the kitchen. The whole main level looked sophisticated and modern without coming across as sterile. Bale was very serious about making sure each tiny house looked like it could easily be "home" to someone.

"The challenge with this place," he said, pointing toward one end of the house, "is the bathroom. Because I gave so much real estate to the kitchen, the bathroom is a little smaller than I'd like."

Molly followed Bale through the tiny house, taking in all the perfect details—the carpentry around the wheel wells, the little extra storage spaces tucked in every conceivable space, the moveable kitchen island—before they arrived, in a few feet, in front of the bathroom.

Molly stopped dead in the doorway.

"Wait!" she said, putting her hand on Bale's arm.

Thor, who had followed her toward the bathroom, shot off in the other direction at the sound of her voice. Bale turned to look at her.

"Is there a problem?" he asked.

"Not exactly."

"So..."

"It's just that...I'm having trouble designing a workable bathroom for the tree house," she said. "I don't want to steal any of your ideas."

"You can't steal my ideas," Bale said, "if I give them to you."

Chapter 4

Bold
Clear
Confident

Bale's innovative tiny house sparked Molly's imagination, and she returned to working on her thesis. After trying and rejecting many media, including the extremely modern 3-D approach, Molly settled on making her tree house out of an ultralight wood fiberboard that was easy to cut and form. After much trial and error, she found a board that was rigid and strong enough to be carved and shaped into the tree but, when damp, could also be molded into the various minute house design elements.

Molly had been hard at work incorporating one of Bale's space-saving bathroom ideas, a toilet that pulled out from under a vanity, with limited success.

"Damn it," she said, as a delicate chain she was constructing broke in two.

"Shit," added Galileo.

Molly sighed. After countless hours of trying to break Galileo of his swearing, her frustration at her lack of progress had her cursing like a sailor. She really wasn't in any position to castigate him.

But she needed to be firm. An African Grey was hard to train, but even harder to un-train.

"Don't swear," she said, pointing her fine-point pen at him.

"Bite me."

The mental tussle with Galileo took her out of her zone. She stretched to unkink her muscles, which tightened with the detailed work required to build a miniature tree house complete with moving parts. Taking a deep breath, she willed herself to count her tips, hoping to find enough money to pay at least one of the three months' rents now due.

She opened the carved box in which she tossed her tips every night. When she first started working at Crabby's, by week's end, the box was overflowing with ten- and five-dollar bills. Now she only saw a smattering of ones. She felt fear travel up her spine. Even with the promise of the tree farm job, her landlord had already warned her that he would have to start the eviction process if she didn't pay up. Some of her friends at Crabby's told her that she could probably fight the eviction for a few months, but she didn't want to do that. It wasn't the landlord's fault she didn't have any money.

Molly looked around the apartment. It was just a nondescript furnished one-bedroom on a busy road—or as busy a road as there was in Cobb, Kentucky. She could certainly vacate quickly. She prided herself on traveling light. She only had a suitcase or so full of belongings.

And the tree house.

And Galileo.

Maybe she didn't travel as lightly as she thought.

She quickly dug her pen out of her purse. Time for her affirmation words! She closed her eyes and visualized what she needed to write. Concentrating on what she had been accomplishing the last two weeks, rather than focusing on the negative, she opened her eyes and wrote:

Bold
Clear
Confident

She closed the cash box without looking at it.

Positive thinking was not for the faint of heart.

The alarm on her phone sounded, reminding her that tonight was what Crabby was calling his "Grand Closing." As nervous as she was about the future, she was looking forward to the party. Most of the town would be there. Except Bale. She knew Bale was on one of his tiny house convention circuits, which took up more and more of his time. He was bringing several of his tinies with him and didn't expect to be back for almost two months.

"These conventions are a necessary evil," he had said to her one day as he was heading out of town. "I wish I could just stay in one place and work on my designs."

Molly looked at the model of her spectacularly unfinished tree house and sighed. He was preaching to the choir. If only she had no worries but her thesis.

But then again, who really had that sort of fairy-tale life?
Quinn?

He seemed to live a magical existence flying in and out of town in Old Paint, dipping over the town as he made his way throughout the South, taking orders for his trees. Nothing signaled the start of the holidays in Cobb like Quinn flying through the air with his first haul of evergreens. While that sight was still months away, Molly was excited about being part of the process that made that vision possible. Once the party was over, she'd be ready to start at Quinn's—and she couldn't wait. She hoped she wasn't going to be too busy taking orders to get a chance to speak to Quinn tonight. They really hadn't nailed down the particulars—when she'd start, what she'd be doing, or how much money she'd make. As she brushed her hair, it occurred to her that these were details she should have hammered out sooner.

No wonder I'm poor.

She stole a look at her cash box, the closed lid offering no relief from the grim reality inside. Coaxing Galileo off the open perch and into the cage, Molly was ready for her last shift at Crabby's—and her new life as Quinn's...Quinn's...assistant? She exchanged her pleasantries with the bird, then slipped out the door, Galileo's "Bite me" sounding as encouraging as a kiss from her mother when Molly left for school.

Ever since the day her alternator died, when she put the key in the ignition, she expected the car not to start.

But it always did.

Good old Bale.

She wished he was going to be at the party tonight. A big event in town wasn't the same without Bale. He was such a *fixture*.

Pulling into Crabby's parking lot at sunset, Molly realized she had started to take the old place for granted. She sat in her car and really looked at the restaurant. There was no denying the building had seen better days. All the servers had started calling it "Shabby Crabby's," but the place had its charm, sitting right on the Kentucky River. This was especially true at dusk, when its worn edges were softened by the fading light.

Molly shook herself. She had no time for sentimentality. After tonight, she would be working side-by-side with Quinn. She caught a glimpse of herself in the rearview mirror and stared sheepishly at her reflection.

She actually had no idea what she was going to be doing for Quinn. The farm was huge, and it was possible she wouldn't see much of him. But, as a new employee, she could certainly find excuses to seek his counsel. Or, she realized, she could offer advice as well as ask for it. After almost two years working on her tree house model, she knew quite a lot about horticulture.

Perhaps that's why Quinn offered her a job in the first place.

She took a Bold, Clear, Confident breath and walked through the kitchen entrance to Crabby's for the last time.

Crabby insisted the employees wear their starched "Crabby's" white shirts. He was wearing a tuxedo shirt, bow tie, and jacket over his "good" jeans. The staff could already hear the buzz of guests in the restaurant and out on the deck.

"So, Crabby," Manny said, as everyone grabbed trays of champagne and appetizers. "What's next for you?"

Since the big announcement two weeks ago, there had been much speculation as to what Crabby had in mind for his future. Would he stay in Cobb? Would he retire? Start a new venture somewhere? Everyone in the kitchen pretended to busy themselves, waiting for an answer.

"Bought an RV," Crabby said, straightening a few glasses on Molly's tray.

The staff waited for more, but that appeared to be all the explanation they were getting.

Molly caught sight of "Bold" on her hand—and decided to go for it.

"An RV?" she asked. "Why not a tiny house? You'd have your very own conversation starter everywhere you went."

"Do I look like I want a conversation starter?" Crabby scowled.

He had her there.

"Now everybody get to work," Crabby said.

The staff blinked as Crabby left the kitchen.

"Not even a 'thank you'?" asked Naomi.

Although one of the old guard—she'd been waitressing at Crabby's for ten years—Naomi was the most gregarious of Crabby's staff. She always had a smile on her perfect face. She took Crabby's grumpiness personally.

"When has Crabby ever said 'thank you'?" Manny asked, shaking his head.

The group laughed. Sean, one of the younger waiters, suggested they all grab a glass of champagne from each of their trays and toast Crabby.

"Should we go get him back in here?" asked Helena, a middle-aged bartender who always had a kind word for everyone—no matter how drunk they were.

"Are you kidding? He'd just be annoyed he was out twelve glasses of champagne," Sean said. He lifted his glass solemnly toward the door Crabby had just exited.

"To Crabby...I've worked in worse places," Donna said.

"I'll drink to that," Manny said, clinking glasses with Helena, who never took her eyes off the door in case Crabby came back and caught them.

"What are you so worried about, Helena?" Manny asked. "What's he going to do...fire us?"

Molly looked around—these people were her family away from Iowa. She was really going to miss them. But it was a small town. It wouldn't be the same, but she knew she'd run into them here and there.

And it's only seven-and-a-half months until Christmas. Maybe some of them would stop by Quinn's farm in December.

The thought of Quinn made her hands shake. Her champagne glasses made little pinging sounds as they wobbled on the tray.

Molly gripped the tray boldly and confidently—and followed the rest of the waitstaff into the restaurant.

Crabby's had been such a staple in the town, it was hard to believe this was the last event. As Molly approached with her tray, each little cluster of guests was reminiscing about events great and small that happened in the restaurant. Everything from christenings to bar mitzvahs to Tinder dates took place inside these walls.

Or on the deck.

Molly thought about all the ladies who came in for breakfast before heading off to Bale's to pick up their tiny houses, excited to start their new lives. Molly had to admit, the thought of working with Quinn gave her a taste of that excitement.

Going in and out of the kitchen, Molly and the rest of the staff kept pace with the guests. Full glasses of champagne were picked off the tray and empty ones appeared in their places.

Naomi was sitting on a stool in the kitchen, compact mirror in hand, examining her teeth for lipstick, when Molly swung through the door for champagne reinforcements. Helena was refilling her own glass and chatting with Donna, who was sitting on a stool rubbing her feet.

"Maybe Crabby has the right idea," Donna groaned. "I'm getting too old for this myself."

"I never said I was too old for this," Crabby's voice came from out of nowhere.

"Hey, Crabby," Molly said, startled. "I didn't see you there."

"Apparently," he said.

"Donna didn't mean any disrespect," Helena, the peacekeeper, said, her cheeks burning.

"Let me just clarify something," Crabby said. "I'm not retiring. I'm just not going to be in the restaurant business anymore."

The women looked at the door as it swung shut behind him. Donna looked at Helena and Molly.

"Is it just me," Naomi said, "or was that the lamest clarification of all time?"

The women laughed. They hoisted their trays into the air, preparing for another spin around the restaurant. As soon as Molly was through the door, she saw him.

Quinn was standing at the bar.

From the look of things, he'd been there awhile. He was deep in conversation with a few of his poker and drinking buddies—and he wasn't drinking champagne. Molly knew his drink. She'd poured a few over the years. It was called a Rusty Nail, which was scotch and a lemon peel on the rocks. Most men would be hammered if they downed one, but she'd seen Quinn knock back two or three to no ill effect. The only way Molly knew he'd had a few too many is when Crabby would, without a word, take Quinn's keys at the end of a long night.

Quinn caught her looking at him. Before she could look away, he called to her.

"Jane," his voice rang out through the crowd. "Come say hello."

Molly felt it was fate. Her tray was empty and it was easy to stow. She needed to talk to Quinn about when she would start and what exactly her job would be and what it would pay. And he was at a party and enjoying himself. They could have a very casual conversation.

She walked up, a bright smile hiding her nervousness.

"Hey, Quinn," she said.

"Hey there, Molly," he said. "I was just thinking about you."

That's a start!

"Any reason?" Molly asked, annoyed that she resorted to "coy"—a word she would never write on her hand.

"Not really," Quinn said. "Just wondering what you were going to do with yourself once this place is history."

Chapter 5

The world was spinning. Molly grabbed the table next to her to steady herself. What did he mean he was wondering what she was going to do with herself? She was going to work on the tree farm! She took a deep breath. Now was not the time to shrink from the situation. She had to face it head on.

"The last I heard," she said, as casually as possible, "I was going to start working for you."

"Is that right?" Quinn said.

He didn't seem annoyed or embarrassed. Neither was there a dramatic smacking of the forehead as if his memory had just been jogged.

"Where did you hear that?" he asked.

"From you."

She noticed everyone around them was very quiet, silently sipping their drinks or exchanging glances with one another. But she was Clear and Bold if not Confident. She was not going to slink away.

"I promised you a job?" he asked.

"Yes."

"Well, then, I guess you have a job," he said.

Molly could feel herself—and the tension in the room—relax.

"Did I say what it was going to be?" Quinn asked. "This job?"

She was about to remind him about planting seedlings, but suddenly remembered him talking about a task he didn't relish—cataloguing all the old trees on the property.

"Yes," Molly said quickly. "I'm supposed to catalogue all the old tree stumps on the property."

"Huh," Quinn said, looking into his drink. "That does sound familiar."

Molly could tell everyone within earshot was waiting to hear what he said next.

"Well, if that's what I promised you, then that's what you'll do."

"Thanks, Quinn."

"When would you be..."

"I can start tomorrow."

"Great. See you tomorrow at..."

"Ten. We said ten."

"Okay. See you at ten."

"Thanks, Quinn."

"Hey, what are friends for?" Quinn said, offering a dazzling, if a bit lopsided smile.

Molly smiled.

We're friends!

She picked up her tray, ready to finish out her shift. Several of the locals gave speeches about how much they would miss Crabby, the man; Crabby's, the restaurant; or both. Crabby, the man, looked as if he were suffering through the well-wishing. When he'd had enough, he handed Molly the keys.

"Lock the place up when everybody's gone," he said.

"What should I do with the keys?" Molly asked.

"Give them to Quinn," Crabby said. "He's going to sell the place for me."

Without another word, Crabby slipped out the back door and was gone. Molly looked at the keys in her hand.

Sell the restaurant?

The words came as a complete shock. She wondered what she'd been expecting. She had wrapped her head around the idea that there would no longer be a Crabby's but she hadn't envisioned it being sold. Would someone buy it and open a new restaurant? She looked around the place as if she'd never seen it before. The building had seen better days, but the back deck with the beautiful view of the river was still enticing. Would someone bulldoze the place? Maybe build a private home here? The possibilities were endless.

Molly took comfort in the thought. The possibilities for the plot of land on the Kentucky River were endless. The possibilities for Crabby, as he drove away in his RV, were endless. The possibilities for her at Quinn's farm were endless. She looked down and smiled at the keys in her hand. It would be no big deal to hand them over to her *new boss* in the morning.

Molly returned to the kitchen. Loading the tray, she felt happier than she had in a long time. She made a vow to keep up her positive thinking.

She added a slick of bright red lipstick, gave herself her most dazzling smile, and returned to the patio.

"Hello, Molly."

Molly's dazzling smile froze.

It was Professor Cambridge.

"Heh...heh...hello, Professor," Molly squeaked. "What are you doing here?"

The Professor cocked his head slightly to the side. His frown didn't seem to have party mode.

"I'm here to pay homage to the end of an era," he said. He frowned around the room. "Like everyone else here, I suspect."

She flinched at her own obtuseness. She wondered how she could be worse at small talk than a civil engineering professor. Why did she *think* he was here?

She said a silent prayer.

Please don't ask about my thesis.

"How is your little tree house project going?" he asked as he daintily took a drink from her tray.

She felt the tray shaking in her hands. She stared down at the drinks, trying to collect herself. Her father had always said, "Don't sit on bad news." Should she tell him it wasn't going well and throw herself on his mercy? Ask for yet another extension? She still had seven months.... Maybe by some miracle, she could get it done on time. She could lead with that, so she didn't seem entirely hopeless. Taking a deep breath, she looked up, ready to meet his gaze. Professor Cambridge was engrossed in conversation with another guest.

Molly felt a tingle of chagrin. She really was the worst at small talk. But she was relieved to have dodged that particular bullet.

After the party ended, Molly walked through the empty restaurant. She locked the front door and sat on the deck overlooking the river. As excited as she was to start on a whole new adventure at the tree farm, closing up Crabby's was bittersweet. The staff, the clientele, even grumpy old Crabby himself had become her family away from home. Cobb was a small town and she knew she'd keep up with many of the people she'd met here, but change was in the air.

It was almost midnight. The river was as dark as the sky, but she could hear the current tripping over rocks. It was a sound Molly had always loved. She smiled. She would miss that sound.

Her phone buzzed. Reaching into her back pocket, Molly dug it out and checked the screen to find a new text message from Bale.

Bale: You guys still partying?

Molly responded, fingers flying over her screen: Did you ever hear of anyone partying 'til midnight in this town?

Bale: Forgot it was midnight! On West Coast time. Sorry for the late text.

Molly: No worries. Just locking up. What's up with you?

Bale: Defending my little place in the world at a big RV show.

Molly: Sounds very David and Goliath.

She added a slingshot and something that looked like a monster winking.

Bale: Not sure David wins this time. J

Molly smiled. She knew Bale only had a rudimentary understanding of emoticons and emojis, so adding a J must have taken a lot of work.

Molly: Careful with your slingshot. Don't put out a windshield.

Bale: You have a lot of faith!

Molly: I do!

Bale: Car okay?

Molly: Thanks to you, yes. BTW, I start work tomorrow for Quinn.

Molly waited for a response. She could see the tree little dots undulating, indicating that Bale was writing. But no response came. She was about to type again when his response popped up.

Bale: Sounds good. Wow. No more Crabby's. End of an era.

He added a L and, apparently for good measure, a roller skate and a hamburger.

And the beginning of a new one, Molly thought as she returned her phone to her pocket.

Molly drove back to her apartment. It crossed her mind that Bale didn't seem particularly excited about her new job. But then, why should he be? It wasn't like she was doing anything as interesting as traveling the country selling tiny houses. She shook her head. Bale was always so nice to her, encouraging her to come up with more and more innovative ideas for her thesis and helping her out with her unpredictable car. She hoped by the time Bale got home—whenever that would be—she'd be on a little more solid footing than she'd been for a while. She wanted to impress him after years of floundering and leaning on his advice and car repair skills.

She was buzzing with expectations for the future. Although she'd been on her feet for hours, she was too amped to sleep. It had been a while since she'd felt any creative juices trickling, let alone flowing. Money problems, wrapping up at Crabby's, the anticipation of her new job on the tree farm, all had shut her down.

But that was all behind her!

She flicked on the light and made eye contact with Galileo, who gave her his annoyed look—cocking his head to one side and staring at her coldly with one eye.

"Have I been ignoring you?" she purred as she looked around the living room.

"Bite me," Galileo said.

"I wasn't talking to you," she said as she sat at the table that held her tree house model.

She studied it. Bale had helped her design the perfect black walnut tree. She thought back to the day they sat for hours after Crabby's had closed, sketching trees. Molly always felt she was firing on all cylinders when she was creating things that were both practical and beautiful. She could tell Bale felt the same.

Molly had drawn a soaring, slim tree with limbs branching up and then cascading down again like an umbrella.

"That's good," Bale said, but she could hear a reservation in his voice.

"But in real life, it wouldn't hold the house I have in mind," Molly sighed, tossing down her pencil.

She looked at Bale. Whether he meant to or not, he kept her honest.

"I know I need a really strong trunk," Molly said. "But it still has to be beautiful."

"I go through that every time I design a tiny house," Bale said. "How do you make something safe and functional that is also aesthetically pleasing?"

Molly stared down at her designs. None seemed quite right.

"Look, you know the main thing is the trunk, right?" Bale said.

"Right."

Bale sketched out a tree. Its trunk had a generous base that split into four sections as it soared skyward, long branches spreading like fingers flexing for a fight.

"That's good," Molly said approvingly. "This tree means business."

Once she'd settled on the tree, Molly tried several approaches for her house. Her first prototype was dubbed "Cubes and Tubes." It was made of several different-sized wood and glass cubes linked by interconnecting tubes. The design didn't lend itself to plumbing—and Molly was determined to create a tree house that not only had a kitchen but a bathroom. Next up, she'd created a version with a steel-frame tower. This worked with her theory of running pipes down the base of the tree and over to a septic system. But the tree and all that steel seemed at odds with each other.

She loved her new design. She thought back to a slow late-afternoon shift when Bale was sitting at the counter. They were discussing their various theories of making miniature houses. Molly confessed her design was not going well. She told Bale she was drawn to engineering because it wasn't just about form and artistry. Civil engineering was about coming up with practical as well as aesthetic solutions. Pouring a third cup of coffee for Bale, she told him that creating plumbing for her thesis model was her biggest hurdle, but she needed to conquer it. And she was getting nowhere.

"I think you're working too hard on this," Bale said. "You need to step back and look for the simple solution."

"There isn't a simple solution!"

"Sure there is. You've come up with all these twists and turns trying to figure out how to outsmart gravity. How's that working out for you?" he asked.

"What's your point?"

"My point is, you can fight this all you want, but gravity always wins. Look, it's not my thesis..."

"But if it were?"

"I'd start with the biggest challenge...which is the plumbing, right?"

"I think we've established that. Yes."

"I'd put the bathroom on the ground."

"On the ground? That would be cheating!"

"Says who?"

"Then it wouldn't be a tree house!"

"It seems to me that you are trying to get a degree so you can solve problems in a new way. That's what I'm doing too with my tiny houses. But you need to accept the laws of nature—even with a flight of fancy like a tree house model."

"You sound pretty sure of yourself."

"I've spent the last few years testing this out. Yes, if you have all the money in the world, you can probably design a tree house with a chef's kitchen and an *en suite* bathroom. But is that what you're trying to do?"

"No, I'm trying to design a tree house that would work for—"

"For the same people who are interested in living tiny," he said. "And that means a different kind of artistry."

"I'm not sure how to do that," she said.

"For one thing," Bale said, "start with the fact that the tree is in charge of the design, not you."

"I thought gravity was in charge of my design."

"No, gravity is in charge of your bathroom."

"My mistake," Molly said, frowning and pouring a cup of coffee for herself.

"I'm no expert," Bale said. "I mean, I start with a trailer bed and work from there. But you have a tree. Take your design cues from it."

"What if the tree doesn't want a bathroom on the ground floor?"

"I'd guess a buzz saw could be a good bargaining tool," he said as he paid his bill.

Molly smiled as she stared at her new design. Surrendering to the challenges of the shape and structure of the walnut tree led her in unexpected directions.

She started with the bathroom on the ground floor, tucked into a hollow at the back of the tree. Because she was following the contours of the trunk, the bathroom was misshapen, like a gossamer hut in a fairy tale. Molly found it strangely beautiful. From there, the tree house came to life. Part steampunk contraption, part fairy-tale castle, the levels started to soar through the branches.

Molly took up where she'd left off—creating a porch off the living room on the third level. Much like an actor creating the backstory for her character, Molly created a life for her tree—a life that included a view of the Kentucky River. It all seemed so real when she was working on it. Molly designed a curvaceous porch, one supported by the black walnut's strongest branch. Since the living room was so high in the air, Molly added a wooden safety fence.

She took a peak at Galileo, who was sitting on the perch in the opening to his cage. The bird didn't really need an enclosure, but the five-foot-tall cage was a flight of fancy. It was one of Molly's first projects, and while Galileo might not be impressed, she was very proud of it. When she worried about having to downsize, she wondered where she would put the gigantic cage. Now, with the promise of a job on the tree farm, she wouldn't have to worry. As if reading her mind, Galileo said:

"I love you, Quinn."

"You need to stop saying that," she said, pointing at the bird. "Quinn is going to be my new boss. I can't have you humiliating me. Stick to 'bite me.'"

Molly shook her head. As if Galileo's signature "Bite me" hadn't embarrassed her enough over the years. The time the African Grey said "Bite me" to her tenth-grade math tutor—not to mention the time he managed to teach "Bite me" to a four-year-old that Molly was baby-sitting—would pale in comparison to the imagined scenario of a romantic encounter with Quinn and having the African Grey prematurely blurt out the obvious.

"'I love you, Quinn' stays between us," Molly said sternly. "Do you hear me?"

"Bite me."

Chapter 6

Open
Discover
Willing

Molly woke with the sun. She'd hardly slept. The thought of working with Quinn every day was a dream come true. Of all the people who were going to be unemployed, he'd chosen *her* to come work at the farm. She tried not to read anything into it, but, frankly, it was hard to ignore the evidence that he was at least aware of her.

She knew she should spend every waking moment on her tree house model, but instead she'd spent the whole previous night researching anything she could find on Christmas tree farms. She'd vamped her way into a job she knew Quinn dreaded—mapping out old tree stumps on the farm—but she didn't really have any idea what that meant. She'd studied up and determined that April was the month Christmas tree farmers started establishing new trees. For every Christmas tree harvested in the late fall and winter, one to three seedlings are planted the following spring. To avoid erosion, the best way was to plant new seedlings between old rows of tree stumps.

She couldn't wait to impress Quinn with her knowledge. She dressed in jeans and a cotton plaid shirt. As she envisioned herself stomping around old tree stumps, which probably held bugs, she donned her most serious hiking boots.

Galileo rustled in his cage. He and Molly rarely spoke in the morning—he was not a morning bird. But Molly was too excited to keep quiet. As she got out his food pellets, cubed an apple for him, and refreshed his water, Molly asked his opinion.

"What words should I write on my hand today?"

Galileo reached into his bowl, delicately selecting a sunflower seed and cracking it open. He ignored her.

"I'm thinking 'Open,' 'Discover,' and 'Knowledgeable,'" she said, grabbing her pen.

She wrote "Knowledge" and stopped.

"Do you think that's overly confident?"

She was met with a munching sound.

She rubbed out the letters.

"I think 'Willing' is a better word for a new employee."

She looked down at her hand.

Open.
Discover.
Willing.

She looked at Galileo.

Munch.

"Okay. See you later," Molly said, heading out the door. "You have a good day."

Munch.

"Come on, Galileo," Molly said sternly. "You know better than that."

The African Grey looked at Molly sideways.

"Shit," he said.

"No."

"Bite me."

"No."

"Crap," Galileo said. "I love you."

"That's better."

As Molly closed the door, she could hear him add:

"Quinn."

What a difference a few hours of daylight could make. Cobb was a small town, and she was through Main Street in two stop signs and one red light. She usually sped down the deserted street before dawn, always late to open Crabby's for breakfast. Now, at 9:45 in the morning, the town was humming with pedestrians already engaged in their day. Waving at some familiar faces, she turned left at the edge of town, excited to be inching closer to her new life.

Quinn's Christmas tree farm wasn't much to look at in late April. While the rest of the South was nudging into spring, the evergreens looked bored as soldiers waiting for action. She turned on to the dirt road that led to the office and Old Paint's helipad. Molly's heart beat faster as she saw Old Paint hunkered down on the helipad and Quinn's truck parked in front of the office. She took them as omens that Quinn might be around. The silhouette of a man, backlit among a close row of trees, waved as she approached. Molly squinted—the dark outline of the man's arm shooting across the sun made a windmill effect. She couldn't tell if it was Quinn, but she waved energetically anyway.

The silhouetted figure was using a weed whacker around each of the trees. Molly frowned. Just last night, she'd read that mowing between trees started in April and continued through October. In October, the final big push of getting the trees ready for sale started. If she knew this beforehand, she could have told Quinn she wanted to be one of the mowers. Talk about job security. Getting the seedlings in the ground would only guarantee her work through spring.

She'd made a list of other jobs she might suggest for herself to Quinn, but decided not to get ahead of herself. She'd almost written "Do Not Get Ahead of Yourself" on her hand but decided that was not positive.

The man with the weed whacker turned off the machine, dusted off his hands, and headed toward her. She smiled brilliantly, still not sure if it were her new boss or not. As far as this job went, she was in it to win it! She toned down her smile. Her radiant smile might scare off a stranger.

Her smile turned to confusion. The sun had shifted, revealing the man walking toward her. It wasn't Quinn. It was Manny!

"What are you doing here?" Molly asked. Realizing her shock might come across as rudeness, she added, "This is sure a surprise!"

No lie.

"Quinn offered me a job last night!" Manny said. "How cool is that?"

Quinn hired Manny? She rummaged around in her brain for some way to spin this so she still felt special, but she came up empty.

"*Very* cool!" Molly squeaked.

"Yeah," Manny said. "I wasn't sure what I was going to do after Crabby's closed. Guess Quinn took pity on a couple of strays, huh?"

Molly bit her lip, trying to not say "Bite me" in Galileo's raspy voice.

A door banged open behind them.

Molly and Manny turned at the same time to see Quinn, aviator sunglasses already perched elegantly on his nose, coming at them. Molly thought he lit up when he saw her, but perhaps that was just her own radiance reflected in his shades.

"Hey, Jane," Quinn said.

Molly tried to decipher if he was surprised to see her.

"Hey, Quinn," she said, trying to sound casual. "I'm here, right on time!"

Quinn nodded vaguely. She knew she sounded ridiculously perky. Quinn stared at Manny.

"Hi..." Quinn started, a question mark clear in his intonation.

"Manny," Manny offered.

Molly noticed Manny didn't seem offended by Quinn's lack of recognition. Maybe just having a job was enough for Manny.

Maybe it should be enough for me.

Molly made a vow to herself. No more romanticizing Quinn's motives. He hired her to do a job and she would do it! She would think of him the way she thought of Bale—a smart and helpful friend. She studied Quinn. She wondered if he was as smart as Bale. But he gave her a job, so he was definitely helpful. That would have to do.

She turned her attention back to the conversation between Manny and Quinn.

"I found the weed whacker in the tool shed," Manny said. "So I thought I'd just get to work mowing the rows of trees until you came out."

"Good thinking..." Quinn cocked his head to one side. He seemed to be struggling.

"Manny," Manny said again.

"Good thinking, Manny," Quinn said in a slightly stronger voice.

"I was thinking I'd do the rows of smaller trees first," Manny said. "Then move on to the larger ones."

"That sounds good," Quinn murmured.

"I can also hand-weed the trees that are set aside for landscaping, if you'd like."

"Uh, sure," Quinn agreed. His head snapped up and he looked at Manny. "Oh, yeah. You. You're the one with the cousin in the tree business, right?"

"That's right," Manny said proudly.

He had a cousin in the tree business? Of all the lousy luck.

Molly found herself being envious of Manny's well-informed tone. Perhaps she should have written "Knowledgeable" on her hand after all.

Quinn turned to Molly.

"Where am I going to get coffee now that Crabby's is closed?"

"I guess you could stop in at Cora's," Molly said, offering up the only suggestion she could think of, the only other spot in town open for breakfast.

She reddened when she remembered Quinn was banned from Cora's, having been caught several years ago making out with Cora's twenty-year-old daughter in the pantry. This happened long before Molly arrived in Cobb, but it was part of the town's lore. Word was that Cora was upset because the pantry was where she and Quinn had their own romantic encounters. Molly refused to believe half the stories she'd heard about Quinn. If he were half as busy with the town ladies as the locals made him out to be, he'd never get any work done.

"Maybe I'll head over to Beamer's in Burgoo," Quinn said, looking up at the sky.

Manny and Molly looked at each other. Burgoo was another little town on the Kentucky River, but it was about thirty miles away—hardly close enough for coffee.

"I could make coffee in the office," Molly said, wondering if he was too shy to ask.

"Nah," Quinn said. "I'm really thinking a cup of Beamer's coffee is just what I need."

"Okay," Molly said hesitantly.

"Want to come with me?" Quinn asked Molly.

"Sure," Molly said breathlessly. She saw a cloud pass over Manny's face, and added. "We can talk about my new duties."

Quinn seemed to pick up on her thoughts and turned to Manny.

"You can hold down the fort?" Quinn asked.

"Sure can." Manny puffed with pride.

"Want us to bring you anything?" Quinn asked.

Molly was thrilled at Quinn's use of the word "us."

Quinn gave Manny a manly smack on the shoulder as Molly headed toward the truck.

"Where you going?" Quinn called to her.

Molly spun to face him in confusion.

"We can't spend all day on the road. Besides, Manny's coffee would get cold," Quinn said. "Let's take the chopper."

Molly tried to act casual as she buckled herself into the safety harness and put on the noise-cancelling earphones. Quinn hopped in the pilot's seat.

"Got any sunglasses?" he asked.

Molly dug in her purse and held up a pair of oversized Armanis she'd gotten from her mother for Christmas. Quinn gave her a thumbs-up, a few words of caution about how the helicopter worked, and away they went.

Molly noticed a corroded hole at her feet. Old Paint really was a mess, but Molly loved watching the ground receding further and further. She looked at Quinn, who seemed totally in control as they sliced through the sky. She looked at the clouds above.

This was as close to heaven as she had ever imagined.

Chapter 7

When the chopper touched lightly down back at the tree farm, she could barely remember her trip to Burgoo. Once they were back on the ground, Quinn handed Manny a cup of still-hot coffee, then waved to Molly and Manny before ducking back into the office. If it weren't for the steaming cup curled in Manny's hand, she might have thought it had all been a dream.

"We didn't talk about what I should doing," Molly said to Manny, although he hadn't asked.

"Quinn seems to run a pretty loose ship," Manny said, shrugging. "Seems like he wants a few self-starters."

Was this a tip—or criticism? Molly arched an eyebrow and waited for further illumination.

"Just get on with it," Manny said as he blew on his coffee and returned to work.

Molly took in a deep breath. She peeked over at the office, but there was absolutely no movement coming from within.

She scanned the horizon. Quinn had been chatty in Burgoo, filling her in a little about the farm. Quinn's farm was three thousand acres—large by Kentucky standards.

"I came to Cobb almost by accident," Quinn had told her over breakfast at Beamer's. "I'd just gotten out of the service…. I'd been a helicopter pilot and I was bumming around, looking for something to do. So I thought I'd come see Uncle Crabby. I figured I might be able to help out at the restaurant."

"You worked at Crabby's?" Molly asked, elated that they might have such an intimate connection.

"Never got the chance," Quinn said. "I had just hit town when I won Old Paint in a poker game and—"

"You won a helicopter in a poker game?" Molly almost choked on her coffee.

"Yeah," Quinn said, smiling nostalgically. "It was quite a game. Anyway, so now I needed Uncle Crabby to not only take me in but take my helicopter in too."

"Wow. I can't imagine him doing that."

"Yeah. He couldn't imagine it either. Gave me the boot."

"Just for having a helicopter? That's unreasonable even for Crabby."

"Well, to be fair, I was supposed to be working my first shift when I organized the little game in the backroom. Put up a 'Closed' sign when I thought Uncle Crabby would be gone for the day."

"Yikes."

"'Yikes' is one word for it. Anyway, appealing to my uncle's higher nature—"

"Crabby has a higher nature?"

"Not really, but he's afraid of his sister—my mom—so he got me a job on the Christmas tree farm. It was November. They would be harvesting the trees—and they needed a helicopter."

"Why?"

"I won Old Paint from their last pilot."

Molly decided she'd walk the farm, making a map of areas she saw where new seedlings could be planted. The gentle rolling landscape undulated with pine, spruce, and fir trees of all sizes. She worried that Quinn might already have a map of the farm and know where the seedlings were to be planted. But to know that, she'd have to ask—and if Manny was right, if Quinn wanted a self-starter, he would think less of her. On the other hand, if he already knew where the seedlings were going, and Molly wasted precious hours mapping out an already mapped-out farm... He might think less of her.

Molly wished she'd asked Bale when he would be coming home. He would have an answer to this conundrum. He seemed to have answers to all conundrums. As Molly traversed the farm, she noticed that the trees were all planted in rows, but there were clearings here and there, where she presumed trees—in all height ranges—had been selected in past holiday seasons and had been harvested.

Molly's phone vibrated in her pocket, surprising her. It was so quiet back among the trees that she forgot all about cell service. It was Bale.

"Hey," Bale said. "Just checking in. How's the new job going?"

"Really fun," Molly said, trying to contain her giddiness. "I went for a helicopter ride."

She knew she sounded like a child, but she didn't care. How many people start their new jobs flying through the air?

"That does sound fun," Bale said. "But don't lose focus."

"Oh, it's not like that," Molly demurred. "It was just coffee."

"I meant, don't lose focus on your thesis."

Molly could feel her ears turning red with embarrassment. Just because she was fantasizing where that helicopter ride might lead, there was no reason why Bale would be.

"I've got to get back to work," Molly said hurriedly and quickly jabbed at her phone to disconnect.

She had walked for about a half hour, studying the different kinds of trees, when she realized she'd lost track of exactly where she was. She looked up to find herself among much older, wilder-looking specimens. Their branches were unruly and there were different kinds of trees bunched together—not only evergreens, but walnut and magnolias as well. She was in a forest! She realized she might not even be on Quinn's property anymore, and, even if she were, he wouldn't be interested in planting seedlings under the thick shade of these ancient, inhospitable-looking trees whose bark seemed to announce there was no room for interlopers.

Molly sat down under the canopy of a large evergreen and studied the forest. Kentucky was known for its softly rolling hills and lush, sprawling horse farms, but it wouldn't take long for the land to return to a thicket of dense trees given half the chance. She stood up, ready to return to a more plausible part of the farm, when she noticed a few pieces of wood hammered into the trunk of the large tree she'd been sitting under. She looked up—it was a handmade ladder, climbing all the way into the needles.

She could see a platform high up in the branches.

Was this a tree house?

Dizzy with anticipation, she tested the first few rungs. They seemed solid enough. She gauged the platform to be about thirty feet in the air—just the height she'd chosen for her model. She knew she shouldn't climb up a makeshift ladder without anyone knowing where she was, but she couldn't resist. She looked at her cell phone. She didn't have any reception. If she were to get stuck in the tree—or worse, fall on some rotten timber—nobody would know.

She grabbed onto the ladder and took a step.

Her right hand, with the words "Open," "Discover," and "Willing" written on it, was on the rung above her, daring her upward.

She took another step.

And another.

Molly was halfway up the tree when one of the steps gave way beneath her. She managed to catch herself, but closed her eyes, hugging the tree as she listened to the step smashing against the trunk of the tree, then crashing to the ground. When everything was still, Molly steadied her nerves and took another step upward. She tried to think of something to take her mind off the climb.

She remembered Bale saying that everything could be a lesson. If she didn't die investigating this tree, she knew she'd spend extra time on her own version, creating a non-scary ascent. She started thinking about various ways to launch oneself into a tree, then she hit her head on something—and realized she was at the top.

She looked up. She could see the bottom of the platform and the top of the tree through a square opening. She grabbed onto the sides and pulled herself through, using all the Pilates upper body strength she could muster. Maybe there was a perfect hidden tree house up here. She might be able to fix it up and present it instead of a model. That would blow her professors away! She realized she was being silly. She wasn't even sure her professors would have any interest in a real tree house.

Her heart started beating wildly as she hoisted herself up. She knelt on the platform, touching the wood around her to see if the base seemed solid enough to hold her. Steadying herself, she stood up, raising her eyes in anticipation.

The place was a complete dump.

She'd risked her life for this?

She knew all along there was no way an evergreen—no matter how large—could sustain a tree house the scope of her model. But she had expected something—she hated to admit it—magical.

She sighed and gingerly made her way around the platform. There was a rickety, small, lean-to shed made from old, misshapen boards. Sunlight passed through the shanty, throwing streaks of light through the shadows. The place was not rain- or windproof. No windows. There were boards missing both in the walls and floors. There was no safety railing. She shook her head. A twelve-year-old could have designed this place. It occurred to her that it might have *been* designed by a twelve-year-old, and perhaps she shouldn't be so judgmental.

There was a space between the tops of several commingling trees where she could look out and see all of Cobb. The sight was breathtaking. The Kentucky River wound lazily through the town. She could see Crabby's patio and deck snug up against the riverbank, devoid of people and furniture. A reminder that nothing in life stays the same.

She stayed away from the edge. While she realized the lack of a barrier was a safety hazard, she had to admit, it did give the place an expansiveness she knew her model lacked. She looked out over the town. The platform and little shanty certainly weren't going to win any design or engineering awards, but the structure did give off a feeling a *freedom* she knew her own model lacked.

Plexiglas?

The idea of an invisible barrier had her itching to return to her model and take out the railing. She wanted to discuss this new idea with Bale. She knew he would love it. Every one of his tiny houses, built on wheels and ready to hit the road, had freedom as a starting point.

A bird twittered, surprised to be making eye contact with a human on its own turf. She thought about Galileo and how much she'd love to bring him here—he'd blow this bird's little mind.

She could feel herself relaxing. The stress of losing one job and starting another, not having enough money to pay the rent and other bills (she realized she still didn't even know what Quinn was going to pay her), and the ever-nagging sensation of not giving enough attention to her thesis seemed to flow out of her as she stared out over the town. Everything was silent, except for a soft whisper among the trees that they had company. She hated to admit it, but she could sit up here all day, just letting the forest surround and inspire her.

The realization that Quinn wasn't paying her to sit in a tree and soak up inspiration smacked her like a flyswatter. She had to get back to work. She looked at the wooden ladder she'd used to get up. It looked even scarier going down.

Taking a deep breath, she backed down the ladder one rickety step at a time. She'd always been afraid of descending a ladder—something that used to make her brother, Curly, furious when they were kids. She would always get herself stuck up a tree or on the roof and he'd be sent to fetch her. When her foot reached for the missing step and Molly found herself pawing at thin air, she could see Curly's annoyed face—and it made her laugh.

The laughing stopped abruptly as she lost her footing and crashed the last four feet. Molly laid sprawled on the forest floor, wondering:

If an idiot falls in the forest and no one hears her, did she really fall?

She raised herself up, propping herself on her elbows to assess the damage. The ground was soft with pine needles. She appeared to be unharmed. Perhaps, at least metaphysically, she didn't really fall.

At least she didn't have to cop to it!

She looked around for landmarks, knowing she would want to come back and stare out at the view. She picked out two interlocking walnut trees to the east and three straight-as-sticks pine trees to the west as her markers and headed back to the more manicured—and less dangerous—rows of evergreens.

She was walking among the stumps of several rows of harvested trees when Quinn appeared beside her.

"How's it going out here?" he asked.

"I think seedlings could go here," Molly said, trying not to feel guilty that she'd spent the last hour daydreaming. She indicated the area. "And I found a few other areas that look good."

"Good work," Quinn said. "So…um…I was wondering…"

"Yes?" Molly asked.

Quinn graced her with one of his magnificent lopsided grins. Molly tried to keep breathing. Was he going to ask her on a date? She thought about misinterpreting Bale's words, but maybe she had been on the right path after all.

She replayed the morning in her mind. The flight in the helicopter was wonderful. Breakfast seemed to have gone well. Maybe she should invite him over to her place. She rejected that instantly. Galileo was sure to tell him he loved him.

"I was wondering what you're doing tomorrow?"

He *was* asking her on a date!

"No plans," Molly said with a shrug.

She wondered if she sounded pathetic, like she had no life. She tried again.

"Nothing important," she tried again, looking accusingly at the evergreen when she noticed a tiny splinter in her thumb.

She stuck her thumb in her mouth, then yanked it out. She wouldn't want Quinn to think she was trying to look seductive while on duty. Perhaps she should remind him she had substance.

"Just working on my thesis," she said, immediately regretting it. "Not that I can't put that aside for a few hours."

Quinn looked at her, a confused look on his face.

"I meant, what are you doing *here* tomorrow?"

Chapter 8

Bale and Thor walked through the Golden, Colorado, Tiny House Show, checking out the competition. Bale had to admit, his own Tiny Dreams houses held up pretty well. He waved to a silver-haired man in jeans and cowboy boots. He didn't know the man, but most of the veteran builders recognized each other on sight, having spotted each other over the last few years at convention centers, stadium parking lots, and county fairgrounds. The man waved back and returned to attaching an outside storage unit to one of his own tiny houses.

Bale swung himself into one of the four tinies he'd brought to the show. It was his steampunk model, inspired by his conversations with Molly about her tree house. He often told her their relationship was like two people working on a still life in an art class. They looked at the same object but saw different ways of capturing its essence. They bounced ideas off each other, taking their collective vision and applying it to their different worlds.

He let out a deep sigh. If only Molly had some interest in seeing him outside of their imaginary art class. But he knew the signs—more specifically, he knew when there were *no* signs. Not that Molly had rejected him. But it was obvious her enthusiasm for him lay in their mutual interests rather than anything along romantic lines. All romantic roads apparently led to Quinn's tree farm.

His thoughts were interrupted when a young woman knocked on the door.

"Hi," Bale said, letting her in through the dark, distressed door with its signature handle shaped like a squid tentacle. The handle had been Molly's design, but when she decided it would be too hard to make in miniature for her thesis model, she gave the idea to him.

"It's all about the sweat-to-glory ratio. If I ran with every idea that came into my head, I'd never get my project done. I've got to go with the big idea and leave the details until I get the actual tree house built," she said. "As if that's ever going to happen."

"It will happen," Bale assured her. "If I can get tiny houses built, I know you'll see your tree house realized."

He was relieved she didn't ask how he knew that.

But the curvy, tactile handle was always a big draw at the tiny house shows—as were the other ideas she'd given him, including fashioning large old keys into kitchen cabinet pulls and using copper plumbing pipes rich with a green patina to make shelf brackets.

"I love your houses," the woman said, her eyes gleaming with the possibilities of a whole new life. "They look like they're out of fairy tales."

"Thank you," Bale said.

Whether they saw the concept of a tiny house as a way to be less burdened by debt or wanted to live in a fairy tale, he loved the different reactions people had to his creations.

"Can I look around?"

"That's why I'm here," he said. "I'm Bale Barrett."

"Violet Green," she said, shaking his hand.

She was beautiful. He went through the search engine in his mind to see if he should say something about her violet eyes—was that why she was named Violet? He decided against it. Hadn't every man on earth used that as an opening line? Should he try for "Violet" and "Green" both being colors? No…that was probably overdone as well. He settled on "Nice to meet you."

He looked at Thor, whose blank expression fairly shouted, "That's the best you can do?"

Violet's brilliant eyes played over the house. She ran her hand over the kitchen countertop.

"The workmanship in here is the best I've seen," she said.

"Thanks," he said. "I'm going to step outside. If you have any questions, let me know."

Did he see a shadow of disappointment on her face? Or was that wishful thinking? It didn't matter. He was in a professional situation and would handle himself accordingly.

When he first started showing his houses, as soon as a customer walked in, he felt as if he were taking up too much space. It was as if he were inflating as the prospective client toured the miniscule dwelling. Bale had learned that a tiny house only got tinier when two people who didn't know each other occupied the space.

He called Thor and the two of them headed outside, but not before Thor got his kiss from their latest visitor.

"That's how it's done," Thor's stubby, wagging tail seemed to say as they clomped down the tiny house steps.

Bale sat on the front step of the tiny house, wondering what Violet was thinking about all the details. He had learned to be patient. Molly had once said that just as every woman can't wear the same hairstyle, not everybody was meant to live in a tiny house.

Experience had taught him she was right. Even though it meant losing a sale, if he felt a person hadn't thought through the immense decision of getting rid of almost all their possessions, Bale would counsel her (there were some "hims" and a few couples, but most of his customers were women) to take her time. His shop would always be in Cobb, Kentucky, and there was no rush. The last thing he wanted was for someone to wake up one day on the road in one of his lofts and say to herself, "What have I done?"

"It's bad for business and bad for my soul," he'd told Molly.

There is a beautiful woman yards away, possibly buying one of my houses...Why am I think about Molly? he asked himself.

Violet popped her head out the tiny house door, smiling.

"This is just fantastic," she said. "I really feel at home in here."

Violet had obviously given a lot of thought to the possibility of living tiny. She stepped outside and sat on the front step next to Bale. She'd done her research and was asking all the right questions.

How big a truck did she need to tow this particular tiny house?

Did the tiny house have off-grid capabilities?

Would the insulation withstand freezing temperatures?

She told him she was a traveling nurse and ping-ponged around the country.

"I've actually sold quite a few homes to traveling nurses," Bale said.

"I know," Violet said. "You've got quite the reputation."

Bale looked at her in surprise.

"As a great tiny house builder!" Violet laughed, not the least bit embarrassed. "Wow, I'm an idiot."

Bale looked to Thor—could he go anywhere with this?

Thor sent a telepathic, unequivocal "No."

"How big—or small—a house are you thinking?" Bale asked.

"Maybe two hundred fifty square feet max," she said. "It's only me, but I want to feel like I'm home. So I want a kitchen, a stackable washer-dryer, a decent bathroom, and room to move around."

"This place is a little bigger than that," he said.

"I know," she said wistfully, glancing back at the house. "But it's so damn cute."

"These houses are all prototypes," he said. "We can work on a smaller one if you'd like."

"Really?" she said, her eyes lighting up. "I'd love that. Could you make it green on the outside?"

He wondered if she was flirting with him.

"I'm surprised you don't want it painted violet," he said, proud of his agility to think on the spot.

"My truck is violet," she said with a wink.

Okay! In the world of tiny houses, this would *definitely* be considered flirting. Wasn't it?

Wouldn't this be the perfect opportunity to ask her out to dinner?

But what was the point? If he couldn't stop thinking about Molly, it wasn't fair to anybody to have even the most innocent of dates.

Besides, those dates rarely ended as innocently as either party had claimed.

They exchanged business cards. In a world where she could have just looked him up online, it felt like an intimate gesture. He promised Violet that when and if she decided to buy one of his Tiny Dreams, he was easy to reach. She shook his hand and said she'd stay in touch.

Bale sat staring out the window, absently rubbing the red patch of spiky fur between Thor's ears. He'd just let a beautiful woman walk away—and for what? He knew he was being ridiculous. He was just torturing himself, thinking about taking a bolder step with Molly. If she somehow returned his feelings, his life would be complete. But he'd be making the biggest mistake of his life if he scared her away. He'd rather stay friends than lose any connection with her.

He was only a few years older than Quinn, but he felt much more...

He thought about the words Molly wrote on her hand every day. He tried to think of a few of his own.

Mature?
Steady?
Solid?
My words suck.

The fact of the matter was that even though he built tiny houses, which to some might seem eccentric, at his core, Bale was a grown-up.

And being grown-up is *never* sexy.

No matter how many he built, a tiny house paled when compared to a helicopter.

* * * *

Molly drove home in total humiliation. How could she have been so lame? Of course Quinn only wanted to talk about her job—she did work for him, after all. She fought with herself all the way home. On one hand, she was an employee. On the other hand, she was an employee who went on a helicopter ride for breakfast in the next town. She didn't even remember what she'd said. She must have sounded at least a tiny bit coherent, because Quinn never took his eyes off her while she blathered on about her big plans for the seedlings. Those gorgeous eyes just made things worse.

She drove past Bale's Tiny Dreams. Half his houses had gone with him to Colorado and the lot was locked. The place looked as forlorn as she felt. When she'd been sitting on the platform high up in the trees, she felt so full of creativity. She couldn't wait to get home and work on her model.

But as soon as she stepped foot back on earth, reality came crashing down.

She still didn't know very much about her job or her salary. The only thing she was sure about were her hours. Quinn said ten in the morning until three in the afternoon sounded about right for his seedling seeker.

"That's five hours," Molly had said.

"Oh, is it?" Quinn asked.

Quinn looked surprised. Was he making things up on the spot? He suddenly looked serious.

"Well, there'll be an hour for lunch, of course," he added.

Molly was thunderstruck. She wanted *more* hours, not less. A chill went down her spine when she calculated. Even if Quinn paid her slightly above minimum wage, she wouldn't have enough money for much more than coffee and birdseed. She really had to work up her nerve to ask Quinn about the details.

Maybe she could look for another part-time job.

But where?

Molly parked her car and peered out the window, making sure Mr. Detman wasn't nearby. She was late on the rent again and she knew she was getting dangerously close to being evicted. She glanced at the path between her parking space and the walkway to her apartment.

All clear.

She quietly got out of the car. Pulling her hoodie over her head, she strode purposefully toward the path. Once she was on the path, it was only twenty steps to her front door. She started counting down....

20, 19, 18, 17, 16, 15...

Molly's step quickened. She was going to make it!

14, 13, 12, 11...

Mr. Detman intercepted her halfway between the parking lot and her front door.

"Hey there, Molly," Mr. Detman said, peering at her under her hood. "I wasn't sure it was really you hiding under there."

"It's me," Molly said.

She wanted to add, "And I'm not hiding," but refrained. She was trying to live up to positive thoughts, and that sounded rude and petulant. Plus, she *was* hiding.

"I just need to talk to you about your rent," Mr. Detman said sorrowfully, wagging his head.

"How are the budgies doing?" Molly asked, trying to distract him.

"They aren't as much fun as I hoped they'd be, frankly."

Molly took in a breath. Grateful as she was to steer the conversation elsewhere, it annoyed her when people wanted their birds to be fun. Birds were regal and an honor to care for. You could learn a lot from birds, but they would never be a barrel of laughs.

"If you want fun, get a dog," she wanted to say.

But she didn't. She really did feel sorry for her landlord, but he just wasn't realistic.

"I'll bring them a wooden chew toy from Pammy's Pet Palace," she said. "I'm working over at Quinn's now, and get off work before the stores close."

She hoped the hint that she had a new job would help matters. But it didn't.

"I have to serve you with an eviction notice," he said, his hangdog expression worthy of a basset hound. "Seven days to quit."

"Seven days," Molly gasped. "I thought I'd have six months!"

"Well, if you call a lawyer.... You might buy yourself some time."

"Then I'll call a lawyer." Molly's mood brightened.

"You'll cause me a lot of trouble if you call a lawyer."

Molly's momentary elation of holding up her eviction in court vanished. She didn't want to make any trouble for Mr. Detman. It wasn't his fault she couldn't make ends meet.

"The new tenant in 12B left a bunch of boxes in the carport. You're welcome to them."

He handed her an envelope.

"Thank you," she said.

Thank you?

"And don't worry about that chewy toy," Mr. Detman said, as he walked away. "You should save your money."

Molly spotted her words of affirmation. They seemed so childish. As if words could save her. She slapped her own hand in anger.

She put her key in the door. Today had started so well. A helicopter ride with Quinn. Finding the secret tree house. And now this. Couldn't things go her way for more than a few hours at a time? She put her head against the door and cried.

She was so tired of crying; she was so tired of worrying.

She was so tired.

She let herself into the apartment, but she hesitated before turning on the lights. Her electric bill was seriously delinquent, and she was parceling out electricity as if it were caviar. In the dark, she could hear Galileo rustling around. She braced herself for one of his insults, but he must have heard her crying outside the door, because instead he greeted her with her father's sweet rendition of the soothing Irish classic "Too Ra Loo Ra Loo Ra."

The tears came hotter and faster.

Chapter 9

Molly had gone to sleep hoping that things would appear less dismal in the morning.

They didn't.

Galileo had gotten over his wave of empathy and woke up swearing. Trying to sort out what she should do and where should she go, Molly fed him in a daze. She tried out a few different scenarios on the African Grey.

"We could fight the eviction," she offered.

Galileo looked at her sideways.

"I know," Molly sighed. "I mean, it's not Mr. Detman's fault I haven't paid the rent. Why should he be punished?"

Galileo turned his feathered back on her.

"I know it's not my fault either," Molly pleaded. "I don't know why I can't make ends meet."

She chopped up a carrot for him,

"We could go back to Iowa," Molly said. "Mom would be thrilled to see us."

Galileo ruffled his feathers.

"Okay, she'd be thrilled to see me," Molly rephrased.

Molly's mom was not Galileo's biggest fan. Besides, Molly hadn't exactly left home with her family's full confidence. Curly never seemed to make a mistake, while Molly's throw-stuff-against-the-wall-and-see-what-sticks approach to life had served up her share of failures. Her family would be happy to have her home, she knew that. But there would be whispers of "Oh, poor Molly," which she couldn't stand to even contemplate.

She needed another plan.

Molly could tell she needed to come up with her positive words or her mood was going to tank. She closed her eyes and inhaled. She let out her breath slowly and evenly.

"Inhale, exhale. Inhale, exhale," she commanded herself.

The words floated into her mind.

Resilience.

Spirit.

Agility.

She opened her eyes. Agility! That's exactly what she needed. She pictured herself as a running back, dodging the tribulations of life.

Eviction—dodge left.

Car troubles—dodge right.

Thesis stalled—

Her breath caught. She tried to imagine not being tackled by this one and determinedly kept the goal in sight. Molly visualized her victory but could feel the other team bearing down on her. She tried to keep her mind focused, but she felt her victory slipping away as she rummaged through her purse looking for a pen. She couldn't get positivity on her hand fast enough.

"Where's my damn pen?" Molly called out in frustration, dumping her purse on the table.

"Bite me!" Galileo squawked.

For such an unpleasant bird, Galileo hated conflict.

"Sorry," Molly muttered, pawing through the flotsam and jetsam.

The contents of her purse, strewn across the table, were glaring evidence of her disorganized life. There were four tubes of lip gloss, scraps of paper with ideas for her tree house, more scraps of paper with doodles for concepts she wanted to share with Bale, at least five pounds of pennies, and a set of keys she'd never seen before.

She picked up the keys. She studied them in a patch of bright sunlight flooding through the window, hoping the intense brightness would make the keys give up their secrets. She turned them over in her hand several times.

Then she remembered.

These were the keys to Crabby's restaurant.

Crabby's.

Closed.

Unused.

Vacant.

Restaurant.

She held them up to Galileo in triumph.

"I know where we can go!"

* * * *

Orchestrating a tiny house migration from Cobb, Kentucky, and back again took all of Bale's concentration. After the last of the tiny houses were returned to the lot, the houses stabilized, and the drivers paid, Bale finally had a moment to relax. He let himself into the office. Thor scooted in ahead of him. By the time Bale snapped on the light, Thor was already curling up in his favorite chair. Bale took a seat behind his desk, which was only clean for moments at a time. He always cleared both his literal and virtual desktops before leaving town. As soon as he returned, chaos reigned again.

He dropped his messenger bag in front of him and started emptying it. He pulled out his sketchbook full of the new ideas that usually sprung up right before he fell asleep. Several of the younger tiny house builders told him he should get a laptop with drawing capabilities, but Bale couldn't see any advantage to that. It was hard enough to wake up enough to draw a simple sketch, let alone be laptop conversant enough to render any kind of useful image.

The fact that Molly also used an honest pencil and pad gave him the courage of his convictions. Of course, she was making her thesis tree house model from some newfangled medium, but he felt he could still hold his head high as long as someone legitimate was still drawing on paper.

He tried to shove Molly from his thoughts.

He rummaged in one of the deep pockets of his bag. He pulled out a fistful of business cards and stacked them. He might not be ready to tackle computer drawing, but he was a master of the virtual Rolodex. On top of the pile, he saw a white card with a background of barely visible purple flowers. He studied it.

Violet Green
"Have Sphygmomanometer, Will Travel"
Phone: 202-555-0166
Email: VGreen@green.name

He had no idea what a sphygmomanometer was but figured anyone who needed a traveling nurse might be amused. He went to type in her information but couldn't stand it. He googled "sphygmomanometer" and found it was a fancy name for a blood pressure monitor.

"Cute idea," he thought.

He typed in "How to Pronounce Sphygmomanometer" and practiced saying it a few times. If he ever saw Violet again, he might impress her by knowing how to say it.

His phone vibrated, making a racket on the desk. Papers jumped in surprise and the stack of business cards toppled in surrender. Thor blearily lifted his head, saw there was no need for action, and went back to sleep. Bale looked at the phone. It was a text from Molly.

Molly: A little bird told me you were back in town. When can I see you?

Bale sat back in his swivel chair, staring at the phone in his right hand. He had Violet's card in his left. Maybe now would be a good time to move on? Stop torturing himself about Molly? Maybe he shouldn't do anything—he'd been unlucky in love. The one time he threw caution to the wind, he got burned. Not that the woman, whose name was Summer, did anything wrong... Their relationship was new, and she was just still in love with someone else. She let Bale down very gently.

But let down he had been.

He stared at the phone.

A woman he was in love with was in love with somebody else...that seemed to be the story of his life.

He texted back.

Bale: Pretty busy right now. Chat soon.

Chapter 10

Calm
Vision
Foresight

In the morning Molly found herself weirdly calm at the prospect of moving out of her apartment and into Crabby's. She hummed as she stirred a pot of chicken double noodle soup. It was as if she'd spent so much time trying to make ends meet—while knowing deep down that was never going to happen—that, weirdly, the eviction letter seemed to free her. She was proud of herself. She hadn't panicked—or, at least, she hadn't panicked for long. And now she had a plan. True, it was a plan that involved trespassing, but it was a plan nonetheless. There would be no more lying awake at night wondering what she was going to do.

"We're going to make this work," Molly said to Galileo.

"Amen, brother," Galileo replied.

Molly was about to correct him, but she saved her breath. If she had to cure Galileo of saying "Bite me," "Shit," or "Amen, brother," a gender mix-up seemed the least of her concerns. Galileo looked at her sideways, a look Molly knew meant he was waiting for her to correct him. She bit her tongue. Her father had taught the bird lots of attention-getting sentences, everyone laughing every time the bird cursed. She'd read that not rising to the bait would (possibly) stop the African Grey from uttering antisocial comments. But it was all a crapshoot. Besides, if she had to stop just one of Galileo's utterances, it would be "I love you, Quinn."

And she couldn't blame that one on her father.

As she sat on the couch sipping the mug of steaming soup, she looked around the apartment. She couldn't just walk away, leaving poor Mr. Detman holding the bag—or bags. This was a small town. People would talk. She'd have to make it look as if she had a place to go. That meant she'd have to pack everything she'd accumulated since she'd arrived in Cobb and move it to Crabby's. Doing that without raising a few local eyebrows wouldn't be easy. Her mood plummeted as she took inventory. How had she accumulated all this stuff? When she moved to Cobb, she had one suitcase full of clothes and Galileo in a small traveling cage with an expanding perch. Every pot, dish, lamp, and pillow—not to mention Galileo's enormous cage—had been carefully chosen since her arrival in Kentucky.

She could feel the tension in her shoulders mounting but pushed the anxiety aside. There would be plenty of room for everything at Crabby's. She wouldn't be homeless forever.

Tears sprung to her eyes.

Did she actually just think that word?

Homeless?

She took deep breaths as she considered the implications. There was no way around it... She would be "minus"—or "less"—a home. She closed her eyes. Would Crabby's be her new home? She decided she could provide a safe place for Galileo and herself—and that was all that really mattered. She'd have four walls—and a walk-in refrigerator.

She made a note to go get those boxes Mr. Detman had mentioned.

She turned her attention to the tree house model sitting on the coffee table, limbs patiently outstretched, waiting for attention. She studied it. She still loved her steampunk design, but her foray into the tree house on Quinn's farm made her look at the model with new eyes. When Molly was in the tree, looking out over Cobb, the simplicity of the lean-to and platform made Molly feel as if she were part of the tree. Even though she had taken down the safety railing on her model and replaced it with a transparent material, her tree house, with its turrets and curved porches, felt heavy—a foreign object in a forest. She stood up and walked around the model, trying to decide what she could alter. She thought she should make all the windows bigger, letting in more light. She took a tiny knife and cut away at some of the windows. That was a good start! She felt she should go for broke and decided to add another level to the model. She grabbed her sketchpad and added a widow's walk as high as she could make it. She'd perfect the addition on paper, then add it to the model later.

She envisioned a tiny room where you could feel as if you were part of the earth's plan.

Her phone, attached to a power cord across the room, rang. *It must be Bale*, she thought as she dashed to retrieve it. She hadn't heard from him in…forever. She couldn't imagine what could be keeping him away. He must be super busy. It wasn't like him not to be in touch.

It flashed through her mind that he had always seen her at Crabby's, when he popped in for breakfast after returning from a show. Was it possible their friendship would end now that she was over at Quinn's? The thought stabbed surprisingly deep.

The phone continued to ring. She yanked it from the cord and looked down at the screen.

It was her brother, Curly. Molly smiled. She'd been avoiding calls from home, afraid she'd blab about her lousy situation. But now that she had a grasp of the immediate future, she wouldn't have to out-and-out lie.

"Hey," Molly said.

"Hey," Curly said. "How are things with you and Galileo?"

"Couldn't be better," Molly said.

She frowned. Did she have to *start* with an out-and-out lie? What was wrong with her?

"You've been pretty quiet since you said you lost your job at Crabby's."

"I didn't say I lost my job." Molly bristled.

This is why she started with a lie. Her family always walked on the dark side.

"You didn't?"

"No. Not at all. The restaurant closed. That's very different."

"Except for the money part. The money part is exactly the same."

"Whatever," Molly snorted.

She hated when she resorted to "whatever."

"So what's up with you now?" Curly asked.

"Oh, lots," Molly said. "I'm moving to a…a different place…and I got a new job. It's really fun. I'm outside all day and we never work past dark."

"Wow! That is lots!"

Her brother sounded so happy for her. She could feel herself warming to their conversation. She knew her brother wouldn't exactly judge her if she told him the truth, but he never seemed to have a misstep, and her life was one blunder after another. How could she tell him she was about to be homeless and had no idea how much money she was going to make?

She prayed he'd change the subject.

"How is the tree house going?"

"It's good," Molly said. "Working at the tree farm has given me new inspiration."

"Don't get distracted and start making all kinds of changes," Curly counseled. "You know how you get."

"How do I get?"

She stared at the model with the new transparent safety rail and larger windows, avoiding even looking at the new addition sketched out on the notepad.

"You get distracted and then don't follow through," Curly said.

"You sound like Mom."

"Yeah. So? You sound like Dad, always living in a dream world."

Ever since they were kids, sibling arguments usually dissolved into the two of them hurling insulting comparisons to their parents.

"Whatever," Molly said. "How are things with you?"

"Great."

Of course they were.

"Got a promotion at work," he said.

"That's good," she said.

Molly felt a slight tingling in her stomach. Maybe he had money to burn. Maybe she could tell him she was in dire straits.

"Yeah," he said. "Bought a little condo. Finally. Of course, I don't have a red cent left, but I'm in the game, you know?"

Molly didn't know. She was so far from the game she couldn't even see the players.

"Congratulations," Molly said. "I'm happy for you."

She tried to tamp down any less-than-kind feelings. "Envy," "resentment," and "bitter" were not words she wanted to associate with. It wasn't Curly's fault nothing ever went wrong in his life.

"Do you want to talk to Galileo?" Molly asked.

"Sure," Curly laughed. "Put me on speaker."

Molly tapped the speaker icon and walked over to the African Grey's cage.

"Say hi to Curly," Molly said, holding up the phone.

"Bite me!" Galileo said.

Curly imitated a rooster. Galileo cocked his head, then repeated the sound. Curly cheeped like a tiny chick, and Galileo responded in kind. Curly barked like a dog.

Galileo looked at Molly.

"Oh, he wants a reward," Molly said, handing Galileo a sunflower seed.

"Diva," Curly said.

Molly quickly tapped the speaker off. The last thing she needed was for Galileo to start a stream of profanity the neighbors might hear.

"Okay, gotta go," Curly said.

"Thanks for calling," Molly said.

"Look Mols… I know you're getting your master's and you're pretty much stuck there in Kentucky…"

"I'm not *stuck* in Kentucky!" Molly said hotly.

"That's not what I meant. All I'm saying is, you're welcome to come home anytime. Okay?"

"Okay. Thanks."

"Whatever," Curly said—and hung up.

Whoever got in the last "whatever" won.

Molly put the phone down. She sat on the couch, hugging her knees. She thought about the conversation with her brother. As much as she hated to admit it, she knew Professor Cambridge wasn't big on changes to an approved design (not that he ever really approved of her design to begin with). She pictured his sour face as she presented her new ideas. But she knew in her bones she was on the right path. She hadn't felt confident in her design for months, and it felt good to be back on track.

She picked up her notepad as she mentally switched gears. She flipped to a clean page and started to map out the floor plan of Crabby's. She was surprised to find, even though she'd worked there for years, she couldn't visualize every inch of the place. She'd seen enough movies to know you had to have a map of the place down cold before you broke in.

Not that she was breaking in.

She had a key.

She set her phone alarm for pre-dawn. She chose the "Chicken Dance" as her wake-up music. Turning the volume to high, she returned the phone to its charger out in the living room. She knew from experience that having to get out of bed and turn off the "Chicken Dance" was less painful than trying to ignore it and get a few more seconds of sleep.

Molly thought she had just closed her eyes when the "Chicken Dance" started playing. She vaulted from the bed and ran to the phone, panting as she shut it off. She and Galileo stared at each other, Molly daring him to burst into song.

She won.

She quickly brushed her teeth, brushed her hair into a ponytail, threw on a baseball cap, dressed in dark clothes, fed Galileo, and tiptoed to the door. As she closed it, she heard Galileo start to sing.

It was the "Chicken Dance" melody, of course.

"Bite me," she whispered hoarsely as she locked the door behind her. She'd have that song in her head all day!

Molly made her way to her car, unlocked it, and slid behind the wheel. She'd taken the car's behavior as an indicator of the day ahead. Car starts, good day. Car coughs and dies, bad day. Her car started.

She made her way through the darkened street to Crabby's. She looked right and left, making sure she had the road to herself. She realized she'd made this trip in the dark every time she opened the restaurant for breakfast, but it had never sent her pulse racing as it did now.

Just pretend you are on your way to Crabby's like it's any other day.

This bending reality was new for her. It wasn't really encouraged in civil engineering. She wondered if she should have chosen theater arts as a major instead.

Parking around back, Molly let herself into Crabby's office. She wanted to make sure she had electricity, so she snapped the light on and quickly off again. The office had a long wall of windows, but they faced the river, so she felt she was pretty safe with a momentary flicker. She closed the curtains and quickly opened them again. What if someone noticed the difference? She used her phone's flashlight to look around. She knew the office pretty well, but she was certainly looking at it with a new objective. She wanted to stay as hidden as possible. Even though it had a perfectly serviceable couch, she was worried that the windows would present a problem. Anyone strolling down the footpath by the river could see into that room.

Maybe she could crawl onto the couch after dark? She should have a plan B just in case.

She walked through the dining room, kitchen, walk-in refrigerator and freezer, garage, and storage areas.

The storage area had no windows. She found a nook around a corner in the storage area. You'd have to be exploring the entire place before you'd look here! It would be the perfect place to hide her stuff—Galileo and herself. If she found she didn't have the nerve to use the couch, she had an unopened, inflatable pool float she could use for sleeping.

She locked the door and returned to her apartment, full of purpose. She rummaged through the hall closet, looking for the pool float. The only reason she'd purchased it was that it had a large parrot on it, and she couldn't resist.

She wondered if Galileo would be unhappy in a dark storage area for… she didn't know how long. Could she move him into a hidden but more light-filled area of the place during the day?

What if someone heard him?

The calmness that had settled over her started to slip away. She'd have to play it by ear, she decided. One of the few good things about having a talking pet was that he would not hesitate to announce his dissatisfaction.

She heard Galileo moving back and forth on his perch.

"Have I been ignoring you?" Molly asked.

"Bite me," the African Grey said.

Molly stretched and walked over to the cage. She held out a sunflower seed. He took it in his toes and swiftly cracked the hull with his beak. While he was busy munching, Molly looked at the cage in dismay. How was she going to get this monster cage out of the apartment and into Crabby's? She couldn't ask anyone she knew to help or her secret would be out. Galileo didn't really need his fancy cage—he spent most of his time with the door open, hanging out on the perch. For an ornery bird, he really was well trained about staying where he was supposed to be. She knew he'd be fine with downsizing, but she was sure he liked the aesthetics of the cage as much as she did.

One drama at a time, she told herself.

She went to the parking area and picked up several boxes. Returning to her apartment, she passed several neighbors. The boxes raised eyebrows and there were lots of questions. Molly made up answers as she went along. By the time she'd reached her front door, she had created her story:

She was moving to a less expensive apartment over near Burgoo, she said. This news was greeted by sympathetic or annoyed eye rolls from neighbors, who agreed their apartments here were overpriced. Now that she was working with Quinn (always looking for a place to slip in his name), it was only twenty-five minutes more to drive to the tree farm. Lots of people drove that far. And besides, she'd added with a toss of her ponytail, even though starting her car was still a crapshoot, if for some reason it didn't start, she could always give Quinn a shout and he'd pick her up in the helicopter.

She realized she might have gone too far with that last statement, but she was building her fantasy life, and in that Quinn was center stage.

Chapter 11

Determination
Fortitude
Grit

Molly knew her new words were going to have to sustain her through several busy days. Mornings were spent packing the apartment box by box, loading the trunk of her car, and taking things surreptitiously to Crabby's. Crabby actually had a shower in the bathroom off the office. She knew she would have to use water sparingly. She wouldn't want the water bill to go up on her account.

She had *some* pride.

There were more immediate problems. She still wasn't sure what she was going to do with Galileo's cage—she thought about trying to push it down the street in the middle of the night, but Crabby's was five miles away. It didn't seem likely that no one would notice.

She made sure she arrived at the tree farm in plenty of time to accompany Quinn for a helicopter ride over his spread, dipping deep into the trees and pointing out the work she'd done the day before. Then they'd hop over to Burgoo, grab breakfast and coffee-to-go for Manny, and she'd return to her work on the farm.

She always spent time in her secret spot, the lean-to in the towering evergreen she now thought of as her tree fort. She never tired of watching the land and trees below her and the river lazily winding off to her right side. She'd also repaired an ancient rope hoist that could carry heavy bundles from the ground into the tree. Not that she needed a hoist. It was just good to figure out the mechanics of the thing. Civil engineers were like that.

Although from her perch in the tree she was looking down at the earth, she couldn't really compare the sensation of sitting quietly by herself in the tree fort to flying over the land with Quinn in the helicopter. Zipping through the air at dizzying speeds with Quinn was electrifying, while sitting alone in the tree fort was soothing and contemplative. She'd brought a sketchbook and spent her lunch hour drawing.

Bale would drift through her mind. It had been almost a week since he'd come back to town. She should stop by his lot as soon as she was settled at Crabby's. She wasn't proud of it, but she'd also brought a pair of binoculars to the lean-to. She brought them to keep an eye on Quinn down at the office, but found, to her astonishment, that she could also see all the way to Bale's Tiny Dreams lot. She could see him playing fetch with Thor, greeting potential customers, and working in his shop. Nothing out of the ordinary. Except he seemed to be avoiding her.

She stopped at Gilbert's Groceries for supplies. One good thing about hiding out in a deserted restaurant: there were plenty of cabinets and lots of refrigerator space. She'd decided that there would be no cooking—she knew the aromatic smells wafting out of Crabby's would draw the locals like bees to flowers. But she could load up on fruit, juices, cheese, crackers, lunch meat, bread, almond milk, and cereal.

By the time she needed to vacate tomorrow, she'd only have the tree house model and Galileo to relocate.

And that damned cage.

As she loaded her groceries onto the conveyor belt, a familiar voice asked:

"Do you want to purchase any bags?"

Molly looked up. It was Manny. What was he doing here? He was wearing a crisp white shirt that said "Gilbert's Groceries."

"Hey, Manny," Molly said.

"Hey, Mols," he said. "So, do you want to buy a bag?"

Buy? A? Bag? Molly's couldn't wrap her brain around the inquiry. There were so many more important questions right now. Such as: Why was her new coworker at Quinn's moonlighting as a bagger at the local grocery store?

She tried to focus.

"No thanks," she said, pulling her backpack from her shoulders and handing it to him. "I can put everything in here."

Manny nodded, and started stuffing her purchases into the lime-green backpack. She quickly eyed her groceries as they were swallowed up by the gaping drawstring mouth, wondering if anything screamed that her lifestyle was about to change.

The groceries seemed innocent enough.

She paid with her credit card, holding her breath while the cash register's computer took its time deciding if the transaction was going to be approved.

It was. She let out her breath and returned her focus to Manny. Life was certainly one adventure after another when you had no money.

"Can you take a break for a minute?" Molly asked suddenly.

Manny looked at Doris, the ancient cashier with her bright red lipstick perpetually partying in the fine lines around her mouth. Doris shrugged. Manny appeared to take that as approval, and he paid the shrug forward. Molly shouldered her backpack and they left the store together.

"What's new?" Molly asked, hoping Manny would jump in with some specifics to her vague inquiry.

More shrugging.

"I mean," Molly asked impatiently, "why aren't you working at Quinn's?"

"I am working at Quinn's," Manny said. "But I… I never asked how much money I was going to make. Got my first paycheck two days ago and…"

Molly bit her lip. She hadn't asked either. It seemed rude somehow. Besides, it couldn't be less than they made at Crabby's.

"It's less than we made at Crabby's," Manny said. "Without the tips… way less."

"We'll get tips when the busy season starts," Molly offered.

She knew she was grasping at straws.

"That's six months from now," he said. "So I got another part-time job here. It's not ideal, but with the two gigs, I can make the rent, food…you know."

She did know.

"I guess I'll find out what I'm making when I see Quinn next," Molly said.

This statement seemed to brighten Manny's mood.

"Oh, you didn't ask either? Cool, I thought I was the only loser."

"No. You're not the only loser."

Manny shrugged again and went back into Gilbert's. Molly got in her car—which started—and headed up to Crabby's, her mind reeling. Even with the news that she might not be making as much money as she'd hoped, she refused to be distracted and kept her wits about her. She waited until nobody was on the road and then pulled into the parking lot, steering quickly around back to hide her car. As she turned off the motor, a thought jumped into her head.

She smacked the steering wheel.

"Damn it!" she said.

She forgot to get a copy of her one key. She didn't want to get a copy made in town, in case anyone might ask her what she was doing. Thinking back over her life, she could not remember one instance when anyone had ever questioned her about getting a key made, but you could never be too careful in a situation like this. She thought about getting a copy in Burgoo, but she was always with Quinn when in Burgoo, so that wasn't going to happen.

She could always get a key made tomorrow.

Not that she really needed a spare. One thing about having Curly as an older brother: she'd learned all kinds of practical things—like picking a lock. Not that Curly would ever use his powers for evil.

Was she evil, using Crabby's without permission?

Best not to go there.

She opened the trunk of her car and started to unload her boxes. She let herself into the back, balancing her boxes on one knee while she hit the light switch. The storage unit flooded with light. She dropped off one of the boxes and headed to the kitchen with the groceries.

She'd just stepped through the door between the back storage area and the hallway that led to the kitchen when the lights suddenly went out.

Molly froze.

She quietly put the grocery bag on the ground.

I'm glad I brought the nonperishables. If I have to make a run for it, at least I won't leave fresh food that would attract ants—or worse.

She listened. She could hear footsteps outside, but no voices. She flattened herself against the wall as she saw one of the door handles jiggle. Then she heard sounds she couldn't identify: a quick clank followed by a heavy swoosh and a snap. She heard the same rotation a few more times around the building.

Clank!

Swoosh!

Snap!

As the sound got further away, Molly crawled to the nearest window. Kneeling on the floor, she lifted her eyes to window level and peeked out.

Molly sat back against the wall, hyperventilating.

It was Quinn. He was making his way around the building, attaching heavy-duty locks to all the doors and windows! Molly had to get out before she was locked in.

She crawled along the floor, mentally saying goodbye to twenty dollars' worth of crackers and cereal, and headed for the back door. She glanced in at her possessions hidden in the back corner of the storage unit. Unless

Quinn was doing a thorough inspection of the place, her stuff was probably safe for now.

She leapt out the back door just as Quinn made his way around the building, several U-shaped locks draped over his arm like a bunch of gaudy S&M bracelets. One look at the locks and Molly knew her lock-picking skills would never measure up. There was nowhere to hide. Quinn was looking right at her.

"Hey, Molly," he said. "What are you doing here?"

"I'm..." Molly had to think of something quickly.

What the hell could she possibly be doing up here? Except...

"I was looking for you," she said.

Quinn gave her his lopsided smile. She knew the answer made no sense, but Quinn did love to talk about himself.

"Well, you found me," he said.

"Yeah, I guess I did," she said. "Well, I've got to go."

Molly took a stepped to her car, but Quinn stepped in front of her. She looked into his heart-stopping eyes.

"What did you want?" he asked.

"Want?"

"Yes. You said you were looking for me. You must have wanted something?"

Molly thought this could all be an amazingly seductive conversation if she were somebody else, but right now, she could feel perspiration starting to circle her underarms and down her spine. She couldn't have willed an enticing comment if her life depended on it.

"Oh," Molly said. "Yes. I guess that's true. I must want something."

Quinn waited, locks clenched on his forearm.

"Do you want me to guess?" Quinn asked with a smile.

"No! I was looking for you so I could give you *this*..."

She held out the key, covering her bets should Crabby ever mention giving it to her. Quinn took it, looking at it disdainfully.

"I can't believe my uncle relied on this little key to secure his restaurant," Quinn said, shaking his head. "The old goat."

"Yeah," Molly said. "What an old goat."

She felt disloyal, but what could she do?

"I have to get this place locked up," Quinn said. "I heard rumors that lights were going off and on here. I want to make sure some homeless guy doesn't take this place being empty as an opportunity to squat."

Squat.

Molly cringed. What a horrible word.

Molly stood rooted to the spot.

"Anything else?" Quinn asked.

Molly decided she might as well go for broke.

"Yes," she said. "I saw Manny today. He says he needed to get a part-time job at Gilbert's."

"So he said."

"So…I was wondering…since I've been working for you for two weeks myself…"

"If I was going to pay you? And how much?"

Molly gulped.

"Yes," she squeaked.

"How much do you need?" Quinn asked, pulling out a roll of bills from his pocket.

"I don't know." Molly stared at the money. "I was hoping for…"

She paused. What could she ask for?

"I want you to be happy, Molly," Quinn said, peeling off several bills. "I worry about you."

He handed her the money.

"I better get going," Molly said. "Thanks for the money, Quinn."

"No problem," Quinn said. "I had a good night last night at the tables. Happy to spread the love, you know?"

Molly got in the car. She counted the crisp Benjamin Franklins in her hand.

She started the engine and headed out of the parking lot. Her first paycheck wouldn't cover the back rent, but she might be able to rent a room somewhere for Galileo and herself. She looked sadly at the restaurant in the rearview mirror as Quinn made his way around, locking every possible entrance.

Unless Quinn discovered her stuff in the storage area.

She decided to stop and see Bale. Driving across town, she found herself following a violet Ford F-150 truck. Molly knew the truck didn't belong to a local and she could see that there was a woman behind the wheel. She watched as the truck turned ahead of her into Bale's Tiny Dreams.

The way Bale snapped to attention when he saw the truck didn't look as if this were business as usual.

Molly drove past the lot.

Chapter 12

Molly was frantic by the time she pulled in to her apartment complex. By tomorrow night, she needed to hand Mr. Detman the keys—or fight the eviction. She knew she could buy herself some time, but the eviction was totally valid. She was over three months late with the rent. It was easy to make excuses for storing stuff at Crabby's ("It's not hurting anybody") and taking cash instead of a payroll check ("I can settle with the IRS at the end of the year"), but she just didn't want to keep chipping away at her ethical core.

But she had nowhere to go.

Molly opened her trunk and looked inside. She had the perishable groceries, the inflatable pool float, food for Galileo, her binoculars, and a heap of clothes and two large beach towels. Upstairs, she had Galileo in his oversized cage, a portable cage and perch, and her tree house model. That was it.

Maybe she should consult a lawyer? Try to stay in the apartment? But all her stuff was at Crabby's. There didn't seem to be any real solution. A voice startled her out of her deliberation.

"Hi, Molly."

It was Mr. Detman.

Just looking at him made her feel guilty.

"Hi, Mr. Detman," she said.

"Are you all set?" he asked in his hangdog way. "For tomorrow?"

Molly decided she needed to make a decision here and now. She basically wanted to say, "Bite me," but knew that wouldn't solve anything. She wasn't exactly sure what she was going to say, but finally—looking down at "Determination," "Fortitude," and "Grit" still a ghost on her hand—she made her decision.

"Yes," she said. "I'll be leaving first thing in the morning."

Why had she said that? She needed all the time she could get.

"I mean," she quickly backtracked, "I'll be leaving after work tomorrow. If that's okay with you."

"That's fine," Mr. Detman said. "I wish things could have worked out differently."

"Me too."

Boy, was that the understatement of the year.

Mr. Detman turned to leave. Molly slammed her trunk and called after him.

Was she really going to say this?

"Mr. Detman, I was wondering if you might be able to keep the big cage for me for a while. I don't have room for it...."

She was about to say "in my new place," but decided "I don't have room for it" worked just fine.

"Seriously?"

"Yes. I think Romeo and Lancelot would love it."

"I'm sure they would," Mr. Detman said, sounding as shocked as Molly felt. "That's very kind of you. And I understand it's just on loan until—"

"Exactly," Molly cut him off. "I'll leave the cage and the keys when I... when I finish moving out tomorrow. Thanks."

"Thank you! I can't wait to tell the boys. Maybe they'll come around a little more when I show them their new digs."

Molly's heart squeezed. What was she going to do with Galileo? He hated the small cage.

Mr. Detman disappeared into the complex. Molly grabbed some cheese and the inflatable float and headed up to her apartment to face the music.

And her African Grey.

She flicked on the light and stared at Galileo. She didn't have the heart to tell him the bad news. She gave him a few sunflower seeds along with his nightly vegetables, knowing full well that when she uprooted his life, he would not remember this goodwill gesture.

* * * *

The sun found the weak spot in Molly's blackout curtains and poked her in the eye with a long slender ray. Molly sat up, aware immediately that this was her final morning in a real bed. As she thought about the words she would write on her hand on her very last morning in the apartment, she paused to choose them carefully. She knew she needed words that would spur her to action—nothing wishy-washy like "Kindness" or "Laughter." She needed robust words that would get her facing her challenges fearlessly.

Fearless.

That was a good word.

She followed up with:

Motivated.

She had to stay strong and motivated. This wasn't an easy task considering what a train wreck her life was right now. Even if she was facing an uphill battle. She just needed to think outside the box. She looked at her hand. To fit "Thinking outside the box," she'd have to start writing at her elbow. "Think outside the box"? "Think outside box"? She bit her bottom lip in frustration. She needed to think outside the box right now! She smiled as she uncapped her pen. The word she needed was:

Innovative.

She looked down at her hand:

Fearless

Motivated

Innovative

They were exactly the words she needed.

"Get ready for an adventure," she called to Galileo as she headed out the door.

"Amen, brother," Galileo said from his perch.

Molly felt guilty that she used such an upbeat tone, hoping to fool Galileo with false cheer. African Greys were among the most intelligent of birds and easily picked up on human emotion. If Galileo understood that Molly was giving away his beautiful cage, he'd be cursing like a sailor.

Molly made sure she was at the tree farm early, in case Quinn wanted to head over to Beamer's for breakfast. It was impossible to tell when Quinn would show up. He prided himself on being "flexible with time."

He was standing by Old Paint, one foot up on the landing skid. He smiled as she pulled in front of the office. She got out of the car as nonchalantly as she could.

"Hey, Quinn," she said.

"Up for a ride?"

* * * *

Flying above the countryside with Quinn made everything better. They never talked in Old Paint, just exchanged appreciative glances as they pointed out the sun glinting off the river or chestnut-colored thoroughbreds racing across a blue-green field. Life always seemed surreal when she was with Quinn. It was only when she was literally set back on earth that the reality of her life smacked her upside the head.

"The usual?" called Marni, Beamer's redheaded waitress.

Quinn nodded with a grin and a thumbs-up as he escorted Molly to "their" table. Molly loved that she was getting to be a regular. It crossed her mind that at the end of day today, she and Galileo would be out on their ears, but thanks to Quinn she had enough money to get a hotel room for a day or two, until she could figure things out.

"So, Molly," Quinn said as the coffee was poured.

Molly stiffened. He sounded very serious. Was he going to ask her for a date? At least, a more official date than Beamer's?

"Wow, the coffee is really hot this morning," Molly stalled, suddenly nervous. "Maybe some cream will cool it down."

Molly asked Quinn to pass the bowl of creamers. She usually stayed away from highly processed food items, but this appeared to be an emergency.

"Oh, they have French vanilla," she said, wagging a little cup of creamer at Quinn. "My favorite."

Quinn sat looking at her, tattooed arms folded across his chest. Marni set their breakfast plates down.

"Would you like anything else?" Marni asked.

"Not at the moment, beautiful," Quinn replied with a wink.

"Oh, you," she trilled. Marni flushed to match her hair. Her finger bounced off Quinn's arm as she poked his bicep.

Molly watched the interaction with interest. Quinn couldn't possibly be flirting with Marni, could he? She had to be a million years old—or at least fifty. Quinn flirted a lot. But Molly didn't take it seriously. After all, he wasn't having breakfast with anyone else. He wasn't flying in his helicopter with anyone else. He wasn't overpaying anyone else to identify stumps and plant seedlings.

"So, Molly..." Quinn began again when Marni had sashayed away.

"Yes," Molly said, then added, to show she understood this might be serious, "Quinn."

"You've done a great job with the seedlings and the transplants."

Oh my god! He's firing me!

* * * *

"This is a pleasant surprise," Bale said as Violet Green stepped out of her truck.

He was surprised how much he meant it. He had not expected to connect with her again so soon.

"I've got a new job in Tennessee," she said. "I thought I'd stop by on my way and check out your merchandise."

Bale opened his mouth and shut it again. He wasn't sure what to make of that statement. Was she flirting? Should he say something like, "What did you have in mind?" But maybe she wasn't being flirty. Maybe he should just be all business.

He really hated these situations.

"Come on into the office," he said.

That sounded safe enough.

She smiled. That seemed to be a good answer. As she locked her truck, Thor came bouncing up.

"Thor!" she said, kneeling down to Thor-level. They drenched each other with kisses. "How's my darling man? Did you miss me? I missed you."

Bale ran his fingers through his hair. Was she really talking about him, not Thor? He looked at his dog, who stared back at him, as if to say, "Get over yourself. This is about *me*."

Bale was more than willing to go with that. It made him much less nervous. As they threaded their way through the tiny houses, Violet seemed to appreciate every model they passed. Bale's nerves calmed. He could talk about tiny houses—why they were getting popular, what made his special—forever and never get tongue-tied. That was one of the reasons he felt so at home with Molly. There was always so much to talk about.

He tried to shove Molly from his mind. When she wouldn't go, he managed to visualize her heading into a maze that would at least keep her occupied for a few hours.

He turned his full attention to Violet.

Chapter 13

"Are you okay?" Quinn asked. "You're white as a ghost."

Molly could only nod.

"Do you need some water?" he asked.

"No," Molly said, hoarsely. "I'm fine. Really. So…we're done with the seedlings, huh?"

"Yep. Time to move on."

"Of course," Molly said. "I get that."

Breathe, breathe, breathe, Molly told herself.

"You know, once the big push of getting the seedlings and transplants is done…"

"You've got to prune—metaphorically."

"Exactly. I knew you'd understand."

"I do," she said. "I'm just surprised it's so soon."

"It really isn't that soon," Quinn said, adding sugar to his coffee. "In June, we need to start pruning the trees over two feet tall, so they grow into the perfect shape for a Christmas tree."

"Wait," Molly said, putting her hand on Quinn's arm. "You're talking about pruning *trees*?"

"What else would I be talking about in June?"

Molly took her hand back. She knew Quinn must think she was acting strangely, but she wasn't about to blurt out that she thought he meant it was time to prune *her*! Why put any ideas in his head? She relaxed.

"I could help with that!"

"I don't think so," Quinn said.

The tiny whisper of hope evaporated like a soap bubble.

"I could! I can prune," Molly said. "Seriously. I…"

She tried to come up with some sort of skill she had that remotely translated to pruning Christmas trees but couldn't think of anything.

"It takes a trained eye and a practiced hand."

Molly looked down at the table. So he *was* firing her.

She still needed to be out of her place tonight, and now she wasn't going to have a paycheck. She was getting further and further behind on her tree house and she was not going to get any "pet owner of the year" award, not knowing how she was going to take care of Galileo.

How could her life suck this much?

"So I was thinking," Quinn interrupted her thoughts. "Maybe you might be into fir cone picking?"

"Fir cone…?"

"Fir cone picking," Quinn said, sipping his coffee. "You know what pine cones are, right?"

"I do."

"Pine cones grow on—wait for it…"

Molly smiled. She could happily wait all day.

"Pine cones grow on pine trees. Fir cones grow on—"

"Fir trees. See? I'm halfway there already," Molly said. She took a sip of coffee, then added, "I guess this is a dumb question—"

"Frankly, when it comes to Christmas trees, all questions are dumb. I mean, how are you supposed to take this line of work seriously?"

"I take it seriously."

"And that's why I love you."

Molly froze. Did Quinn just say he loved her? She wanted to jump across the table and say she loved him too, but he appeared to still be speaking. Had she even asked her question, "Why are we picking pine—or fir—cones in the first place?" She must have asked, because he was answering. She tried to focus on his words.

"It takes a ton of time, but cones sap energy from the trees. We need the trees to be focused on growing big and strong, so Daddy can turn a hefty profit."

Quinn rubbed his fingers and thumb together in the classic "money" gesture. Molly tried to smile. She realized someone would have to be out of his mind to work with trees all year long just for the love of it but she sometimes forgot that.

"And people don't want cones on their Christmas trees," Quinn added. "They're really sticky, especially the ones growing on the Fraser firs. And too many cones hog all the room for ornaments."

"I'd be happy to pick cones," Molly said. "That sounds fun."

She was telling the truth. Even though she was relieved to the point of turning into a puddle on Beamer's floor at still having her job, the thought of interacting with the trees on another level sounded wonderful.

"It can get pretty hairy," Quinn said. "Some of our Fraser firs are forty feet tall."

Molly was well aware of that. Her tree fort was in a Fraser.

"Oh, I know you've got some big trees on the property," Molly said, but stopped herself from going any further.

Why introduce *her* tree (and tree fort) into the conversation? Besides, she really wanted to get back to that "I love you" part.

"So…Quinn," Molly started in the most smoldering tone she could muster in a coffee shop at nine in the morning.

As she leaned toward him, Marni appeared with the check and the coffee pot.

"Fresh coffee," Marni preened. "I made it just for you."

"And that's why I love you." Quinn winked.

* * * *

"We've been talking for three hours," Bale said.

"Really? Oh, I'm so sorry," Violet said, pushing back the guest chair in Bale's office. "I didn't mean to take up so much of your time!"

"Not at all. It's just that my dog is looking at me like he's ready for some food."

Bale and Violet both looked at Thor, who stared blankly back at them.

"So, that's his 'I'm hungry' look?" she asked.

"That's pretty much his everything look," Bale said. "But I can read his every mood. Both of them."

Violet laughed.

She had a great laugh.

"Hang on while I feed this beast," Bale said.

As soon as Bale stood up, Thor thundered to his feet and raced to the door.

"He eats in the workshop," Bale called back to Violet. "I can meet you out in the lot if you want to check out some houses."

Violet gave him a thumbs-up and smiled.

She had a great smile.

Bale felt happier than he had in a long time. He loved to spread the joy around, so he skipped the dry food and gave Thor his favorite: stinky gourmet anchovy, sardine, and salmon mix. As soon as Thor dove in, Bale headed out to the lot to find Violet.

He studied her as she walked among his creations. She really seemed to appreciate the artistry in each one, touching the steel rivets on one house and the red flower boxes on another. A traveling nurse wasn't exactly the perfect match. On the other hand, Molly was always right around the corner, and that hadn't worked.

He stopped himself. He was getting better at not thinking about Molly but he certainly couldn't say he'd mastered it.

Violet must have felt his eyes on her, because Bale found her staring right at him.

"Can I buy you lunch?" he suddenly asked. "Thor isn't the only one who needs to eat. There isn't anything fancy in town, but…"

"Lunch sounds great!"

"Great. I'll get my keys."

"I've already got mine," Violet said, holding up her keys and jangling them.

"Sounds good to me."

Bale opened the driver's side of the purple truck, and watched Violet's long legs climb in. Violet snapped open the passenger-side lock and Bale slid in.

"Where to?" Violet asked. "You're the local."

"There's a good burger joint, Chinese, Indian, a microbrewery, and Thai."

"No pizza?"

"Pizza?"

"A traveling nurse can tell everything about a place by the pizza."

Did this mean she wanted to check the place out? He grinned.

"We have great pizza," he said. "Hang a left to Main Street, then turn right and go to the stop sign."

Violet pulled a pair of mirrored aviator sunglasses from the visor and slipped them on.

"Love the shades," Bale said.

"I know," Violet said, pulling onto the street. "Very badass, right?"

"My exact thought."

"You have to know how to take care of yourself when you're on the road as much as I am," Violet said. "Looking like a badass helps."

Bale nodded. He wondered if Violet liked being so independent. Or if she might, sometimes, want someone to take care of her. He looked over at her. Not that she gave any indication of needing any help.

He didn't have to give directions twice. As Violet headed confidently down Main Street, Bale spotted a car at the side of the road with the hood up. He closed his eyes and put his head back.

It was an old blue Buick Lucerne.
Molly.

* * * *

Molly stared down at the engine.
Why? Why? Why?
Now that she was a few bucks ahead, was her car going to eat it all?
"What seems to be the problem?" The familiar voice wrapped around her like a favorite old sweater.
"Bale!" Molly cried as she spun around. "Thank—"
She stopped, mid-exuberance.
The beauty in the purple truck was leaning against her vehicle, watching Bale.
Were they *together*?
"This doesn't look good," Bale said, indicating the engine.
"No, it doesn't," Molly said, unsure of what exactly she was referring to.
She and Bale stared deep inside the engine compartment.
"The car sounded like somebody was hammering on the engine," Molly said. "And there was smoke coming out the exhaust."
Even though he was not looking at her, she could practically feel Bale grimace.
"Get me a rag," he said. "I want to check the oil."
"I just put oil in it," Molly said. "I'm not that lame!"
"It still sounds like you ran out of oil."
Molly rummaged in the trunk until she unearthed a roll of paper towels she kept just for this purpose as well as a plastic bottle of oil. She handed them to Bale.
She waited until Bale turned to face her. He didn't need to tell her the car was in trouble. It was written all over his face.
"There's no oil," Bale said, showing her the dipstick. "I'm pretty sure the engine froze."
"Oh no," Molly said, staring at the dipstick, willing it to drip. "Can we just put some more oil in?"
"I think it might be worse than that."
Molly bit her lip.
"Look, Molly, I'm on my way to lunch with a client," he tilted his head slightly in the direction of Mama Long Legs. "But I can come help you out in an hour or so and we'll figure this out."
"I'm on my lunch break. I have to get back to work."

"I'm sure Violet wouldn't mind running you back to the farm before we have lunch," Bale's said, his eyes flicking to the woman standing by the truck.

Violet?

"Don't be silly," Molly said. "I'll call Quinn and just let him know I'll be late. I'm sure he'll be cool."

"Isn't he always?"

Molly looked down Main Street. There were certainly plenty of places she could kill an hour.

"Go ahead and have lunch," Molly said. "I'll be fine."

"You're sure?"

"Very sure," Molly said. "I'm just grateful you came by."

"You have my number if you need me."

Molly watched Violet's truck head down the street and stop in front of Pietro's Pizza. She watched Bale hold the door for Violet, putting his hand on the small of her back and guiding her inside. Molly thought this was highly unprofessional but stopped her disapproval when she thought of how many unprofessional fantasies she'd had about her employer at the Christmas tree farm. She blushed. Her scenarios started further along than a hand on the small of her back.

She realized she was hungry. And she did have an hour to kill. She thought about heading to the pizza parlor. But she decided a visit to the same place Bale was entertaining his...*client*...seemed a bit too desperate. She decided she'd better save her money until she found out what the car was going to cost. She fished around in the seats and pockets of the car, unearthing $4.27. Not enough for a pizza anyway. Deciding she didn't want to run into Manny, she popped into the little convenience store, choosing a giant ice cream sandwich and a bottle of iced tea that was on sale. As she took her selections to the front of the store, she was surprised to see a familiar face at the cash register. It was Naomi, looking exactly the same as when she worked at Crabby's, except she'd changed her bright red lipstick to a dazzling pink.

"Hey, Naomi," Molly said. "I didn't know you were working here."

"It's not Crabby's," Naomi said with a shrug. "But it's a job, right?"

"Right," Molly said.

"I hear you're over at Quinn's with Manny," Naomi said.

Molly frowned. She felt special working for Quinn. Adding "with Manny" to the equation dulled the sparkle.

"Yeah," Molly said. "It's a pretty sweet gig."

"I'll bet." Naomi arched a tweezed eyebrow. "That Quinn's a hottie."

Molly smiled.

Now that was more like it!

Molly sat on the hood of her car, watching for the purple truck to head in her direction. As soon as she saw the truck go into reverse and onto Main Street, Molly busied herself with her phone. She could hear the truck getting nearer. Molly tried to act as casual as she could, waiting for the truck to stop and Bale to come to her…she was thinking "rescue" but changed her mind to "aid." It made her feel less out of control.

But the truck didn't stop. It headed down the street and turned toward Bale's lot. Molly jerked her head up. Did Bale forget about her?

The crushing feeling that she was completely alone overwhelmed her. Tears sprang to her eyes. Okay, maybe she wasn't a long-legged beauty in super-tight jeans. And okay, maybe she wasn't even as alluring as Naomi with her pouty lips. But Bale was her friend. Wasn't he?

She stared down the street, bereft. The purple truck was almost out of sight.

Her phone vibrated in her hand. It was a text from Bale.

Bale: Going back to get my truck. I'll tow you over to Altro's A-Plus and we'll see what's up.

Molly wiped away the tears and smiled. He'd added two eyeballs, a brain, and a fountain pen.

Chapter 14

Violet pulled into the lot, rolling smoothly to a stop in front of Bale's. Thor shot out the office's doggy door, hurling himself against Bale's leg.

"I love that," Violet said. "The way a dog acts like he hasn't seen his human in ten years."

"I've been gone an hour," Bale said, kneeling down to receive Thor's adoration. "I think that's ten years in dog years."

"He's a good guy. I bet he's good company."

"He's the best," Bale said.

He immediately mentally kicked himself. Couldn't he have settled for "man's best friend" instead of insinuating that Thor was better company than she?

"You have any pets?" Bale asked, straightening up.

"Not right now. My job makes it impossible. I never know if I'm going to be able to find a pet-friendly building or not," Violet said, taking her turn at petting Thor. "That's one of the reasons a tiny house would be perfect for me. I miss having a dog."

Violet stood up. She and Bale were standing very close to each other. She stared at him frankly.

"I better get going," she said. "I've got a long drive. And you've got to go help your…"

She let the sentence dangle. It took a few seconds for Bale to understand he was meant to finish it.

"Oh!" he finally said. He looked up the road. "You mean Molly."

"Yes. You have to go help your Molly."

"She's a friend."

Violet arched a perfect eyebrow.

* * * *

"The piston rings are worn out and the oil burned with the gas. It just froze up," Albert Altro said, wiping his hands on a flashy pink rag. "The engine is going to have to be rebuilt."

"That sounds expensive," Molly said.

"It is expensive," Albert said.

She wished Bale was still with her. He'd said he'd stick around until she heard the diagnosis. As they walked to the waiting room, he told Molly he was leaving on another road trip with his tiny houses, but he really wasn't busy for the rest of the day. She stopped in her tracks.

"But you just got back," she said.

"This is a busy time of year," Bale said. "The road shows are getting more and more popular."

"But you just got back," Molly said. "Sorry, I know I just said that."

Molly felt a shimmer of doubt—why hadn't she seen him since he got back? Was he taking Violet with him? She shook off her thoughts. Violet wasn't any different from any other client.

Or was she?

"You don't have to wait," Molly said. "You must have a million things to do to get ready. With your new client."

"That's okay. Violet's committed to buying a tiny house from me, but it will be an ongoing process. She's on her way to Tennessee for a short-term nursing gig."

Tennessee. That was only one state over, but the distance sounded promising.

"She's in no rush," Bale continued. "We're going to stay in touch, so we can collaborate on the design."

"Is that all you're collaborating on?" Molly asked, shocked she'd used her outside voice.

"Pardon me?"

Luckily, she must have muttered, because Bale didn't seem to have understood her.

"Nothing," Molly said.

Bullet dodged!

"She really liked the steampunk model," Bale said, warming to his subject. "I gave you full credit for your ideas."

"Not necessary," Molly said, but she was happy he'd mentioned her.

"I think you'd really like her."

I don't want to like her.

"Glad to hear she's got good taste," Molly said.

Molly finally convinced Bale he didn't need to stay and, metaphorically, at least, hold her hand. She stood on her toes and kissed him on the cheek, surprising them both. Molly sighed as she watched him drive away. She was perfectly capable of standing on her own two feet, but she always felt better when he was around.

Bale was probably the best friend she'd ever had.

Molly returned her thoughts to Albert and the problem at hand.

"Now what do we do?" Molly asked Albert.

He shrugged. "I guess that's up to you."

"Is the car worth fixing?"

"The car hasn't been worth fixing since you've owned it," Albert said. "So I guess the question is, can you afford a new car?"

"No," Molly said. "Not even an old new car."

"Okay, then I guess we fix this one. You're in luck. I just took in a junker that happens to have a decent engine. I can drop it under your hood and have it for you in two days."

Molly swallowed hard. Not only did she not have the money to pay for an engine, she needed to get herself and Galileo out of the apartment tonight!

"Can I put this on credit?" Molly asked.

She knew this was a stupid question—who extended credit these days?

"Sure," Albert said. "I'll put it on your tab."

"I don't have a tab."

"You do now."

Apparently, people in small towns still trusted their neighbors.

"Thanks, Albert," Molly said, trying to control her shaky voice. "This means a lot."

"No problem." Albert smiled. He loved to do his New Jersey gangster impression and added, "I know where you live."

Not for long.

After tonight, *she* didn't even know where she lived.

"This is a huge relief," Molly said, pulling out her phone.

"And I can lend you a car," Albert said. "It's nothing fancy.... well, actually, compared to your car, it is fancy. Anyway, I can set you up."

Molly waved as she drove out of the shop in a nondescript beige car. She'd been vague in her phone call to Quinn, merely stating, "It's Molly. Can you give me a call?" She looked at the dashboard and located the clock. She wondered, in her disguised automobile, if she could probably sneak onto the tree farm without Quinn noticing she was two hours late coming back from lunch.

Her luck continued to hold. Quinn was nowhere to be found. Molly headed up to her tree fort, ready to study up on evergreen cones—pine, fir, and otherwise. She climbed up quickly, noticing the smattering of cones clustered around the base of the tree. She sat cross-legged, trying to focus on her Google search on Fraser firs. A little guilt crept in. Quinn wasn't paying her to study about cones, just to gather them. But Molly had always been a student of whatever she was working on. In the long run, she felt it made her better at whatever job she was tackling. She read on:

To grow evergreen from seed, gather large brown or slightly green cones. Cones should be closed. An open cone has probably already released its seed. She also noted that only female Frasers produced cones.

She tried to read more but found herself worrying about her own circumstances instead. She had a few hundred dollars in her pocket until next payday, but was it practical to spend any money on a hotel or renting a room when she was going to have to pay off an engine repair?

She found herself looking out over the beautiful view instead. Everything looked so different in the trees. The world looked so big. Bigger than it looked on the ground. And it didn't look anywhere near as scary from forty feet in the air. Everything just looked perfect. She relaxed as she took in the world below her. Her heartbeat slowed.

She wished she could stay here forever.

The thought hit her so suddenly, her phone almost toppled through a crack in the lean-to's flooring.

Of course! She and Galileo could stay here until she could figure things out.

She took out a pen and wrote on her hand. Her fingers trembled with excitement.

Imagination
Creativity
Resourceful

As she scrambled down the makeshift ladder, she tried to convince herself that this was a bad idea. She got as far as admitting it wasn't a sensible idea. There was no water, no electricity, there were holes in the roof and floor, there was no furniture. But for every argument against it, she had an answer. She'd take some of her cash and renew her membership at the gym, where she could shower. She'd charge her phone in the tree farm's office and in her car. Everybody did that! As far as electricity, she'd have to be careful about light anyway. Somebody noticing a bright spot in the trees after dark would be a sure giveaway. She was used to sitting in the lean-to for hours and never noticed the lack of furniture—and she had the blow-up pool float in the trunk of her...

She stopped climbing and froze. All her clothes and the pool float were in the trunk of her car at Altro's A-Plus. Could she stop and pick up her things without causing suspicion? She started down the ladder again. She'd have to risk it. The thought of living in the tree made her heart soar. And she was sure living there would be the best possible inspiration for her thesis.

She jumped in her loaner car and headed to Altro's.

She played over what she would say when she got there. Albert would probably say, "Hey, Molly. Forget something?" and she could launch right in to needing to get stuff out of her trunk. It would be ultra-casual.

Molly was happy to see the garage was still open. She waved to Albert as she pulled into the garage.

"Hey, Molly," Albert said.

So far so good.

"Couldn't stay away?" he teased.

Molly sighed. Why couldn't people just stick to her script?

"Hey, Albert," Molly said.

She could hear her voice shaking. She thought about a movie she'd just seen. A woman was going to break into a museum and steal a valuable jewel. She was cool as fresh hotel sheets, charming the curators and guards. Why couldn't Molly be like that? She plunged ahead with her own lines.

"I need to get some stuff out of my trunk."

"Knock yourself out," Albert said, returning to the underbelly of a Fiat. "Key is in it."

Molly loaded her belongings into the loaner and headed to the gym. In ten minutes, she had her renewed membership card in hand.

Everything was going smoothly. It was as if the universe was agreeing with her that this tree-fort thing was a great idea.

Now to convince Galileo.

Chapter 15

"Bite me," Molly finally said to Galileo.

She'd spent a half hour trying to coax the African Grey into the traveling cage. Molly's hope would soar as he started walking to his perch. She would extend her forearm, like an old-fashioned gentleman offering a lady his arm for a promenade. Galileo would cock his head to one side, hesitating as if deciding whether to accept her invitation. He would then turn his back on Molly, heading nonchalantly back into his big cage, where he would hang upside down and taunt her with a maniacal pirate's laugh.

She'd given up and packed the few final things that needed to go with them into the loaner car. The thought of her precious tree house model packed in the car while she negotiated with Galileo tied her stomach in knots. She needed to get Galileo into the cage. She didn't want to navigate the tree fort's ladder at night, much less move in a bird, a cage, and her model.

Mr. Detman knocked on the open front door. He tiptoed in and looked mournfully at Molly.

"We're sure going to miss you around here," he said.

"Thanks, Mr. Detman. We'll miss you too."

"I see you're ready to go."

"Almost," Molly said, trying to be polite but in no mood for small talk. "But if I don't get Galileo into his traveling cage, we might not get out of here tonight."

Molly had outfitted the travel cage with his favorite toys and a few treats. But Galileo stood firm in his upside-down posture. Mr. Detman walked over to Galileo and studied him.

"He's a fine bird. If he doesn't want to leave, he can always stay with me. I'm sure Romeo and Lancelot would love a new brother."

Molly saw Galileo's head snap around.

"That's not a bad idea," she said, speaking very clearly. "Maybe he would like to stay here."

Galileo hopped into the traveling cage without another complaint.

The sun was splashing around in the sky as Molly drove to the tree farm. She was grateful for the remaining couple hours of daylight in which to get settled. She couldn't remember if there was a gate and was relieved to see the road to the larger evergreens was wide open. She headed to the base of the tree fort. Standing at the base of the tree, looking up the ladder, she'd wished she'd thought of this great scheme a few weeks ago. Getting Galileo up the ladder was going to be tricky. She would have shelled out enough money to buy a new travel carrier that converted to a backpack. She put his cage on the ground so he could watch her prepare their new home. He amused himself by imitating all the bird and insect sounds around them as Molly availed herself of the pulley.

She climbed up and down the ladder several times getting all her other possessions in place. She'd hoist a load with the pulley and then fasten the rope at the base of the tree before climbing to the landing. Once she made sure her footing was secure, she'd lean out, grab the parcel hanging in midair, and, without looking down, pull it into the tree fort. Once she had almost everything inside, she inflated the pool float, put her bags of clothes and food in the lean-to, set up a lantern for emergencies, and put Galileo's traveling perch together. She climbed down the ladder. She had only to get her tree house model and Galileo into the lean-to and she'd be all set.

Knowing she'd have to send the model up to the tree fort with the pulley, Molly had packed the tiny tree house carefully in a large box, then carefully wrapped the box in sturdy rope, knotted expertly at the top. She slid a substantial carabineer through the knot. She attached the carabineer to the pulley, tested the strength of her connection, and started to pull. It was surprisingly heavy.

"Be careful!" Galileo instructed from his cage—a sentence he'd picked up watching the Animal Galaxy Network.

"I am," Molly hissed, realizing she sounded like a pouty teenager arguing with an overbearing parent.

"Bite me."

She ignored the parrot and focused on the precious box inching its way into the rapidly darkening sky. She could feel her palms starting to sweat but couldn't let go of the rope to wipe them dry. Maybe it was fatigue, but the model seemed to be getting heavier as it neared the fort. Her muscles strained as she hauled on the pulley ropes, one hand after another. The box was above her now. She needed only to guide it into the fort.

A gust of warm summer air suddenly blasted through the trees. Molly could feel the wind grab the box containing her precious project. The box, suspending in midair, bent to the whim and will of the air coursing around it. The box swung back and forth above her. The pulley creaked in protest. Molly could think of nothing to do but to try to hang on as the wind pulled at the box.

"Be careful," Galileo said.

Molly could feel the rope slipping through her tired fingers. For a fleeting moment, she pictured the box crashing to the ground. All her work, the sacrifices, the student loans—all for nothing. How would she explain this to Professor Cambridge? The thought of his disapproving sneer gave her a burst of energy. She wrapped the rope around her hands and forced herself to the ground, bending in a yoga child's pose against the wind. She realized if she lost control now, the box might come crashing down on her. Could it knock her out? Could it kill her? She was so tired of everything. In her exhaustion, she wondered if maybe she could just let go of the rope. She wouldn't have to face the uncertain future after all. She closed her eyes and hesitantly started to loosen her grip, letting the rope burn her hands.

Through the wind whistling in her ears, she made out the faint strains of "The Female Highwayman." She didn't know whether her father's voice was coming to her through Galileo or her heart, but she knew he was telling her something.

He was saying she couldn't give up. She had to be true to her mythic heroine from long ago. She had to be tough and she had to be strong. Her father always said she could be anything she wanted to be. But he never said it was going to be easy. As she opened her eyes and sat up, pulley rope now tight around her hands, the wind died down as suddenly as it had started. She looked up at the box, which swayed gently high above the ground, like a graceful hula dancer.

She stood up. Her new resolve invigorated her as she reached out to pull the miniature tree house in its box up to the landing and tied off the rope. Once she'd climbed up the ladder and pulled the precious box safe inside, she headed back down.

One last hurdle and she'd be all set to call the tree fort home. She looked through the cage at the bird.

"Okay," Molly said, looking him in the eye. "There is no denying that this is going to be very weird. But I can't carry your cage up the ladder. And I'm not sending you up the pulley, so we've got a problem."

"Amen, brother."

"Yeah. Anyway, here's what going to happen. I'm going to send the cage up by the pulley. You need to sit on my shoulder. We'll climb up the ladder and pull the cage in. Got it?" Molly said. "And no biting."

Galileo had a habit of biting her ear whenever she had him on her shoulder. Her father used to say it was because the bird was humiliated at having to act like an accessory. Molly found that a little sophisticated in the thinking department. She didn't care how smart Galileo was. If Galileo bit her on the way up the ladder, she might lose her grip and crash to the ground. Molly anticipated Galileo might give her some trouble and she could not afford for him to fly off into the evergreens. Before she'd left the apartment, she'd half-clipped his wings. He couldn't fly away but he'd have enough control so that if he fell, he could sort of glide to the ground.

She trusted Galileo to obey her. He knew when she was serious.

Molly took a deep breath and opened Galileo's cage.

"Come on," Molly pleaded, holding out her arm. "Please don't mess with me."

"Shit," Galileo said in surrender as he flapped out of the cage and onto her arm.

Galileo climbed up Molly's arm and settled on her shoulder. She could hear him rustling near her ear. She knew biting her would be hard for him to resist. She needed to reinforce the seriousness of the situation.

"Don't you dare bite me," Molly snarled at him.

"Bite me," he rasped back.

But he behaved all the way into the tree fort.

Molly set him down on his freestanding perch. Staring accusingly at Molly, he crab-walked sideways for four steps, which took him from one end of the perch to the other. Molly looked around the lean-to. She knew what the African Grey was thinking. What delirium had led her to think this was a good idea? The floor had holes in it; the walls leaned to one side.

She convinced Galileo to get in his cage. His look said that this place was not up to his standards. It was as if he had lived at The Ritz and now was expected to make due with a one-star motel. She took a few toys out of her purse and put them in the bottom of the cage to amuse him. She flipped a sheet gently over the cage, knowing he would settle down.

"I don't like this either," Molly said soothingly to the covered cage. "We've just got to hang out here until I figure something out."

As she crawled onto the pool float and pulled the blanket around her, she hoped she could figure something out fast.

* * * *

Bale and Thor were up before dawn, making sure the four tiny houses Bale was taking to the convention in Arkansas were all set to travel. He'd decided on the Victorian, the Little Cabin, the Mid-Century Modern with the sloped roof, and the Colonial. Taking four of the tiny houses with him left six models just sitting there on the lot, including the steampunk model that so entranced Violet.

Bale prided himself on running a one-man show, but his business was on the verge of being more than he could handle. He had part-time help, men and women who would do finishing work when he had more than one house to build at a time, and there were the drivers who went on the road with him, hauling the tiny houses to the latest convention and then returning to pick them up. He always had his eye on expansion. Maybe now was the time.

He gave each of the drivers final instructions and watched as the strange little caravan headed into the early morning light. He had his own tiny house that he and Thor traveled in—a school bus he'd outfitted with all the bells and whistles. The bus was always a conversation starter—as if being the purveyor of tiny houses wasn't enough. He'd always get orders for school bus conversions when he was on the road.

Making sure the lot was secure, Bale whistled for Thor to hop in the bus. Patting down his jacket in search of his keys, he felt his phone go off. After more frantic patting down of jacket and pants, he found the phone but had missed the text.

It was from Violet.

Violet: Arrived safely. Geography was never my strong suit, but isn't Tennessee on your way to Arkansas?

Bale stared at the phone. He hated to admit it but seeing Molly yesterday had set him back. Looking down at the text, he realized he was at a crossroads: either man up and tell Molly he loved her or move on. He took a deep breath, put the phone back in his pocket, and jumped in the bus.

With Thor impatiently riding shotgun, Bale sat for a few minutes deciding what to do. A left turn would take him toward town and to Molly's apartment; a right would send him to Arkansas by way of Tennessee.

He heard a buzzing overhead and looked up to see Old Paint sailing through the sky. Bale looked at Thor.

"Think we can turn Molly's head in this bus?" Bale said, ruffling the red thatch between Thor's ears.

He put his indicator on, signaling a right turn away from Molly's apartment.

In four blocks, he swung the bus around. It was now or never. He could tell Molly what was in his heart and if she...

Laughed?

Ran away?

Or even worse, just felt sorry for him?

Then he could be on his way. At least he wouldn't have to face her for a while.

Pretty sure those emotions were Molly's only options, Bale felt himself losing his nerve. He came to a turnout and once again headed away from Cobb.

He thought about his early days, when he took the leap and started Bale's Tiny Dreams. He smiled as he remembered coming up with the name. Yes, the houses were tiny, but his dreams were huge. Taking every ounce of nerve and every dime of savings, he'd faced financial hardship for years. But he never gave up. He always told himself "Failure changes nothing; success, everything" and lived by those words.

Wasn't Molly worth the same risk?

As his phone vibrated, reminding him he still needed to respond to Violet, he headed back to town.

* * * *

Molly woke on the pool float but realized her hip was still asleep. The enormity of her situation came flooding back, but the pool float wasn't comfortable enough to hide in. She peeked over at Galileo's cage, still covered with a sheet. She knew she had to face him but knew it was going to be ugly. She also knew she deserved his wrath.

Standing up and doing a few stretches made her feel a little more human. She rummaged around in the grocery bag and broke off a few pieces of broccoli as a peace offering. Still in pajamas but wearing a pair of boots against the splintery floor, Molly pulled the sheet of the cage and gave Galileo her brightest smile.

"Who's a good bird?" Molly crooned and waved the broccoli. "I have a treat! Who wants a treat?"

Galileo turned his back on her. He hated baby talk.

Molly knew to leave Galileo alone when he was in a mood. He could ignore her for hours, just to be sure that she got the point that he was angry with her. She opened the cage and put the broccoli down. She checked to make sure there was no way out of the lean-to and decided to leave the cage door open. Scooting the freestanding perch near the open door so he could pull himself up as he saw fit, she stared at his back.

"I'm going to enjoy the view," Molly announced. "I'll be right outside."

No response. Molly hated the silent treatment, but when it came to Galileo, all she could do was wait it out.

Rummaging around in the grocery bag, Molly dug out a granola bar and headed outside. She gasped as she looked across her new neighborhood. Everything was covered in a thin layer of dew, making the world look completely at ease with itself. The only sounds she could hear were subtle noises of the trees coming to life—birds chattering and squirrels rustling.

At least, she hoped they were squirrels.

The silence of the morning was broken by Quinn's helicopter buzzing through the air. Molly drew back into the shadows as a precaution, although she knew the tree fort wasn't visible from the air—she'd checked that out over and over again on flights to and from breakfast with Quinn. She looked at her phone. The battery was almost dead. She needed some coffee and to brush her teeth. Quinn wouldn't be around for another hour or so, but Manny would have the office open by now. She'd be able to get herself together by the time Quinn arrived if she got a move on.

"Okay, look," Molly spoke sternly to Galileo, who was sitting on his perch, but turned his back when she came in. "I have to go to work."

Molly could feel herself blushing. True, she was going to the office, but not to go to work. Why was she lying to a parrot?

"So you're going to have to go back in the cage for an hour," she said.

She opened the cage door. At home, Galileo would crab-walk over to his cage and pop right in. His little body language let her know that was then and this was now. She was making new rules, but he didn't have to live by them.

"Seriously, dude," Molly said. "This is hard on me too."

No response.

Molly had learned very young that while it might be a good idea to keep your cool when arguing with humans, it was much better to let a bird know your emotional state. If a bird loved you—or in Galileo's case, tolerated you—it was more likely to cooperate if it knew how you were feeling.

"Try this," Molly said, letting Galileo in on the fact that she was at her wits' end. "Pretend you're a dog. Now pretend I'm just going away for a little while and I'm just going to crate you."

Galileo turned around and faced her.

"Please just give me a break," she almost sobbed.

Galileo crab-walked over to his cage, hopped in, and pulled the door closed. As she locked him in, Molly couldn't help but laugh.

"Thanks, buddy," she said, covering him with the sheet. "Just chill. I'll be back soon."

Molly grabbed a small backpack with her morning necessities, including her phone charger, and headed to the door.

"You'll be safe, I promise," she said.

Before she headed down the ladder, she heard Galileo bark like a dog. No one could say the bird didn't have a sense of humor.

* * * *

Bale pulled the bus into Molly's apartment complex. As he turned off the ignition, he saw the complex's manager pushing across the asphalt a huge cage on little wheels. Bale was pretty sure the man's name was Mr. Detman. It was a small town, but he had never really had much reason to socialize with Molly's manager. He wondered if this place was some sort of bird sanctuary. He knew Molly had a giant cage just like that, too. As the man wheeled the cage closer to the bus, Bale knew it was Molly's cage, or Galileo's cage more specifically. Was this man stealing the cage in broad daylight? Bale stepped into the man's path.

"Morning, Bale," Mr. Detman said.

Bale was continually surprised that people in town knew him. But when you run a tiny house emporium, word gets around.

"Good morning," Bale said, putting his hand on the cage.

Mr. Detman stopped, as if to chat. Bale thought that Mr. Detman had pretty strong nerves for a thief—especially an old thief.

"Isn't that Molly's?" Bale asked, thrusting his chin toward the cage.

"Was," Mr. Detman said, his eyes running lovingly over the bars.

"Was?"

"Yeah. She gave it to me to watch for her," Mr. Detman said. "I have two birds who can use it."

Mr. Detman whipped his wallet out and showed Bale a picture of Romeo and Lancelot.

"Aren't they something?"

"Yes, beautiful," Bale said distractedly. "Why would she need you to watch Galileo's cage?"

"She didn't need it anymore."

"Why?" Bale asked in alarm. "Has something happened to Galileo?"

"No, nothing like that," Mr. Detman said. "She just moved to a smaller place and didn't have room for it."

"She moved?"

"Yeah, over by Burgoo," Mr. Detman said. "She didn't tell you?"

"No, she didn't."

"Huh. I thought you two were friends."

"So did I."

Bale returned to the bus. He watched Mr. Detman wheel the cage up a winding path until he was out of sight.

Chapter 16

Molly walked into the office as Manny was putting on a pot of coffee—a chore he'd assigned himself when he'd started working at the tree farm. He looked surprised when Molly walked in.

"You're early," Manny said.

"I have new hours," Molly said.

That wasn't exactly a lie. She didn't say *Quinn* had anything to do with her new hours.

Manny seemed satisfied with the answer, poured himself some ink-black coffee, and offered her a cup.

"That's okay," Molly said, peering into the oily coffee pot.

It occurred to her that she was probably going to have to get used to less-than-gourmet coffee, but she was going to take all these new steps one at a time.

"How are things at Gilbert's?" Molly asked.

"Did you know I went to college?" Manny asked abruptly.

"Pardon?"

"I said, did you know I went to college?"

"No, actually, I didn't."

Should I have known that?

"You went to college too, right?"

"Right. Actually, I'm still in school. I'm in graduate—"

"My point is," Manny interrupted, "you and I are both college graduates, with student loans up the butt, and we've got these…these jobs that have nothing to do with what we studied."

Molly wasn't sure what to say.

"What did you study?" she decided was a good question.

"Bagpiping."

Molly stared at him. Was he kidding?

"You have a degree in Bagpiping?"

"Yes," he said. "From Carnegie Mellon."

"Oh. Well, I think maybe that's a hard major to market in Kentucky."

"Tell me about it."

"What about…you know, going someplace they need bagpipers. Like Scotland."

"They don't need bagpipers in Scotland," he said sullenly.

Mercifully, Manny downed his coffee and headed out to the trees. As soon as Molly was sure he wasn't coming back, she plugged in her phone and iPad, then raced into the bathroom for a quick scrub.

When she'd accomplished all that could be done without a shower and her drawers full of cosmetics, Molly studied herself in the mirror. She had to admit, with a hot pink baseball cap to hide her wonky hair and a pink-and-white sleeveless—and wrinkle-proof—top, she didn't look like someone who'd slept in a tree. She slicked on some lip gloss as she heard Old Paint settling onto the helipad behind the building.

She rushed into the office, yanking various cables from her electronics. She had them stuffed in her bag just as Quinn walked in.

"Hey, Molly," Quinn said. "You're early."

"I have new hours," Molly said before she could stop herself.

"Cool."

That was easy.

Molly smiled. As messed up as her life was right now, it was always so exciting to see Quinn.

"Ready to go get some breakfast?" Quinn asked.

Molly's smile faded. She couldn't go to breakfast! Galileo was spending his first day in the tree fort. She would have to check on him several times to make sure he was all right. Saying no to Quinn made her stomach hurt but she had to be responsible.

"I'd love to," Molly said.

Quinn cocked his head to one side, his own smile fading.

"I hear a 'but' coming on," he said.

"Yeah," Molly said hurriedly. "I would love to, you know I would. But I want to check out the…the cone situation…since it's my new job."

"The cone situation will be there after breakfast. As a matter of fact, the cone situation will be there until November."

I'll have a job until November?

"I really want to get started," Molly said, knowing how ridiculous she sounded.

Who would be this excited about pine and fir cones?

"Suit yourself," Quinn said, shrugging his shoulders.

She watched him head out to Old Paint. It was all she could do not to run after him. He'd been so good to her. What if he held this against her? That was crazy, she told herself. She was a good worker, and Quinn valued that. Didn't he?

She stood in the doorway to the office, watching Quinn's back. He suddenly turned around and faced her.

"Want me to bring you anything?" he asked.

The tension left Molly's body so suddenly, she felt weak at the knees. He did value her. She also realized she'd love some hot food.

"Could you bring me a breakfast burrito?"

"Sure. Bacon or sausage?"

Molly couldn't bring herself to say, "I want some sausage."

"Bacon."

She waved as Old Paint shimmied into the air like an ancient go-go dancer who still remembered her moves. Once Quinn was out of sight, she walked back to the big trees, noticing for the first time how the cone population grew exponentially as the trees grew higher and higher. This early in the season, most of the cones were still on the trees but there was a smattering on the ground. She used to crunch over them without a thought but now studied them as she made her way to the tree fort. Some were like the pine cones you see scented with cinnamon around the holidays—bulbous with gaps between the thick, woody scales. But others were more slender and compact with their scales tightly closed. There was a surprising variety of colors too, from tan to russet to slate gray.

At this point, Molly knew it was important to take the cones off the trees to conserve the trees' energy, but she knew the more beautiful cones could also be sold in the shop during the winter as fragrant fireplace fuel, so it would be important to preserve the pretty ones. Everything about the trees seemed new and exciting. This world, Quinn's world, enchanted her.

She scampered up the ladder, raced into the lean-to, and uncovered Galileo.

"Shit!" he squawked.

At least he was talking to her.

"I know, I know," she said, giving him a carrot. "Want to hang out?"

She opened the cage and waited. He was still giving her the cold wing.

Molly wasn't sure how much Galileo understood her actual words, but she knew he understood intonation. Molly stuck a handful of sunflower seeds in her pocket and continued chatting at him.

"I have to get back to work pretty soon. If you want to come out, it has to be now," she said in her most serious voice.

Galileo digested the information while chomping on the carrot. Without looking at her, he pulled himself onto the perch. Molly tried not to smile. She kept her voice serious.

"I could take you to look outside," she said, putting out her arm. "It will blow your mind."

She had no idea what he was making of this conversation, but when he finished the carrot, Galileo climbed up on her arm. She stretched out her arm, the signal that he should climb up to her shoulder. He did so without a word. With him firmly on her shoulder, Molly left the lean-to and walked out onto the platform.

"Shit!" Galileo said.

Molly took that to mean he wasn't very happy with the new environment. It made her sad that a bird would feel uncomfortable high up in a sheltered tree, but he was older than she was, and this was his first experience in nature. She wondered if it was not possible to teach an old bird new tricks.

Molly was careful not to take him near the edge, should he decide to stretch his wings. With his half-clip he would certainly survive a corkscrew glide to the ground, but why take chances? After walking him around the platform, Molly took him back inside. He seemed more than happy to get back in his cage. He'd had enough.

"Okay," Molly said, locking the cage. She looked at her phone. She really needed to get to work, to have something to show for her day, but she couldn't resist unpacking her tree house model. Being up in the air like this had ideas crowding her brain. She opened the box, gently removed the packing, and pulled the model into the room.

The model seemed at home in the lean-to. It pulsed with possibilities. The delicate branches stretched skyward, almost as if it were reaching for the sun. She couldn't wait to finish her workday and start working on it.

"Okay, dude," Molly said, tearing herself away from the model and covering Galileo again. "I'll be back as soon as I can. You be good."

"I love you, Quinn."

Molly looked around and blushed, as if Quinn could hear him.

"Can't you just say 'I love you'?" Molly hissed.

"Bite me."

Molly climbed down the ladder, relieved that Galileo seemed to be getting back to his loathsome personality.

She walked back to the smaller trees. She reached in to pull a cone from a white pine, but the needles pricked her. They were not giving up their cone without a fight. Molly went back to the office to get a pair of gloves.

Quinn was in the office when she arrived.

"Your burrito is probably cold by now," he said.

Molly was so worried about Galileo, her food order had entirely skipped her mind.

"I got so involved with stuff, I forgot about it," Molly hedged.

Her stomach growled. Mortified, Molly slapped her hand over her midsection. Quinn laughed good-naturedly.

"If I took as much interest in trees as you did, I'd probably be a millionaire," he said, passing the paper bag across the counter. "You might want to heat it up in the microwave."

Molly opened the bag and peered in. The burrito had taken on the unattractive tinge of cooling refried beans, but she was too hungry to care.

"That's okay," she said. "It's still warm."

"Have a seat. Talk to me."

Molly sat, wishing she'd pick a less ungainly meal. Stuffing your face with a burrito was not the look she was going for. As much as she loved spending time with Quinn, there was very little about her life she wanted to share at this moment. Luckily, Quinn was in a chatty mood, so basically all she had to do was listen. He talked about a few high stakes games he'd recently played—going enthusiastically into detail she didn't understand, not being a poker player—and he mentioned a baseball game he'd bet on.

"Oh, and I talked to my Uncle Crabby yesterday," he said. "He said he's having a good time bumming around the country. Said he even had a marriage proposal."

Molly almost choked.

"That was my reaction too," Quinn said. "He asked how things were up at the restaurant."

Molly, about to take a bite of her cumbersome feast, paused with the burrito in midair.

"What did you tell him?"

"The truth," Quinn said with a shrug.

"Which is?"

"Which is, I haven't been up there," he said. "But I told him I'd check on the place in a day or two."

Molly put the burrito down. The thought of Quinn checking on the place and discovering her stash took away any appetite.

"Hey," Quinn said, interrupting Molly's thoughts. "You know the place better than I do. How about you run up there and check things out? You can do it on company time."

Molly tried to control her breathing as Quinn rummaged around in his desk. If she could get her hands on the keys, she could probably make copies. Even if she couldn't make copies—Quinn's locks looked pretty complex—she could find a door she could leave open that nobody would see and use her own lock to come and go, while still leaving the place secure. In any case, she'd be able to go back to her original plan. As much as she loved the tree fort, Galileo weighed on her mind.

"Here they are," Quinn said, triumphantly holding up the jingling set.

Molly gently put down the remains of the burrito and wiped her hands on her jeans. She took a deep breath. Her pulse beat in her ears as she waited for the cold keys to hit her palm. Just as the keys were within an inch of her hand, Quinn suddenly snatched them back.

"Nah, that's okay," he said, pocketing the keys. "I should do it myself."

Chapter 17

Molly was dizzy with disappointment. She tried to think of a way to make Quinn reconsider, but everything that came to mind would sound suspicious. And the last thing she needed to do was to raise anyone's suspicions.

Easy come, easy go—but even just talking to herself took some convincing.

"I better get working on those cones," Molly said. "Are there any gloves around?"

"You got me," Quinn said, shrugging.

Molly wondered how Quinn kept the farm going. He really didn't seem to have much of a handle on things.

"You up for lunch, since you stood me up for breakfast?" Quinn asked.

"I wish I could," Molly said—and she meant it. "But I need to go to the gym."

"Why? You look great to me."

Molly had a hard time with Quinn's sideways compliments. But, two could play at that game.

"If anybody knows the value of the gym, it's you," she said, blushing to the roots of her hair.

"Maybe we could go work out together."

There was no way she could tell Quinn she needed to get to the gym in order to take a very badly needed shower. That confession would kill this flirtation in its tracks. She wondered if she could do a step class with Quinn and then take a shower. She pretended to stretch and quickly sniffed her armpits.

Nope! She needed to hit the shower *now*.

"I'm meeting…"

Who could she be meeting?

She thought and thought.

"I'm meeting Bale," she said triumphantly.

"Sorry to tell you this," Quinn said. "But Bale is going to stand *you* up."

"How do you know?"

"When I was flying this morning, I saw a caravan of tiny houses taking off and about an hour later, the school bus leaving the lot. Isn't that the secret signal that Bale is off to another convention of crazy tiny house zealots?"

"That's a bit harsh."

Quinn shrugged. Molly found it disconcerting that Quinn didn't seem to understand anyone's passions but his own.

Molly was shaken that she didn't know Bale had left. Why hadn't he called?

She slyly snuck a peek at her phone. No messages. How could Bale just disappear without a word? Were they on the outs? Was this about that Violet person?

"So what do you say?" Quinn asked, interrupting her thoughts.

"About what?" Molly asked, knowing instinctively he wasn't interested in Bale taking off without a goodbye.

"Lunch or the gym?"

Why did her life have to be some complicated? If this were last week, when she had her apartment, Galileo was secure, her car was running, and Bale was still her friend, the thought of having to choose between lunch or a workout with Quinn would have been the stuff of dreams. Now it was just one more thing to stress about. She needed to shower anyway, she decided.

"The gym," she said, knowing the shower could not wait another day. She thought if she checked on Galileo before she left and after she returned, he'd only be alone for a couple of hours. "But I can't be gone long. Those cones aren't going to gather themselves."

"It's only June. The cones are just getting started," Quinn said, looking at his watch. "Okay, see you in two hours? We can stop at your place and you can pick up your gym gear."

Was Quinn coming on to her? Molly envisioned herself letting Quinn into her apartment and him pulling her toward him for a passionate kiss before she even got the door closed. She felt another tweak from the irony fairy as she remembered there was no apartment anymore.

At least she would be spared Galileo saying, "I love you, Quinn," at an inopportune moment.

"I've got my gym stuff in the trunk of my car," Molly said, not untruthfully. "Well, the trunk of my loaner car."

"You have a loaner?" Quinn asked.

Molly brightened. She couldn't tell him everything, but she was happy to share at least part of her story with Quinn.

"Yes," Molly said. "It was terrible! I was—"

She was interrupted by Quinn's cell phone buzzing. He put his finger up for Molly to wait. He answered the phone.

"Hey, doll," he purred into the phone. "Oh, you know, workin' hard, hardly workin'."

Molly could hear tittering on the other end of the line. She felt superior for a few heady seconds, before she remembered she'd done some tittering of her own since becoming Quinn's employee. She looked at Quinn, who was trying to get her attention. She wasn't sure, but she thought she saw him push the mute button on the phone.

"I'll see you in a couple hours," he said to Molly with a wink. He unmuted his phone and walked to his desk, listening to the chatter on the other end of the call.

"See ya," Molly said.

Not only did she now have a place to live and get to see Quinn every day, Molly also loved working on the farm. There were animals and birds everywhere, using the trees for shelter and food. While she knew this would all change in late October, when the trees became big business, it was wonderful to work alongside all the different creatures. It made her feel less weird about calling a tree *her* home.

She made her way back to the tree fort. As she climbed the ladder, she could hear many different kinds of birds singing. She couldn't wait for the day she felt comfortable enough to let Galileo stay outside his cage, so he could commune with his fellow feathered friends. It occurred to her the Kentucky birds probably had never met anything like Galileo. Molly was optimistic by nature, but it was a stretch to hope Galileo would behave himself. He really was one rude bird.

Molly slipped the sheet off Galileo's cage and peered in. He didn't look at her. Back to the silent treatment, it seemed. Molly knew better than to plead with him. Galileo's moods would probably come and go until he accepted their life here as normal. On one hand, Molly loved the idea of staying in the tree forever. Everything she'd ever heard Bale's customers say about living tiny—lack of financial pressure, a more simplified existence, living more closely with nature—was realized in the tree fort. While tiny-house living wasn't for everyone, she figured tree-fort living was for even fewer. But she had no complaints. Luckily, Galileo didn't get a vote.

It might be another story once winter came. She'd have her thesis done in November. The weather usually started to turn in October, but it was possible, if the weather held, she might be able to stay put until then. Armed with her master's, she'd be able to get a real job.

She looked out over the treetops, the river, and the town. Right now, she couldn't imagine a better job. Her miniature tree house caught the sun, bringing her back to reality. She watched how the shadows of the pine needles played over the various levels of the house. She hadn't considered how much the movement of the sun could impact the design. Watching the tiny bedroom plunge into shadow had Molly redesigning the floor plan in a few quick sketches in her notebook before she put fresh vegetables in Galileo's cage, covered him back up (sometimes she was grateful for the silent treatment), and scrambled down the ladder to her car. She popped the trunk, grabbed her gym bag, and ran to the office.

Quinn was waiting inside, leaning against the office wall, looking down at his phone. Molly wondered if he had any idea how amazing he looked in his gym shorts and tight black tank top. He looked up as she approached.

"Hey, gorgeous," he said.

"Hey..." Molly tried to think of something to say.

Hey, hottie? Hey, sexy? Hey, stud?

She cringed just thinking about saying "Hey, stud." He *was* her boss after all.

"Hey, Quinn," she finally said.

"Want me to drive?" Quinn asked.

"Sure," Molly said.

As they walked to Quinn's truck, they passed Molly's car. She thought about returning to her story about her loaner, but she sensed Quinn wasn't really into car troubles. Which was good. Molly needed to forget her troubles, not dwell on them.

Molly looked over at Quinn as he opened the door for her. She hopped into the truck and watched Quinn jog over to the driver's side. He glanced over at her and smiled one of his killer smiles.

Quinn was the perfect antidote. Period.

It was always too loud when they were flying in Old Paint to really talk. Molly was worried she might not be able to think of anything to say as they drove the seven minutes to the gym. She didn't need to worry. Quinn was singing along to a very loud AC/DC song, pumping his fist and smacking the dashboard.

"I love this music," Quinn called over the song. "I need to get pumped for my workout."

"Me, too," Molly yelled back, trying to get in the spirit.

She extended her head back and forth like a turtle coming in and out of its shell and bit down on her lower lip, rock star style. She caught a glimpse of herself in the side mirror.

You look like an idiot.

Quinn pulled into the gym parking lot and shut off the ignition.

"Are you so hyped?" Quinn asked.

"I sure am," Molly replied enthusiastically, although she had no idea to what she was agreeing.

"Cool. Let's do this."

He jumped out of the truck, shadow-boxing as he waited for Molly to grab her gym bag. Quinn punched and jabbed at the air as they climbed the stairs, shoulder muscles rippling seductively. Molly dabbed at her forehead. If her body experienced half the workout her hormones were getting, this would be an effective day at the gym.

"Hey, Quinn," a soothing southern accent greeted them at the door.

It was Matt, one of the personal trainers. Molly couldn't help but notice Matt's biceps were every bit as impressive as Quinn's. But Matt was significantly younger—too young for Molly.

Molly wondered, not for the first time, *When did any guy get too young for me?*

"This is Molly," Quinn said.

Molly was about to tell Quinn he didn't need to introduce them. Molly had been a member of the gym, off and on, when she could afford it, since she moved to Cobb. She'd seen Matt many times over the years.

"Nice to meet you, Molly," Matt said.

Molly smiled and shook his hand. It was easier to think of Matt as too young for her rather than her being too old for him.

"Ready to get this party started?" Quinn asked Matt.

"Free weights?" Matt replied.

"Free f-ing weights!" Quinn said.

They seemed to have forgotten about Molly.

"See you in an hour?" Molly squeaked, afraid she might pierce the testosterone balloon being blown up around her.

"Sure," Quinn said.

She watched the two men walk to the free weight room, chatting animatedly. As Matt opened the door to the room, Molly heard more thumping rock and roll before the door closed and the rest of the gym went silent. She watched as Quinn high-fived other muscular men. Quinn was definitely a man's man, comfortable in a helicopter or gym or at a poker table. She wondered how she might fit into his world.

Although her entire goal was to wash up, Molly decided she might as well do the treadmill. She did have an hour to kill. Even in her rank condition, she'd only need twenty minutes to shower. Plus, a half hour running/jogging/sweating would give her that healthy post-gym glow that Quinn was sure to recognize and appreciate. They could compare workout notes on their way back to the tree farm. And she might just tone up a bit.

It was a win-win.

Molly quickly changed into her gym gear, slung a small towel over her shoulder, and waited for the next treadmill to become available. Molly was surprised how busy the gym was on a weekday. For such a small town, there was certainly a lot of physical fitness going down. Molly watched a woman's athletic green spandex-clad butt bob up and down as she ran full bore on the treadmill. Molly was impressed. She knew she'd never be able to keep up such a pace. The woman slowed to a walk, then shut off the treadmill before turning around and leaping gracefully off. Molly was shocked to see it was Geraldine Murphy, one of the old guard from Crabby's. Emphasis on the Old. How could a seventy-year-old have such a muscular bum?

"Molly!" Geraldine exclaimed. "I'm surprised to see you here."

Molly tried to hold in her stomach under her baggy T-shirt. It was an unspoken gym law that those in shape wore spandex and those...like Molly...wore shorts and tees.

"I'm here with Quinn," Molly said.

This announcement might not have astounded Geraldine, but it certainly impressed Molly.

"Oh, I've heard the rumors," Geraldine leaned in and squeezed Molly's less-than-firm-forearm.

Was the whole town talking about her and Quinn? This was exciting news. Molly's insides quivered, but she kept her voice under control.

"What rumors?"

"That Bale met a gorgeous woman his own age and you've rebounded with the tree farmer."

Molly could feel her jaw drop and couldn't seem to command the synapses in her brain to shut it.

"Bale hasn't met a woman his own age!" Molly said, surprised this was the part of the story she felt compelled to clarify. "You mean the woman in the purple truck? She's a client."

"Maybe," Geraldine said. "But I was having lunch at the pizza place...I was just having a salad...and I saw the two of them. She didn't look like 'just a client' to me."

Molly wondered if Geraldine was hearing rumors or spreading them.

"I better get on that treadmill before I lose it to somebody else," Molly said, having lost all interest in the rumor mill.

Molly jumped on the treadmill and roughly shoved in her earbuds. She tapped the music icon on her phone, looking for something to motivate her. She settled on "Harlem Shake" and angrily set the treadmill control to go rapidly up and down hills. She pictured herself looking as graceful as a fox outrunning the hounds. She took off, her calf muscles remembering the rhythm of long-ago workouts. Why would anyone in town think Bale had thrown her over? She and Bale had never been more than friends. And no one seemed to see her conquest of Quinn as anything to write home about, either.

Small towns!

After thirty seconds, her anger spent, she felt herself getting breathless. Instead of the nimble fox, she worried she looked more like a three-toed sloth who'd already had dinner.

Her heartbeat slowed as she walked at a more realistic pace. Her good humor was returning as well. Maybe a workout with Quinn every few days wouldn't be a bad idea. It occurred to her that a workout would be a perfect cover for showering at the gym.

She smiled at her own ridiculous subterfuge.

She was still smiling when she noticed a changing of the guard on the treadmill to her right. The smile froze on her face as Professor Cambridge, clad in a bright blue tracksuit, grabbed the handles and pulled himself into position. Molly faced straight ahead, hoping the professor wouldn't notice her. Her fingers were shaking as she pushed the control setting to "off." But in her haste, she hit "incline." The machine thrummed with excitement, the rubber conveyor belt under her feet tripling its speed. Concerned that Professor Cambridge would witness her failure should she fall, Molly powered through the run. She finally managed a cool down and the treadmill whirred to a stop. She felt she'd run the Appalachian Trail. Professor Cambridge continued to look straight ahead, planting one foot determinedly in front of the other. Molly stood for a moment, afraid to try her legs for a dismount. With her hands firmly on the handles of the machine, Molly took one step and then the other off the treadmill.

She was safe.

And now she could really use that shower!

Without looking at the professor, Molly headed toward the locker room.

"How goes your little thesis, Ms. McGinnis?" she heard the professor intone.

She turned back to the treadmills. Professor Cambridge didn't turn around and continued to tread.

"It's going well," Molly said to his back.

"That's good to hear," Professor Cambridge said. "Higher education is a terrible thing to waste on frivolity, wouldn't you agree?"

Chapter 18

Renew
Celebrate
Observe

Molly woke the next morning with her affirmation words already formed. She grabbed a pen and wrote the words before they went the way of dreams. She put the pen back in her purse and lay listening to the sound of birds singing. At first she thought it was Galileo, but she eyed the shrouded cage and all was silent there. Struggling from the pool float, she padded to the door of the lean-to and put her ear to the door. It seemed as if the birds were right outside. Opening the door, she saw the birds fly from the platform, soaring into the sky. She was sorry they saw her as an intruder, but asking to be accepted after only two days in the tree seemed too much to ask. Of course, what she really wanted was for the other birds to accept Galileo. She felt like the parent of the awkward kid when they moved into a new neighborhood. She knew it was not going to be an easy road. It made her heart hurt.

She heard Old Paint flying overhead. She instinctively reached out to wave but caught herself and tucked back among the fir needles. As much as she wanted a Snow White moment communing with the animals of the tree farm, she did not want to be discovered by Quinn.

She hated to see Quinn up there without her, but she'd told him yesterday that she wouldn't be able to join him for breakfast today. She was glad he hadn't asked why, because she hated lying. She couldn't very well tell him she had to spend as much time as she could with her cranky bird in a tree fort on his property because she wasn't yet comfortable leaving Galileo alone for long.

Molly went back into the lean-to and pulled the sheet off Galileo's cage. He was wide awake and gave her the side-eye.

"Are we speaking this morning?" Molly asked.

"Bite me."

"Oh, good!"

Molly fed the African Grey and poured some water into his bottle from her thermos.

"If you'd just give this place a chance, I think you'd like it."

Galileo laughed his pirate's laugh, which he knew freaked Molly out. She opened his cage anyway and gave him some space. She knew this was all going to unfold on Galileo's own terms.

She just didn't know what those terms were.

Molly had an hour or so before she needed to check in at the office. Her phone had died during the night and although she didn't know exactly what time it was, she was relieved she didn't have the battery life to call Bale. She didn't really have any right to interrogate him about his whereabouts—or his *whyabouts* when it came to Violet.

She could always use the sound of the chopper returning to the farm as an indication she needed to head over to the office. Molly glanced at her tree house model. Every minute in the tree fort gave her new inspiration. But actually working on the project was not the same as getting one idea after another. When Professor Cambridge asked her about her thesis at the gym, it put the situation in stark relief—her dissertation was due in November and it was now June. She had so many new ideas she wanted to implement—she wanted to rearrange rooms and redirect plumbing—but she had to face it: even if she stuck to her original plan, she was behind schedule.

Molly tried to give Galileo as much time as she could outside the cage, but she could only hold off nature's call for so long. She got Galileo settled back in his cage, covered it, and secured the lean-to. In only two days, Molly had figured out how to get down the ladder without having to watch every step. She knew which ones were just waiting to take her down.

As she walked to the office with her toiletries bag and phone paraphernalia, she slowed to watch a fawn nibbling at a Douglas Fir. Molly pretended to ignore the animal, hoping it would not run away. The deer pricked up her ears and stood perfectly still as Molly walked by, but it didn't run. Molly loved her new neighbors.

Molly beat Manny to the office. After a quick trip to the bathroom to freshen up and pull on a clean T-shirt, she plugged in her phone and she brewed a serviceable pot of coffee. As soon as her phone was sufficiently charged, she checked it, hoping there would be a message from Bale.

There wasn't.

Maybe Molly should reach out to Bale? He might be surprised to hear from her when she didn't need anything, she thought ruefully. Molly wondered if she hadn't been a very good friend to Bale.

The doorknob to the office turned. Molly's pulse started to quicken, but it was Manny, not Quinn, who walked in.

"Early, again?" Manny asked. He looked at the coffee pot. "And you made coffee. Nice."

Manny put a white paper bag on the counter and poured himself a cup. He took a sip and made a face.

"This is pretty weak," he said.

"It is not. It's the same strength I used to make at Crabby's."

"That might be why we closed," Manny said.

Catching a glimpse of Molly's affirmation words on her hand, he added, "Maybe you should write 'Make better coffee.'"

Molly was about to say something, but saw Manny was teasing.

"Donuts," he said, indicating the white bag. "Got 'em at Gilbert's for free."

Molly suddenly realized she was starving. She reached into the bag and pulled out a glazed old-fashioned.

"Why were they free?" Molly asked, popping half the donut in her mouth.

"'Cause they're super old."

"This is horrible," Molly said, coughing on the cement-like donut.

"A perfect complement to your lousy coffee," Manny said. "Anyway, they aren't for humans. They're for the deer."

"Do deer like donuts?"

"Deer will pretty much eat anything," Manny said. "But I'm trying to put food out in the forest behind the farm, so they don't eat the trees."

"I don't think feeding donuts to deer is a good idea," Molly said. "On the farm or not."

Thinking back to this morning, when she watched the fawn delicately munching away on the evergreen, she felt a pang of guilt. Of course, Quinn would not have the warm-and-fuzzies about his trees being eaten.

"Well, if the deer keep stripping the trees, they're going to be…"

"What?" Molly's insides flipped.

"Let's just say it would be better for them if they stayed off the farm," Manny said. He arched his eyebrow significantly. "And for me, too."

Molly was confused. She could well imagine the fate of the deer—at least when hunting season started in September. But what could possibly happen to Manny?

"Quinn wouldn't fire you, would he?"

"If those deer don't stop eating the trees, Quinn won't have to fire me, because I'll quit."

"I don't think the deer mean anything personally," Molly said. "Why would you quit?"

"Some of us don't have the luxury of strolling around the farm looking for pine cones."

Ouch.

"And fir cones," Molly added, knowing how lame that sounded. "I still have no idea what you're going on about."

"Have you ever heard...have you ever *smelled* the deer deterrent Quinn uses?"

Molly shook her head.

"I didn't think so," Manny continued. "Let me tell you, it's strong enough to keep the most insatiable deer from the trees. And if the deer start winning, it'll be my job to smear the stuff around. And I'm already doing most of the heavy lifting around here."

"What about scarecrows?" Molly asked suddenly, ignoring Manny's verbal jab. "Can we put up scarecrows?"

"Why would we do that? Scarecrows scare, well, crows. Not deer."

"I'll research this," Molly willed herself not to say it, but she failed. "I'm sure there is something we can do."

"Don't strain yourself," Manny said as he headed out of the office.

Molly stared after him. She wasn't sure exactly what Manny did around the tree farm. She had to admit, gathering pine cones was going to be good job security until December, but, while it would take away from her tree house model, she knew she could take on some more responsibility.

"Hey, gorgeous," Quinn said, rattling a bag from Beamer's. "Even though you're breaking my heart making me eat alone, I brought you your burrito."

"Perfect," Molly said. "I'm starving."

She opened the bag and took a huge bite. This was much better than a stale donut. Molly thought about talking to Quinn about the deer problem but held her tongue. Maybe addressing it would just make things worse— for the deer.

She'd try to come up with a solution first. It was true this new endeavor would take away from her thesis. But it would also take her mind off her housing situation, her angry African Grey, her lack of funds, and her loaned car—not to mention Bale leaving town without letting her know. Getting her hands on a problem she might actually be able to solve might be just what she needed.

"Get you some coffee?" Molly asked, falling easily back into waitress mode.

"No thanks. I can't stand that swill Manny makes."

"No fear. I made this myself."

"Music to my ears." Quinn gave her one of his killer smiles while handing over a mug.

Their fingers touched when Molly put her hand on the mug to steady it. Neither took their hands away.

Molly poured slower.

The sound of yelling startled them both. Molly put the coffee pot down and followed Quinn outside. Manny was running toward them as fast as his legs would carry him.

"There's some sort of lion back in the big trees!" Manny called.

Molly got ready to run. Galileo was in the big trees! She had to save him. As she turned to go, she heard Quinn's calm voice.

"What are you talking about?" Quinn asked. "There are no lions around here."

"Not only a lion, but a bear," Manny said, putting his hands on his knees and trying to breathe.

Molly and Quinn exchanged a look. Had Manny lost his mind?

"A bear and a lion?" Quinn asked.

"I know you don't believe me," Manny gulped. "But I'm right. I've heard enough lions and bears on Animal Galaxy to know."

"Okay, then, let's go take a look and figure out what's out there," Quinn said. "I'll get my gun."

Molly felt her legs go rubbery. She held onto the wall of the office for support. Galileo knew those sounds from Animal Galaxy too.

He must be in trouble.

Molly slipped away from the office as quickly as she could. Manny was paying no attention to her and Quinn was in the office. As soon as she was out of sight, Molly ran as fast as she could.

As she approached the big trees, she could hear the lion, then the bear, coming from the tree fort. She wiped away tears as she ran. As she started to climb the ladder, Galileo added his most fierce animal sound—a jaguar.

Molly pulled herself onto the platform, her heart stuck in her throat.

The door to the lean-to was open.

She raced inside and gasped.

Galileo was backed into the far corner of his cage, the sheet that usually covered him spread out on the floor. As Galileo let out one threatening sound after another, a large raccoon was trying to unlock the cage. Molly tripped over the groceries that lay sprawled on the floor. The raccoon was fearless. He had obviously been through everything in the lean-to already. He looked at Molly for an instant and went back to work on the lock.

Molly's first impulse was to grab the raccoon by the tail, but she was afraid he might attack. She grabbed a can of hairspray, ran behind Galileo's cage so she was looking the creature right in the eye—and sprayed.

The raccoon reared up, grabbing its eyes, and fell off the cage.

"Shoo," Molly yelled, stamping her feel. "Shoo."

The raccoon blinked angrily through his sticky eyes. On his way out of the lean-to, he grabbed a carrot, just to let Molly know she hadn't won.

Molly turned to Galileo, who was still roaring, the various animal sounds bouncing off the wooden walls. Parrots could die from fright, but her father always said Galileo was too mean to die. From the fire in the African Grey's eye, she hoped her father was right.

"I'm so sorry," Molly said, closing the lean-to's door and opening Galileo's cage.

The bird wanted nothing to do with her.

Could she blame him?

Molly heard movement outside. She grabbed her can of hairspray again, then looked through a crack in the wall when she realized she heard voices. Quinn, shouldering a rifle, and Manny, gesturing wildly, were getting closer.

"Galileo," Molly said in her sternest voice. She had to get his attention. "You have to be quiet."

"Bite me!"

At least he was back to human sounds.

Molly went back to him. Although the cage door was open, the parrot was still pushed back against one wall.

"You need to be very quiet now," Molly said again.

"Shit!"

"I know," Molly whispered. "I know. This is very bad. But you can't let anyone hear you."

This called for more than broccoli. Molly looked around the floor and gathered a handful of sunflower seeds. She held one out to him.

He continued to go through his animal sounds.

"You need to calm down," Molly said, waving the sunflower seeds a little more forcefully.

At last, Galileo focused on the sunflower seeds. He took one and delicately released the seed from the hull. Molly breathed easier, hoping that the men would go away now that there were no more wild animals attacking the Christmas tree farm. She crawled over to the door and listened.

"I don't hear anything," Quinn said from just below the tree.

What if they decide to climb the ladder? How could she explain...any of it?

"I swear, they were right here, Quinn," Manny said defensively.

"I'm sure it was just a deer," Quinn said. "Or a fox."

"I don't think so," Manny said, but apparently losing confidence in his own hearing. "I know that a deer and a fox sound like."

"I love you, Quinn," Galileo said through his seeds.

"Be quiet," Molly hissed, as she crawled back to the cage.

She listened. The only sound she could hear was Galileo munching. When she looked out again, the men were gone. Poor Manny. Quinn must have thought he was nuts.

She looked at Galileo.

"Who's a good bird?" she whispered.

And who is a horrible, irresponsible human?

Chapter 19

Molly's hands were quivering as she punched in Quinn's phone number on her phone. She needed to have the rest of the day off to figure out what she was going to do.

It occurred to her she couldn't very well say, "A raccoon nearly ate my bird while we've been hiding out in one of your bigger trees—oh, and by the way, it was my bird who scared the crap out of Manny with all the wild animal noises."

She decided to hang up, but he answered.

"Hey, Jane," he said.

"Hey, Quinn. So…ummm…I was thinking I might take the rest of the day to figure out a way of keeping the deer off the property."

Way to throw the deer under the bus.

"Okay."

Don't elaborate. Don't explain. Just say thanks.

"I have a couple of ideas that might work. Just…you know…going to research a few things."

"If the problem gets bad this year, we do have that deer repellant."

"I know. But there might be a better way. I think my engineering work might lend itself to this."

"Your engineering work?"

"Yes. You know, I'm getting my master's in civil engineering?"

"Huh."

"I'm building a model of a tree house?" she offered, hoping to jog his memory. "That's why you call me Jane?"

"Oh, yeah," Quinn said. "I forgot that. Anyway, don't wear yourself out. Deer repellant is effective and cheap."

"I won't," she said, hoping he didn't change his mind before she could get off the phone. "Thanks, Quinn."

"No worries. You think on your feet. That's why I love you."

Molly disconnected the call. The low of him forgetting she was getting her degree and the high of hearing him say he loved her (even if he didn't actually mean it) added to her exhaustion.

She decided she needed to change her affirmation words to:

Pithy
Succinct
Concise

Galileo kept his back to her when she approached.

"Look," Molly said, "I know you must hate me right now. Well, I don't know if you hate me or not, because I don't know if parrots actually hate people, but I do know you're disappointed in me. But not more disappointed than I am in myself. When the sun goes down, I'll get you out of here, if you'll just trust me one more time."

Galileo didn't speak. Molly could feel the tears coming. She couldn't believe how many tears she'd shed the last few months as everything seemed to sour.

"You've got spunk, Molly girl," she heard her father's voice say.

She turned to face the cage. Galileo was looking right at her.

"Thanks," she said, biting her lip.

She smiled and opened the latch, which was a little misshapen since the raccoon attack. She held out a sunflower seed as a peace offering. Galileo took it in his claw, then bit her.

"Okay," Molly said, snatching her finger back. "Baby steps."

Molly packed up her few belongings but decided she would leave everything—even the tree house model—in the lean-to instead of taking anything to the car. She didn't want to risk being spotted—and she didn't want to leave Galileo alone for even a minute.

Once she had everything packed, she did spend some time looking into the deer situation. Typing "deer" and "scarecrow" in the search engine on her phone, she managed to find some interesting ideas for making a sort of disguised water sprinkler. Her battery died just as the sun went down.

"Okay, time to go," Molly said as she opened the cage door. "I'm going to send your cage down on the pulley. You know the drill. I need you to climb up on my shoulder and I'll take you down the ladder."

"Bite me."

"This is the last time, I promise."

Could she make this promise? She really had no idea what she was going to do or where they were going to go.

She put out her arm and Galileo climbed on. He shuffled up to her shoulder, digging in his claws a little more than necessary, she thought.

The cage stood empty, which gave Molly an idea. She stuffed the deflated pool float and a blanket inside, and then tied the perch to the outside. At least they wouldn't be without *any* provisions.

Molly took the cage out to the platform and hooked it to the pulley. Being outside agitated Galileo, who screamed jungle animal obscenities in her ear.

"Knock it off," Molly said. "You're going to have everybody up in arms again."

Galileo quieted, and Molly lowered the cage to the ground. She jammed a piece of wood under the doorknob of the lean-to to keep at least the weaker animals from getting inside. She was nervous about leaving the tree house model, but she had to make sure Galileo was safe before anything else.

Molly looked up at the brilliant night sky. She was going to miss living in this tree—she felt it was where she belonged. Would her tree house model ever be realized as a real edifice? She felt like a loser Geppetto wishing his damn Pinocchio could be a real boy. There was no use thinking about that now. She couldn't even get her model finished.

She climbed down the ladder, Galileo clinging to her shoulder. This time his obscenities were in English. Molly could not believe some of the words her father had taught the bird. She unhooked the birdcage from the pulley and then sprinted to the car. She got everything inside, forgetting Galileo was still on her shoulder. She plugged in her phone and noticed she'd missed a call from her brother.

Was this a sign that she should pack it in and go home? She had no home, her thesis was getting further and further behind as new ideas spiraled through her head, her professor had zero respect for her concept, she was driving a loaner and wasn't able to pay for her car when it was ready, Bale seemed to have kicked her to the curb, and Quinn...well, Quinn confounded her at every turn.

She took a deep breath and punched in Curly's number.

He answered right away.

"Hey, Mols." Curly's voice reverberated through the car.

"Is that the horse's ass?" Galileo said in her father's voice.

Molly cringed. It was her own little joke that she taught Galileo to say after Curly had refused to have anything to do with the bird. Molly often regretted Galileo's lack of understanding when it came to humor.

"Hey, Galileo," Curly said dryly. "You sound...status quo."

"Bite me," the bird replied.

Just what she needed—Galileo acting like a complete jerk when Molly was looking to have Curly take them in. Molly shook her shoulder and Galileo popped onto the passenger seat, apparently content with the interpersonal damage he'd inflicted.

"I missed your call," Molly said.

"How are things going?"

"They're...going."

Spit it out!

"I know you're not graduating until December, but..."

"But?" Molly wondered if he wanted her to come home for some reason. Maybe she wouldn't have to admit to being in such ruin.

"Mom and I wanted to start planning our trip for your graduation. I know I told you money is tight, but I didn't want you to worry. We'll make it happen."

"Oh." Molly thought she might have sounded disappointed. She tried a different emphasis. "Oh! That's really good to hear."

Not as good to hear as, "Come on home and forget how you're failing miserably at life," but she thought she carried it off.

"So, you're pretty sure this is going to happen, right?" Curly asked.

"Am I pretty sure *what* is going to happen?"

"Your graduation."

"Yes," Molly said, sneering slightly.

She realized she had a lot of nerve sounding like a surly teenager when she wasn't, in fact, sure at all "this was going to happen." Molly looked over at Galileo. She was glad he'd called Curly a horse's ass.

"Just making sure," Curly said. "Because..."

"Because what?"

She was daring him to say she "never finished anything" or "sometimes things don't always go as planned."

"Because we want to be there to support you," he said. "It's not every day your little sister gets a master's. Maybe you'll even be able to come home for Christmas afterwards."

"Thanks, Curly. I promise I will be graduating in December. And speaking of Christmas, did I tell you I was working on a Christmas tree farm?"

If she was hoping this would make her sound like she had her life together, she failed miserably.

"A Christmas tree farm?" Curly asked. "But it's barely summer."

"Oh, there is a ton of stuff to do on a tree farm all year round."

"Like what?"

"Right now, I'm collecting pine cones. And fir cones. It's really very interesting."

"Sounds it," Curly said in a deadened voice, clearly not finding it interesting at all. "Just don't get distracted, okay?"

She hung up.

"What a complete jerk," she said to the phone.

"Amen, brother," Galileo said from the passenger seat.

After rearranging everything and getting Galileo back in his cage, Molly headed out of the tree farm. She had no idea where she was going.

She stared at her phone. Should she call Bale? It was so weird that he left town without getting in touch with her. Maybe he just got tired of bailing her out. She'd often joked that he should have spelled his name B-A-I-L. She realized she didn't even know where exactly he'd gone. She'd never asked. She hadn't been much of a friend.

Deciding not to add that particular spice to her current stew of self-loathing, Molly started to drive. It was getting late, she'd have to come up with something or spend the night in the car. Which was a great idea if you were camping, but a pretty pathetic move if you weren't.

Camping!

Molly turned the car toward the campground at the edge of town, about two miles past the darkened tiny house lot.

She could hear the gravel crunching under her tires as she pulled up to the kiosk behind two other cars. Who knew camping was so popular in Cobb? Not knowing if the campground took animals, Molly hastily threw the blanket over Galileo's cage. When she turned back, she noticed one car had moved forward. She put the car in gear and inched ahead. Molly saw a woman in a ranger's uniform come into view. As the woman leaned toward the driver's window of the next car, Molly gasped. It was Helena, the bartender from Crabby's. Molly could feel herself starting to panic. She couldn't let Helena see her like this. No real camping gear. No supplies. Not that Helena was known to gossip.

But there was always a first time.

Molly slouched low in her seat and turned the car around.

Now what?

She decided she had no choice. She'd have to spend the money for a night in a one-star hotel. She needed to pull off the road to check her phone—she wasn't exactly sure where the nearest, dirt-cheap hotel was. She realized she was almost in front of Bale's Tiny Dreams. When she saw the lot, she pulled off into the wide driveway to look through her online options.

Molly put the car in park, her headlights on the closed entrance. She smiled at the padlock across the gate. It was the brand Curly had once said was the easiest to pick in the whole world. She shook her head. Bale was so trusting. She would have to tell him about this—if she ever saw him again. She could recommend the monsters Quinn was using at Crabby's.

Molly looked down at her phone. She'd expected to have limited options, but it was far grimmer than she'd expected.

She had zero options.

She leaned back against the headrest and closed her eyes. She was so tired.

She suddenly jolted forward in her seat as if smacked by a fly swatter.

She got out of the car and walked to the gate. She picked up the lock and studied it. It was the easiest type of lock to pick in the whole world. She pulled a bobby pin out of her hair and got to work.

Chapter 20

After successfully picking the lock, Molly drove into the lot, looking behind her at the road, hoping no one was driving by. She pulled the car behind the gingerbread Victorian, shut the car off, and turned out the lights. She could hardly catch her breath. Being homeless was one thing. Being a criminal was another.

Was she a criminal? Bale certainly would understand that she was desperate, wouldn't he? She should call him. Staring at her phone, she remembered she had no idea where he was—or what time zone he was in. And if he was with Violet, he might not want to be disturbed. She decided she'd wait on calling him. She couldn't admit she didn't want to take the chance he'd say she shouldn't be there.

Molly pulled the blanket up on Galileo's cage and peered at him. She could see his eyes gleaming in the dark.

"I hope you appreciate everything I'm doing for you," Molly said.

"Bite me," Galileo said, with more than usual fervor.

"I know," Molly said. "This isn't your fault."

Molly dropped the blanket and opened the car door.

"I'll be right back," she said.

Galileo didn't bother to respond. She hoped he'd stay quiet. The last thing she needed was for him to start with his animal noises. She could just imagine Manny hearing about it and spreading the word that a zoo must have lost several of its wild beasts.

Using her phone as a flashlight, Molly scoped out the few tiny houses on the lot Bale had left behind. Even though she was breaking in, she had her requirements. She wanted the most private of the houses, so no one from the road could see her. She wanted a furnished model. She wanted the steps already in place, since most of Bale's homes were built on trailers, which made the entrance over a foot off the ground

She was about to compromise her list when she found the perfect house. It was a modern steel and wood model with skylights. One end soared higher into the sky, looking like a diminutive tower, an area she knew must be the loft. It was also tucked away behind the office and workshop, where nobody would see her—or hear her. She tried the door.

It was open.

She really was going to have to talk to Bale about this. He really should have a better security system. Anyone could break in.

She looked around the unit. She remembered when Bale first built it. It had a raised kitchen on one end, with a drawer underneath that pulled out to reveal a double bed. She was so grateful she'd seen this feature in action or she'd never have known it was there! She made her way into the bathroom and discovered what she was looking for. The solar panels and the alien-looking toilet meant the tiny house had off-the-grid capabilities. She'd be able to power this house up come morning!

In less than twenty minutes, she'd unloaded Galileo. There was a tiny pull-down table just big enough to hold the cage. It would have to do until morning.

"Things will be better tomorrow, I promise," she said.

Galileo didn't say anything. Was he angry again?

"Say good night, please," she said.

"Good night, please," he replied.

"Always the comedian."

"Bite me."

Molly pulled the bed out from under the kitchen floor. The bed had sheets and a blanket. She fell asleep before her head hit the nonexistent pillow.

After living in the tree and sleeping on the pool float, Molly was used to waking up on the floor. But when she awoke in the tiny house, it still took a minute for Molly to remember where she was. Looking around her, the tiny house was even more perfect than she remembered. The guilt she felt last night was replaced by calmness. Although she loved living in the tree fort, she never felt one hundred percent sure that Galileo was safe there. And the raccoon had confirmed her danger radar. At the thought of the raccoon Molly shuddered.

Molly got up and tucked the bed back under the kitchen floor. She remembered Bale explaining the concept to her when he designed the house.

"It's like a Murphy bed," he'd said. "Only instead of coming down from the wall, it slides out from a big drawer in the floor."

When Molly finally confessed to Bale that she'd broken into his place, she'd make sure to let him know what a great design it was. She knew she should call him immediately. She was overly tired last night and not thinking straight. Breaking in was a bad idea—and not like her at all. What would Bale think?

She started to worry about what Bale *might* think. Maybe he would—quite reasonably—be angry. She checked her phone, which she'd optimistically plugged in last night, hoping for the best. The phone was fully charged. The solar panels were working and she had power. She tried to make herself punch in Bale's number—but she couldn't do it.

She was so tired of all her troubles.

And the tiny house was so perfect.

She reached out to pull the blanket off Galileo's cage but decided she didn't want to hear from him just yet. He could wait another few minutes.

She padded into the bathroom, ran the water, and flushed the toilet. Everything was working! Running water for a quick shower, Molly wondered if she should be using the towels on display. She planned on popping back into the tree fort later in the day to retrieve her all-important model. Just the thought of it being outside of her immediate control brought back the anxiety she'd been feeling over the past few weeks. She would get her miniature tree house and everything else she'd left up there, which included towels. In the meantime, if Bale found himself ready to forgive her break-in, he certainly wouldn't begrudge her the use of a towel. She snapped it off the rack.

Refreshed, Molly returned to check out the kitchen. For a display model, the house was thoughtfully outfitted. While there was no food, there were dishes, cups, bowls, a coffeemaker, utensils, pot and pans, and wine glasses. Molly was impressed by how well everything fit in the miniscule kitchen, but she figured that was the point. Why else have all this stuff in cupboards nobody was using? Whatever the reason, she was grateful.

Finally ready to face Galileo, she pulled off the blanket. She knew African Greys had long memories and she didn't for a minute think he'd forgotten the raccoon attack, but she hoped that, using his bird logic, he might conclude that she was his rescuer rather than the cause of his predicament.

"Good morning," Molly said brightly.

"Feed me, wench," Galileo said, puffing up his chest and speaking in his pirate's voice.

Molly laughed. He hadn't used this expression in a while. She wondered if it was because he always got a rise out of her when he said "Bite me." Maybe he was giving her a break.

Not that "Feed me, wench" was going to win any prizes in the politeness department. But with Galileo you took what you could get.

Molly was starving. She currently didn't have any food except some carrots for Galileo. She remembered Bale had a small kitchenette inside the cavernous workshop. She gave Galileo a carrot, threw on a pair of yoga pants and a light sweatshirt, opened the door, and looked cautiously around. She hopped onto the asphalt and made herself saunter into the large building sitting square in the middle of the lot. The large barn doors were padlocked. She tried the side door. Also locked. She tried two windows in the back.

One of them was not secure, and she crawled in.

Molly gasped as she stood in front of the latest of Bale's creations. It was a tiny red schoolhouse. It even had a little steeple and bell. Molly clapped at the sight of it. There didn't seem to be any limit to Bale's imagination. He had one amazing idea after another. Her own lack of progress on her tree house model flitted into her mind, but she shoved it back out.

The fridge and pantry offered up dull but serviceable breakfast items. Almond milk, cereal, and tea. She pulled out a jar from the cupboard. It was something called Tangy-O—an orange powder. Molly opened the lid and sniffed. The synthetic orange smell made her eyes water. But she made a glassful and drank it while preparing a bowl of cereal. She felt incredibly at home. Once fed, she cleaned everything up. She would go to the store and buy her own supplies so she didn't have to keep sponging off Bale's unbeknownst hospitality.

Molly suddenly remembered an organization specialist named Vivien bought a tiny house from Bale about a year ago. Didn't Bale tell her Vivien had organized all his paperwork and the keys? She rummaged around the office until she found all the keys, neatly labeled and color-coded. She grabbed one marked "Front Gate" with a tangerine rubber cover, one to the back door in a startling blue, and—she was guessing—one in hot pink marked "Tower," which she suspected was the name of the tiny house she'd chosen as her hideout. She felt the hot pink was not the right color for the industrial style of "her" house, but that was a minor quibble.

Bale might be a slacker about keeping the lot safeguarded, but Molly had other ideas. Maybe Bale would even thank her.

Maybe...

She looked at her phone. Even though she'd just eaten, she might actually be able to get to work in time to have breakfast at Beamer's with Quinn. One of the worst parts of this subterfuge was not being able to admit to Quinn what was going on with her life. She didn't want to appear that she didn't have it all together. A woman casting about just to stay afloat didn't seem like the kind of woman who would be of interest to Quinn.

As she got to know him, it was clear he liked things uncomplicated.

Molly walked toward the backdoor and stopped suddenly. There was a three-foot roll of chicken wire leaning against the far wall of the workshop. She had an inspiration, which, if successful, would make Galileo a very happy bird.

She pulled a staple gun, clippers, and gloves off a cluttered workbench (it seemed Vivien could only make so much progress with Bale), grabbed a stack of newspapers, and shoved the chicken wire under one arm. Loaded down, she quietly left the workshop and made her way back toward Galileo.

Molly tried the key in the lock of the tiny house. It fit perfectly.

"Your human is a genius," Molly said to Galileo as she hauled in the chicken wire and other supplies.

"Bite me," Galileo said through a beak full of carrot.

Molly studied the tower vaulting into the sky atop the loft at one end of the tiny house. A ladder accessed the tower. She tried the ladder to make sure it was sturdy and well built. Of course, it was perfect. Bale was a master.

"Watch and learn," Molly said to the African Grey.

Within a couple hours, Molly had closed off the loft by stapling the chicken wire over the opening. She made a door on one end. It was primitive, but it worked and could be easily removed. Climbing inside, she spread newspaper on the floor of the loft and assembled her traveling perch, which she stood near the chicken wire so Galileo could climb the wire from the floor of the loft to the perch. She stood up and spread out her arms. The loft was even bigger than Galileo's large cage, which was now housing Romeo and Lancelot back at Mr. Detman's.

She climbed down the ladder, spent a few minutes begging Galileo to get on her shoulder, then took him into the loft and settled him on his perch. Tugging his cage into place without a pulley system was no easy feat, but she managed to wrestle it inside the loft. She left the door open so he could come and go at will, setting it up with fresh water and vegetables.

"You couldn't do better at the Four Seasons," Molly said proudly.

Galileo eyed his new home. He did not complain.

Leaving him exploring his new surroundings, Molly headed off to work, hoping she might still catch Quinn. She waited in the car until the road was clear, then slunk around the tiny houses until she got to the gate. She had a lump in her throat as she pulled the car through and locked the gate behind her. She was more nervous letting herself out than she was breaking in. It was broad daylight and would be no easier to explain.

As she drove to the tree farm, she saw Old Paint rise into the air, heading to Beamer's. Molly sighed. She'd missed him again—and she was actually hungry from all the work on her masterpiece for Galileo back at the loft.

Molly pulled into the farm and waved to Manny, who was just coming out of the office with his cup of coffee. Molly slowed and rolled down the window, concerned by Manny's tense expression.

"What's up?" Molly asked.

"Deer were at the trees again," Manny said. "Quinn's hopping mad."

"Oh no," Molly said, having forgotten all about the deer amid all her own problems. "I'm… I'm working on that."

"Well, that deer repellant won't spread itself. I'd appreciate it if you worked fast."

Molly figured the deer would probably appreciate it too.

She wondered if Manny was judging her for not having a second job. She sometimes judged herself. But she had to think of her thesis as her second job or it would never get finished. She went into the office and sat down at the computer. Now that she knew Galileo was safe and she could get the rest of her belongings out of the tree later, she settled down at the computer to work on a humane, non-stinky way to keep the deer off the farm.

She grabbed a pen and wrote her affirmation words for the day. They came easily:

Accomplish
Productive
Innovate

Good, solid, employee words!

Her research led her to several conclusions. Her scarecrow idea was a good start, but deer needed more than a stationary object to keep them at bay. She thought back to spritzing the raccoon with hairspray. She would have been happier if she could have just squirted him with water, but at the time, she just needed to get the thing away from Galileo.

Was water the answer? She checked out a few portable sprinkler systems. She knew that Quinn had lots of water available on the farm, which was just off the river. She remembered looking out from the tree fort and seeing a sprinkling of small lakes on the property. So access to water wouldn't be an issue. The problem was, Quinn used drip irrigation. Effective watering, but a completely quiet and motionless system. It wasn't going to disrupt a deer hell-bent on an evergreen snack. She tried various combinations of cute or scary scarecrows attached to a sprinkler, but since the sprinkler head would have to be attached to a hose, nothing was practical for the size of the farm. After an hour, she decided she needed to change approaches.

She was so involved in her research, she wasn't aware that Old Paint was landing until it cast a shadow over the computer. She looked out the window as Quinn and his passenger climbed out of the helicopter. Her heart stuck in her throat as Naomi's bright pink lipstick caught the sun.

Naomi went to breakfast with Quinn?

Molly tried to hide, but too late. Quinn saw Molly through the window and made a circling gesture that she should come out. Molly took a deep breath, plastered on a smile, and went outside.

"Hey, Naomi," Molly said.

"Hi, Molly," Naomi said, leaning into Quinn's body. "I'm surprised to see you here."

"I work here," Molly said.

"Oh, I know that," Naomi laughed.

Molly supposed the laugh was supposed to sound like a wind chime's tinkle, but it came out more like a donkey's bray.

"I just meant I didn't expect to see you at the office. I thought you… scooped up pine cones or something."

"I've been doing some research," Molly said, trying to sound important.

"Molly's our little scholar," Quinn said. "That's why we love her."

"Oh, I know that." Naomi flashed her brilliant teeth.

"Thanks for breakfast," Naomi said, giving Quinn a full body slam as a parting hug. "That was super fun."

Molly watched as Naomi got in her little Fiat and drove away, waving until she was out of sight.

"So, you've replaced me already?" Molly asked.

She meant it to sound flirtatious, but it sounded petty and accusatory. Quinn just smiled.

"I stopped in the convenience store last night and ran into Naomi," Quinn said easily. "We got to talking and I invited her to ride out with me to Burgoo, since you don't seem to be interested in joining me anymore."

Molly knew he didn't owe her an explanation, but she was glad he was giving her one.

"I have seen the error of my ways," Molly said.

This time, she must have gotten the intonation right because Quinn laughed.

"I've been looking into the deer situation," Molly said, hoping to sound studious and indispensable.

"Do you have a solution?" Quinn asked, guiding her into the office.

"Not yet, but I can run a few ideas by you," Molly said.

"That's okay," Quinn said. "This can be your project. When you have something, let me know."

Molly blinked in surprise as Quinn went into the back room. If she'd come up with a few theories about tiny houses or her tree house, Bale would have wanted to hear all about it. She just had to remember Quinn was not Bale.

And maybe there was something to be said for letting her work it out for herself.

Her phone buzzed. She was used to hoping it was Bale, but now she feared it was him. Caller ID let her know that it was Albert from the garage.

"Hello?" Molly said. "Albert?"

"Yeah. Hi, Molly. Just letting you know the car is ready."

"Okay, thanks," Molly said, lowering her voice. "And I can owe you the money?"

"Sure," Albert said. "I know you're good for it."

Clearly, he hadn't had a chat with Mr. Detman.

She hung up the phone as Quinn was coming out of the back room.

"I'm going to go pick up my car later, if that's okay."

"Sure," Quinn said. "I hate car problems. They are always so damn expensive. And you never have anything cool to show for it."

"Seriously."

"Look, Molly." Quinn suddenly sounded serious. "Can you afford to spring your car?"

"Yes," Molly said. She reconsidered. "No. But Albert says I can put it on my tab."

"That sucks."

Molly was confused. Considering her finances, she thought it was great. Quinn disappeared again, returning in an instant with a small canvas bag.

"How much is it?"

"How much is what?"

"The car."

She swallowed hard. This was really a personal question—and to her mind, a personal failure. She told him. He didn't bat an eye.

Instead, he took a stack of hundred-dollar bills out of the bag and handed it to her.

"I can't take this!" Molly gasped.

"Why not?" Quinn asked. "I've been on a winning streak lately and I'm happy to share. Anyway, you work for me, not for Albert. Better to keep it in the family, right?"

Molly didn't remember the rest of the day. She'd gotten her car, she'd picked some fir cones, she'd loaded her trunk with the tree house model and driven back to the tiny house lot, replaying Quinn's use of the word "family" over and over in her head.

Chapter 21

Manifest
Visualize
Attract

Molly woke with the words already in her head. Positive, exciting words seemed to come tumbling into her brain. Her life seemed almost perfect. In the last week, she'd settled into a routine of having civil conversations with Galileo, who seemed to adore his new digs, racing off to meet Quinn for breakfast, working on the farm, and sometimes accompanying him to the gym.

Although Quinn didn't seem terribly interested in the deer situation, Molly continued to do research into the problem. It made her feel a little more like she was doing something productive with her brain. She hadn't come up with much in the way of an inexpensive, reasonable solution, but she made it a habit of shooing the deer away on her rounds, hoping they'd get the hint.

Molly still spent a part of each day in the tree fort, where her imagination soared. She realized she could use the tree fort as a sort of test kitchen for her thesis. She could try out various lever systems and decide which materials might weather better in trees.

Molly had taken over coffee duty at the tree farm, a job that required stopping for milk or sugar, even though Manny worked at the grocery store. Molly didn't mind. The hardware store was right next door, and she was always happy to strike up a conversation with Mrs. Minsberg, one of the proprietresses. Mrs. Minsberg loved the idea of Molly's miniature tree house.

"I have a few couplings you might find interesting," Mrs. Minsberg said, offering Molly a bag. "They're all different shapes and sizes. I was going to toss them, but then I thought, 'Molly might be able to use these.'"

Getting a bag of couplings was better than being handed a bag of candy as a kid.

Mrs. Minsberg also saved cans of paint that had been returned. Molly hauled up cans of half-priced paint and stains, along with treasures from the local junkyard, until she had an entire workshop in the tree. Working with full-sized materials, she found herself coming up with more interesting ideas than she'd ever dreamed possible. She knew she needed to finalize her design or she'd never get her thesis in on time, but the possibilities seemed endless. She kept hearing Curly's "Don't get distracted" admonishment in her ears, but then a new deck stain that looked like dark tree bark with a hint of moss creeping in would catch her eye and she'd find herself... sidetracked.

Curly didn't say anything about getting sidetracked.

She was working away on a shelf made of red-stained pipes when the lean-to was thrown into shadow. Molly looked up in surprise. Had it gotten dark without her noticing the time? The sky suddenly rumbled. Molly looked out the window. Clouds were rolling in fast. A storm was on its way. Molly climbed down the ladder and sprinted to her car. She slammed the door just in time. The clouds released a torrent of angry rain. Molly studied the tree that housed her tree fort. She loved the place but she was happy she and Galileo had another place to call home.

It was still pouring when Molly pulled into Bale's tiny house lot and let herself inside the Tower. After greeting Galileo, she made a cup of tea without hitting her head on the shelf over the stove and watched the storm rage across Cobb. It had taken her awhile to get used to the place. Tiny houses had a steep learning curve—literally. Molly didn't need the dexterity to launch herself into a loft, a requirement of most tiny houses, but this model's fancy bed-in-a-drawer-under-the-kitchen-floor required a certain amount of strength. Molly could feel her biceps getting stronger by the day.

Molly smiled to herself. She used to think of any house not on wheels and over three hundred square feet as a "real" house, but now, safe and warm in the snug little house as thunder and lightning jousted outside, she felt very much at home.

"We are so lucky," she cooed to Galileo.

"Bite me," he said.

The thunder cracked outside.

"Thank God you're not afraid of storms," she said, as she covered his cage for the night.

"Amen, brother," he said gravely.

"It's *sister*," Molly said with a sigh.

Why couldn't he get that right?

Curling up under the blankets, Molly had one final thought before sleep settled over her like a down comforter:

I wonder how long Galileo and I can stay here before we're busted?

* * * *

Bale and Thor sat outside the converted school bus, absorbing the quiet of the grounds. Now that the tiny merchandise had headed off to the next showcase in Missouri, the county fairgrounds where the tiny house convention had been held had an exhausted, sleepy feel to it. The convention had been a huge success. Bale had more orders than he could handle. It would make sense to go straight back to Cobb. But the next showcase lasted only a few days and his inventory was already on the road, so he figured, "Why not?"

It also gave him an excuse to touch base with Violet, since the showcase was going to be located in the Missouri Bootheel, a stone's throw from Tennessee. They'd been Skyping about various ideas for her tiny house but by now, both had given up the pretense that they were constantly in communication over just design ideas.

Bale knew Thor would never tell, so he admitted he also wanted to stay away from Cobb a little longer, because every day he was away, it was easier not to think about Molly. He was holding to his resolve not to text her. And she sure wasn't texting *him*. Maybe more time apart—especially with that time being filled up by Violet—would just about cement the idea that they were better off as friends than…anything else.

From the lack of communication, he was pretty sure he was in this struggle alone. His phone vibrated. Thor looked at it and then at Bale.

"It's Violet," Bale said.

He was happier every time he got to say it.

* * * *

Quinn was leaning against Old Paint when Molly drove up in the morning. Molly looked at her hand. She'd forgotten to write her words this morning, but nothing printable came to mind when she looked at Quinn.

She'd just have to go naked-handed today.

"You ready to ride?" he asked.

"I wasn't sure we'd go today," Molly said. "After that storm."

"What are you talking about? After a storm is the best time to go. The ground looks completely different."

He was right. Molly always felt the world seemed cleansed after a big rain. But yesterday's storm seemed to have slapped the earth silly. The river was pulsing, little puddles had turned into lakes, and potholes dotted the country roads.

Conversations with Quinn had gotten easier over the past week. Molly noticed that Quinn never wanted to talk about anything important or stressful. There were never any discussions about politics or family drama. A quick update on Crabby was usually the most Molly got out of him, but after their breakfast arrived at Beamer's, Molly decided to dig a little deeper.

"So exactly how are you and Crabby related?" Molly asked casually while stirring a hazelnut creamer into her coffee.

"He's my mom's brother," Quinn said. "He was bigger than life. I wanted to be just like him."

"Really?"

Molly couldn't imagine what there was about Crabby, with his forlorn, almost bitter demeanor, that would make a young kid want to emulate.

"He was a helicopter pilot. Really played it up...leather bomber jacket, the whole nine yards."

"No kidding?" Molly almost snorted her coffee she was so surprised.

"He used to take me up with him when I was little. I'd sit on his lap, and he'd let me fly the thing."

"That sounds pretty reckless."

"Runs in the family, I guess," Quinn said with a killer smile.

"So what happened?"

"What do you mean?"

Molly realized she couldn't really say, "When did Crabby become... crabby?" But Quinn seemed to understand what she meant.

"Life is hard sometimes, you know? We all have our coping mechanisms. I gamble when I'm stressed...or when I'm not...and Crabby just lost interest in everything. We all handle it different ways."

Molly nodded. She certainly agreed life was hard. And she knew everyone handled life's ups and downs differently. She wondered if her coping mechanism was avoidance. She'd have to find the opposite of that word and write it on her hand.

The flight back to the farm was uneventful. When she walked around the farm, she was suddenly aware that she knew the differences in the various evergreens. When she first started, all the trees looked the same. She wondered if the lack of stress in her life at the moment was helping her see life around her in a new way. She hoped so. She didn't want to end up like Crabby.

The sting of Bale's abandonment seemed to be easing as well. Which was a good thing and a bad thing. If she was so *dispensable* in Bale's life, how was he going to feel about her...visit...to the tiny house lot?

She drove carefully home from the tree farm, avoiding new potholes created by the storm when she could. She'd gotten so used to driving into the lot, she'd long since abandoned checking for other people on the road. She slammed on the brakes as soon as she got to the gate.

It was open.

It must be Bale.

In the nine days since she'd moved in, she'd rehearsed and rehearsed what she would say to him, but now her mind went blank. Her heart pounded, and her palms turned to marshes of sweat. She knew it was time to face the music.

It turned out she didn't have to face the music, or Bale. As she skirted the corner of the tiny Victorian, she saw the police car parked in front of the office. The uniformed officer had his back to her, hands on hips, staring up at the workshop.

Molly stopped the car. Maybe he wouldn't notice her. She got out as quietly as she could, but as soon as she took a step, the officer turned around.

She knew the cop. It was the deputy named Officer Melon, a man in his forties who was as wide as he was tall.

"Hey, Molly," Officer Melon said. "What are you doing here?"

Molly went through myriad reasons why she was here.

She was driving by and saw the gate open?

She'd thought Bale was back and stopped to chat?

It occurred to her someone must have reported her, so perhaps she should confess?

"I'm staying here watching the place while Bale's away," she said, opting for a version of the truth.

"That explains it," Officer Melon said. "We had a report that there was some activity on the lot, so I thought I'd check it out. How is Bale doing?"

"He's... He doesn't really keep in touch while he's away. You know how that goes."

"Yep," Officer Melon said. "I know how that goes."

He nodded sagely, as if knowing how not keeping in touch goes was the stuff of enlightenment.

"Is there anything else?"

"Nope. That'll do it," Officer Melon said, giving Molly a little salute. As he walked back to the patrol car, something occurred to Molly.

"Officer Melon?"

He turned around, eyebrows arched waiting for her to finish her thought.

"How did you get in here?" Molly asked. "I'm sure I locked the gate before I left this morning."

A smug grin spread across the officer's round face. He walked back to her, eyes darting in both directions to make sure he was not overheard.

"I probably shouldn't tell you this," he whispered, "but that lock of Bale's? Easiest model to pick in the whole world."

Chapter 22

Bale sat at the coffee shop, pretending to look at his phone, while he kept an eye out for Violet. He was sitting at an outdoor table so Thor could keep him company—and for moral support. The waitress had brought a bowl of water for the dog along with Bale's coffee. Bale hoped Thor would hurry up and drink. Thor was a noisy slurper, and when every drop of water was lapped up, his little white beard dripped sumptuously. Bale wanted time to clean him up before Violet arrived and Thor covered her with kisses.

"Come on, little guy, cut me some slack," Bale said to the dog, whose head was deep in the bowl.

Thor looked up and wagged his tail. The bowl was empty.

"Good dog," Bale said.

He wiped Thor's whiskers just in time. He caught sight of Violet's purple truck pulling into the parking lot just as he judged Thor presentable for kissing.

He wished he had someone who could judge *him* presentable for kissing.

"Hi, strangers," Violet called as she walked toward them.

"Hi," Bale said as Thor strained at his leash. "Looks like Thor missed you."

"It's always good to be missed," Violet said as she scooped Thor up in her arms. "Isn't that right, Thor?"

Bale felt himself losing his power of speech. Violet was so incredibly beautiful. She couldn't possibly be interested in him, could she? He thought she gave him every indication that they could move their relationship in a more personal direction, but he had a history of misreading women. Sometimes he was interested and they were not. Sometimes they were interested and he was not. The common denominator was he got it wrong most of the time. Maybe he was misreading Violet. Maybe she only wanted to talk about tiny houses.

"I have some really good ideas," he blurted, hoping to cover his tracks.

Violet looked up at him, surprise and amusement dancing in her violet eyes.

"That's nice to hear," she said, putting Thor on the ground. She studied Bale a minute before adding, "I've got a few really good ideas myself."

* * * *

Expand
Confident
Free

Molly wrote her affirmation words to start her day. It was Saturday. She didn't need to go to the farm. She decided to start her morning by making notes for improvements she was going to recommend to Bale once he returned to Cobb. First and foremost, Bale had to find a way to make the bed under the kitchen easier to slide. Molly also thought the kitchen sink shouldn't be round. Since Officer Melon now knew she was residing on the tiny house lot, Molly had gotten a little bolder about cooking. While circular was certainly an interesting look for a kitchen, the design made it difficult to wash a rectangular pan. She also thought the Tower might be pitched to bird owners as the perfect model. Galileo had more room in this tiny house than anywhere he'd ever lived. He gave her much less sass, feeling that he was the master of all he surveyed.

She'd sketched a few ideas for Bale, hoping her residency would be seen as something positive instead of a break-in. She also adjusted her own tree house to include a tower for Galileo…not that she expected to actually ever see her tree house realized, but keeping the design grounded in reality was part of the thesis. This was not just a concept home—it was a real possibility.

If not for her, for someone.

As she eyed her ever-changing tree house model, Molly sighed.

She envied that someone.

She eyed the clock on her phone. Even though she didn't have to go to work, Quinn had asked her if she wanted to meet him at the gym for a swim. Molly's instinct was to say no—there was no way she was going to look half as good in a bathing suit as he did. But she realized, between the now frequent visits to the gym, the wrestling match every day and evening with the bed, her endless walking at the farm five days a week, and climbing up and down to the tree fort, she actually would look pretty damn good.

Her really cute bathing suits were locked up at Crabby's, but she knew she had at least one suit...somewhere. It was interesting; even with very few possessions, it was still hard to keep track of everything. She dug around in the crevices of her gym bag and the car trunk. She was about to give up when it occurred to her she'd stuffed a bunch of clothes in a pillowcase to use at night as a makeshift pillow. She pulled the bed out from under the kitchen—a concept that still made her head reel—and dumped the contents of the pillowcase onto the bed.

She picked up the rumpled navy blue one-piece with the racer back. It was even more hideous than she remembered. It screamed "This suit means business."

"This is the worst," she wailed. "I'm going to look like an old lady in this!"

"Amen, brother," Galileo called from his loft.

"Bite me," she said.

Molly ran into Bale's workshop and rummaged around the tools. Huffing with disappointment, she went into the office and opened drawer after drawer. Giving up in frustration, she sat down at the big desk.

"That's where you are!" she said triumphantly as she seized the scissors.

She climbed back into the tiny house and grabbed the suit. She held it against her body and made some computations. She put the suit on the little table that came down from a latch on the wall when needed, smoothed it out, and cut the leg holes higher until they had a sexier line.

"This will have to do," she said before grabbing her keys and gym bag.

She heard Galileo offer her his leering pirate's laugh as she hurried to the car.

* * * *

"Oh no," Molly said to herself as she stared at her handiwork in the locker room.

She'd miscalculated by a few inches. She admonished herself—a budding civil engineer should never *guess*. She recalled the carpenters' mantra "Measure twice, cut once." But the damage was done. The leg holes were almost to her waist. She looked in the mirror. She had to admit, she didn't look half bad. But the effect was far from subtle.

Molly took her towel and wrapped it around her hips. She hoped her ponytail would suffice. She may have made her peace with the devil about the bathing suit, but she was not going to let Quinn catch her in a swim cap.

Okay, she could do this. She looked at the clock on the wall. She was five minutes early. She could run out to the pool and get in the water before Quinn arrived.

Now she felt more like an engineer—she had a solid plan.

Taking a deep breath, straightening her shoulders, and holding in her stomach, Molly walked to the pool. It looked deserted, but then she spotted a figure sitting at the far end of the pool. As she got closer, she could see it was Quinn.

Quinn, lounging poolside, in a Speedo. Molly willed herself not to run back to the locker room.

"Hey, Jane," Quinn called to her and waved.

As if she could miss him. With his various tattoos, washboard abs, and the bright red Speedo, he looked like a Chippendale Santa.

"Hey, Quinn," Molly said, giving a little wave back.

She willed herself to go through the motions anyone getting into the pool would do.

Walk to the bench.
Drop the towel.
She tried again.
DROP THE TOWEL.
Walk to the pool.
Don't worry if it's cold.
Get in the water—at least until you cover up the problem areas.
And just like that, she was in.

She took a deep breath and turned to Quinn. He was no longer on the side of the pool. She looked around. Suddenly, she saw a flash under the water. She shrieked as something brushed by her ankle. Quinn emerged from the deep like a really fit Poseidon, popping up right in front of her. She lost her footing and started to fall backwards, hoping the water at least made her look less clumsy. But Quinn caught her and pulled her back to her feet. He steadied her but didn't let her go. He looked at her hand and studied her words.

"Expand, confident, free," he said. "Those are good words for today."

He lifted her hand and kissed her palm.

Chapter 23

Molly was shaking as she let herself into the tiny house. She replayed every minute of her afternoon. She rubbed her chin. The fabulous make-out session in the pool left her with razor burn, which stung, but she was glad she had it or she would have thought she'd made up the whole thing. One minute, she and Quinn were lost in their own watery world, and the next, several of Quinn's friends materialized out of nowhere. They were yelling to him that they had a game going and he'd better get his ass in gear or he'd miss it.

Molly was thunderstruck when Quinn gave her a quick kiss on the forehead and swam to the ladder. His tight red butt was out of sight within minutes, leaving Molly standing in the shallow end by herself.

Galileo greeted her in his pirate voice but clearly sensed her distress and cooed at her instead.

"That's okay," Molly said, passing him a lettuce leaf. "I'm a total jerk."

But Galileo didn't bite.

Molly pulled out the bed and flopped down, her arm over her eyes. She tried to put a spin on the situation, so she could save face. Although she wasn't sure with whom she was saving face.

Herself?

She wasn't ready to sleep with Quinn, she told herself. But herself laughed back—who was she trying to kid? He was her boss and that's always a bad idea, she floated. Maybe he was concerned about that too.

Nice try, came the response from within.

"I'm an idiot," Molly said.

"Amen, brother," Galileo offered.

"Yeah."

"I love you, Quinn."

"I know," Molly said miserably. "Me too."

She tried to work on the miniature tree house, but inspiration deserted her. Molly moped around the tiny house lot the rest of the day. Her phone rang and she jumped. It was Quinn.

Should she answer it?

Of course she should. And she should act casual about the whole thing. Pretend as if she spent every Saturday making out with some guy in a pool who would apparently rather be playing cards.

That sounded more bitter than casual, she had to admit.

She took a deep breath and answered.

"Hey, Quinn."

"Hey, beautiful," Quinn said cheerfully. "Today was fun."

Today was fun?

"How was your card game?" Molly asked icily. She decided to tone it down to frosty. "Did you win?"

"I sure did. You're my good luck charm."

"Glad to hear it."

"So, want to come out and celebrate? We could go someplace nice for dinner."

Molly was tempted. She was always tempted by Quinn. But she was really stung by the rejection at the pool—even if he didn't see it that way.

"I really can't," Molly said. "I've got to work on my thesis."

"Your what?"

"My thesis," Molly repeated. "You know, I'm building a model of a tree house? I know I've told you about it."

"That's right. I keep forgetting that, don't I?"

"Yes."

"Are you sure you don't want to come out and party?"

No! I'm not sure!

"Yes, I'm sure. Sorry."

"I guess I'll just have to celebrate by myself."

"I sincerely doubt that."

Quinn laughed good-naturedly.

"I'll survive until Monday," he said. "Breakfast as usual?"

Molly wasn't sure what to say. She didn't want to seem like a pouting child if he just saw today as a fun but unimportant interlude. She really needed to be more sophisticated—not a skill she thought she'd need in a tiny town in Kentucky.

"I'll see you Monday," she said vaguely as she clicked off.

"I'm an idiot, aren't I?" she asked Galileo.

"Amen, brother."

"I mean, I have to have *some* self-respect. Don't I?"

Galileo refused to get involved. Molly played her own devil's advocate, trying to convince herself that she should be more cosmopolitan, more adult. A make-out session at the gym wasn't exactly a marriage proposal. It meant nothing.

Galileo suddenly started singing "The Female Highwayman" in her father's clear tenor. Molly could just imagine her father's reaction to today's events.

She was right to stay home.

"Okay, knock it off," she said to the bird. "I get it."

Galileo stopped singing and hopped onto his perch to look out the window. His job here was done.

Molly turned off the sound on her phone so she wouldn't hear it in case Quinn called back. She didn't want to weaken and agree to go out.

She strolled around the Bale's Tiny Dreams lot, clearing her head. She missed working on her thesis model in the tree fort. When she was on the ground, the project seemed overwhelming, but the elevation always gave her confidence in her work.

When it was time for bed, she'd done no work on her thesis.

But she'd stood her ground and never looked at her phone to see if Quinn had called. She brushed her teeth and crawled, emotionally exhausted, into bed.

She awoke in the dark to the sound of a roaring lion.

Molly shot up in bed to see Galileo, feathers standing up, swaying side to side and making his wild animal noises.

"It's okay," Molly soothed. "It's okay."

Galileo quieted down.

Molly heard him bark like a dog as soon as she turned her back to him.

"It's okay," she said. "I'm here."

She looked at him. He was still agitated, but he wasn't making any noise. Molly was confused. She still heard the dog barking.

A dog barking? Was she dreaming?

She crawled to the window and saw lights coming into the lot. It was Bale's bus. As Bale relocked the front gate, Thor was running toward the Tower, barking.

Molly ducked down and put her fingers to her lips for Galileo to remain silent.

"Bite me," he groused.

"Please be quiet," she said. "It's a matter of life and death."

Chapter 24

Molly heard Bale whistle for Thor, who was barking and wagging in front of the Tower where she skulked.

"Go away, Thor," Molly hissed through the door.

"Bite me," Galileo said in solidarity.

"Don't help," Molly called over her shoulder.

She peeked over the window frame again. Thor was returning to the bus. Molly leaned her back against the wall, trying to slow her breathing.

This is nuts! Why am I hiding from Bale?

Because you broke into his place of business?

All her justifications as to why it was perfectly fine to trespass now seemed totally absurd. Explaining herself was going to take some time. She glanced at her phone. It was three in the morning. She really shouldn't reveal herself now. Bale was probably tired, having driven all the way from…from…she had no idea where he'd come from. They hadn't texted or chatted in weeks. Since the rest of the tiny houses weren't caravanning onto the lot behind him, she suspected they'd arrive in the morning. She frowned. The fact that he was arriving before the tinies meant he must have been somewhere without them, but she let that pass. The fact that they would probably arrive in the morning was a good thing. He'd be distracted getting all the models back in place. She knew she couldn't evade him, but at least she could minimize how long she had to explain herself.

He would certainly understand.

Bale always understood.

Then why is my stomach in knots?

Even though Officer Melon knew she was on the lot, Molly still made sure to keep a low profile with her car. She prayed Bale didn't see it. She peeked out again and watched the bus's headlights float just above her car. Safe!

Bale parked the bus. Molly hoped he'd get in his truck and go home. She could be packed and sneak out after he left—although there was no way she could get Galileo's loft-cage dismantled in the dark. She'd have to deal with that in the morning. She started to collect her things, but after ten minutes, it appeared Bale was going to spend the rest of the night in the bus. She lay back down, knowing she wouldn't sleep, and waited for dawn.

She woke to the sound of Galileo swearing and the ground vibrating under her. Army-crawling to the window, she saw the tiny houses returning to the roost. Bale was directing each driver, while Thor kept looking toward the Tower. Molly imagined a puzzled look on his blank face.

She looked at her phone. It was six in the morning. She couldn't believe she fell asleep. She calmed Galileo and fed him, keeping out of sight of the goings-on on the lot. She knew the tiny houses fit like pieces of a puzzle. Bale could get them moved in and out or change their positions in record time. She'd just have to wait it out.

She went into the bathroom, putting on makeup and brushing her hair. Although she knew Bale didn't care how she looked, she needed to bring her A game to whatever was going to happen next—and that meant makeup.

Shoving the bed back under the kitchen, she sat cross-legged on the floor. This would be her last night here. Where would she and Galileo go? How had she not come up with a Plan B in all this time? She wondered if Professor Cambridge might have been right. Perhaps she didn't have the brain of an engineer. Not that his opinion mattered right now. What mattered was, she had to face Bale today.

She leaned against the wall and waited for the ruckus outside to die down. It was 7:30 before all the drivers left the lot.

Maybe Bale would go home now that the inventory was safely back in place. She peeked out the door. No such luck. She saw Bale heading for the workshop, Thor at his heels.

"I guess I have to go in there," Molly said to Galileo. "Wish me luck."

"You've got spunk, Molly girl," he offered in her father's voice.

"Thanks," Molly said, "but I'm not sure spunk is enough to get me out of this."

Molly called the tree farm. Not knowing how long this confrontation with Bale might take, she thought the responsible thing would be to let someone know she might be late.

"You've reached Quinn's Tree Farm," came the voice message in Quinn's cheerful voice. "Leave me a message, and if you're not a bill collector, I'll get back to you in a day or two."

Molly shook her head. Quinn could be such a man-child. What serious businessperson would leave a message like that?

And what would a bill collector think?

"Hey, Quinn…or Manny…whoever gets this. It's Molly. I'm still hoping to be on time, but…"

She stopped. There was no way to explain any of this. Not that she wanted to. And she doubted if either of the guys wanted to hear.

"Quinn, I'll text you if I'm not going to make it in by breakfast. Bye."

Molly clicked off. She was stalling. She could have just texted Quinn when she knew how the morning played out. It took Molly three false starts before she could bring herself to leave the tiny house. Realizing she was going to be late for work, she stepped out of the Tower and onto the asphalt. She forced herself in the direction of the workshop. The door was slightly ajar. Molly could smell coffee brewing. Even as nervous as she was, she could feel her stomach rumble and her mouth water. Unlike Quinn, who refused to make coffee, and Manny, who made horrible coffee, Bale made a great cup of coffee.

Molly slowly pushed the heavy workshop door, so it wouldn't announce her. Bale was standing with his back to her at the tiny kitchen that hugged the wall next to the office. Thor was nowhere to be seen, thankfully. He would bust her for sure. Molly tried to make her feet move forward, but she couldn't do it. She started to back out the door, but Bale's voice stopped her.

"I was wondering when you'd decide to stop in," Bale said without turning around.

"How…" Molly began.

At the sound of her voice, Thor bounded in from the office, hurling himself into her arms. Molly busied herself with the dog. She'd have been happy to prolong the homecoming, but Thor finally demanded to be put back on the ground. When she stood up again, Bale was looking at her.

"Thor seems glad to see me," she said.

"Yes, he does."

They both stared at Thor until the dog got bored and returned to the office.

"How did you know I was here?" Molly asked, trying to stall her explanation.

"I ran into Officer Melon on my way in here last night," Bale said, sounding a bit tense. "He said that as long as I was going to have such crap locks on my gate, it was good I had a security guard—even if it was a girl."

"Oh."

"Yeah."

"Did he tell you it was me?"

"No, he didn't have to! I knew it was you. Who else would feel she had the right to break into my place without asking?"

"It's not that I felt I had a right," Molly said, trying to keep offense out of her voice. She really had no room for umbrage. "I just didn't have any other choice."

"Here's a crazy idea. What about asking me? Did that even cross your mind?"

"Of course it crossed my mind!"

"And? Exactly what made you think that was a terrible idea?"

"I don't know," Molly said.

"Do you have a guess?"

"You stopped texting me and you left town without saying goodbye and I... I figured you must be sick of me. I was afraid you might say no."

"Let me get this straight. You thought I might say no, so instead you just moved in."

"Basically, yes."

"I could have you arrested."

Molly froze. She knew Bale might not be pleased with her, but *arrested*? She opened her mouth, hoping some fabulous defense would spring to her lips, but instead she burst into tears, surprising them both.

"Please don't have me arrested," Molly said.

"I'm not going to have you arrested," Bale said, handing her a handkerchief. "And I'd bail you out if I did."

"You would?"

"Which would be wrong on so many levels," he said. "Not the least of which, my name is Bale."

Molly gave him a watery smile. She snuffled into the handkerchief. Staring at it, she wondered if she should hand it back, tear stained and snot filled. Could that possibly help her cause? She tentatively held it out to him, but he waved it away.

"Do you forgive me?" she asked.

"It's not a question of forgiveness. It's just...that took a lot of..."

"Balls?"

"Or whatever."

Now that the heated discussion seemed to have cooled, Thor poked his head out of the office.

"Come on out, mighty warrior," Bale said, frowning, as Thor trotted out. "It's all over."

Molly's stomach flipped.
What was over?
The fight?
Or their friendship?

Chapter 25

"I'm really sorry about everything," Molly said. "I'm sure you want me to go."

"That's very astute of you," Bale replied.

"But if I can impose just a little bit longer…"

"Longer?"

Molly could hear how incredulous he sounded, but she kept going. "If I could just leave Galileo here until I get back from work…"

"Galileo's here?" Bale asked in surprise, looking around as if the African Grey was suddenly going to come flying through the air.

"Not here, here." Molly almost laughed but figured that would not help her case. "He's in the Tower."

"He's in the Tower?"

"Yes," Molly said.

She opened her mouth to say more but found she couldn't come up with any words. Bale didn't know to what extent Molly had made herself at home. Did she want to let him know?

"Really?' Bale asked. "Why the Tower?"

"Pardon?"

"Why the Tower? Why not the Log Cabin or the Victorian or any one of the other models?"

"Is that…seriously your question? I mean, I break into your place and take over one of your most expensive models and you want to know *why* I chose that particular one?"

"Yes. I mean, you're almost a civil engineer. There must have been something that drew you to the Tower. I'd like to know what it was."

The old excitement of sharing ideas with Bale came rushing back. She could see it in his eyes that he felt the same way. If she kept talking, maybe the awkwardness would just blow over.

"I'll show you why," she said, turning on her heels and heading toward the Tower. "It's actually pretty awesome."

Thor trotted alongside, his blank expression signaling he was taking no sides.

"I see you found the keys," Bale said as Molly took the key out of her pocket.

"They were very well organized," Molly said.

"I'm glad that worked out for you."

Molly decided she didn't want to look too closely at that remark. Best to keep moving forward. She stepped up on the first stair, which put her at eye level with Bale.

"Maybe Thor should stay outside," Molly said. "I'm not sure what Galileo will think of him. He's been pretty freaked out lately."

"*He's* been freaked out?" Bale said, but he put his hand up to signal Thor to stay.

Molly went inside, followed by Bale.

"I'll be damned," Bale said, spotting the chicken wire-enclosed loft immediately.

Molly held her breath as Bale walked to the enclosure.

"Hello, sailor," Galileo said in a flirtatious voice.

Where had he learned that?

After the fiasco in the tree fort, Molly refused to play the Animal Galaxy network and chose random TV shows to keep Galileo company when she was out of the tiny house.

Bale was running his hands over the seams of the enclosure.

"I know it's rough," Molly said, "but I…"

She let the sentence trail off. What could she say? *I was limited in my materials*—which were *his* materials.

She decided to just watch and wait for Bale's next move.

"This is great," Bale said. "It's a really good idea. Maybe we can offer an aviary as an option for people thinking about the Tower."

Molly's hopes perked up at the word "we."

Bale spotted the tree house model. He frowned.

"You've made some changes," he said, walking over to study it.

"Yes. Don't you like them?"

Bale looked at the model from all angles.

"I do," he said. "I like the changes a lot. Especially the larger windows."

"But..." Molly said.

"But," Bale said, "it's different, but it's not even close to being done. This is still as unfinished as it was when I left. Even though I can see you've been working on it."

"I know, I know. But when I was living in the tree, I just couldn't leave it the way it was."

"Wait a second! Did you say living in a tree?"

Molly stared at Bale. She might as well confess to everything.

"Want some coffee?" Molly asked. "This is a pretty long story."

* * * *

Molly filled Bale in on all the details of the past few weeks—the eviction, hiding her stuff at Crabby's and Quinn changing the locks, and deciding that living in the tree fort was a great plan, until a raccoon proved her wrong.

"That's when I came here," she said.

"I still don't understand why you didn't call."

Molly wasn't quite sure why she didn't call either, except that she was too embarrassed, so she lobbed the question back at him.

"You didn't call me either," Molly said. "I guess that had something to do with Violet?"

"In a very roundabout way, yes," Bale said.

Although he said no more about it.

"So here we are," Molly said.

"So here we are." Bale agreed.

"I hope you're not disappointed in me."

"Disappointed? No. I'm actually pretty impressed that you have such an array of criminal skills. I'm just glad you use them for good, not evil."

Molly could feel the tension draining from the room. Maybe everything was going to work out—somehow.

"I know I can't stay here," Molly said. "But maybe I could leave Galileo here...maybe not in the Tower, but in your office? He just can't go back to the tree fort. It isn't safe."

"It's not really safe for you either," Bale said. "And how long do you plan on staying up there? Till November when your thesis is due? It starts getting cold before Halloween."

"I can figure something out. I just need to make sure Galileo is safe."

Molly's stomach flipped as she watched Bale shake his head.

"Thor will not be happy sharing the office with Galileo," he said.

"Oh. I understand." Molly tried to keep the quaver out of her voice.

Why she expected Bale to help her out when she'd been trespassing on his property for weeks, she couldn't say.

Except, she had expected him to help.

"I think Galileo should stay right here," Bale said. "I wouldn't feel right taking him away from his palace."

"Really? That would be such a weight off my shoulders knowing he's safe."

"And it would be a weight off mine knowing *you* were safe. You both should stay."

Molly jumped up and threw her arms wide. Bale managed to get onto his feet before she squeezed him in a bear hug.

"Easy, there," Bale said, laughing and coughing. "You've gotten really strong working at that farm, I see."

"I've gotten really strong pushing and pulling the bed out from under the kitchen," Molly said, releasing him. "I have a few ideas how to counterbalance it, so it glides out and back."

"Sounds good," Bale said.

"Maybe I could help you around here," Molly said shyly. "Earn my keep?"

"I was just going to propose—" Bale seemed to strangle on his words but continued. "I was just going to propose something along those lines. But as usual, you beat me to it."

"Sorry."

"Don't be. You definitely have a faster hard drive. It's always impressed me."

Molly thought if she were talking to Quinn, he'd say, "That's why I love you."

But she didn't need Bale to love her. It was enough that he was her safe place.

"What did you have in mind?" Molly asked, settling down on her chair again.

"I'm sort of making this up as I go along," Bale said. "But I've been thinking about doing more work over at my place."

"Isn't this your place?"

"I meant my home," Bale said. "I've got four acres on the river. Plenty of room to expand Bale's Tiny Dreams without investing more capital. I've got too many orders to just work here at the lot. You could keep an eye on this place when I'm not around. Meet customers, show them around. Give me great ideas when they occur to you."

"That sounds perfect," Molly said. "But I have to be fair to you. I do work over at the tree farm. And we're just going to get busier. I don't want to take advantage."

"You broke into my place," Bale said. "You've already taken advantage."

Molly looked stricken, but Bale was smiling.

"Sorry, I couldn't resist," Bale said. "I'm sure we can work things out."

Molly tried to say thank you, but she was afraid she'd burst into tears. Instead, she turned to Galileo.

"We're home," Molly said to the African Grey. "Say hello to our new landlord."

"Hello, sailor," Galileo crooned.

Molly definitely had to curb his TV time.

Chapter 26

As summer turned to fall, Molly's life settled into a comfortable pattern. She would wake up early, feed Galileo, work on her thesis, go to breakfast with Quinn, work on the tree farm, then return to the tiny house lot where she might—or might not—see Bale.

She loved working mornings at the tree farm. They were getting busier as the holiday season inched closer. Late summer saw some labor-intensive days for Manny and Molly, as they helped trim and shear the evergreens, preparing them for market. Quinn kept a casual eye on things, although he made it very clear his only interest in the job would come in November, when he'd haul up to fifteen trees at a time through the air, much to the amazement of the town. He'd effortlessly lower the load into a flatbed truck, then take to the air for more.

Quinn's humor rose when Lady Luck stood beside him at the gambling table and fell when she deserted him. Breakfast conversation could be warm and flirtatious or completely one-sided as Molly tried to distract him from his gloom. She would exchange looks with Marni, the waitress, every time Molly and Quinn entered Beamer's, in the way women had to signal "He's in a mood."

"Have you heard from Crabby?" Molly asked one morning when Quinn was unusually pensive.

"Hmm?" Quinn asked, distracted.

"Have you heard from Crabby? You haven't mentioned him in a while."

"Yeah, as a matter of fact, I did. Conversation didn't go very well."

Molly waited. Was she supposed to ask why? She could never tell with Quinn. He wasn't like Bale, who was so easygoing. She decided to go for it.

"What happened?"

"I asked to borrow some money. He wasn't too happy about it."

Molly felt her throat tighten.

Did Quinn need money? Was the farm in danger? Would she lose her job? Would she lose Quinn?

"Bad night at the tables?"

"More like bad nights."

"Well, Crabby is retired. Maybe he doesn't have any money."

"Crabby is loaded." Quinn barked a sharp laugh. "Everything he touches turns to gold. When I was a kid, he had four helicopters. Got bored, sold them all, and bought a horse ranch. Sold the horse ranch and bought a traveling amusement park. Got tired of that and bought the restaurant. It was one thing after another."

Molly couldn't figure out what was wrong with that.

"Maybe he wasn't bored," Molly said carefully. "Maybe he just saw one good investment after another."

"Everything he did was a gamble," Quinn said. "He was a gambler. Just like me. But his gambles all paid off. So he thinks he's better than me."

"Did he say he thought he was better than you?" Molly asked.

"Not in so many words."

That didn't surprise Molly. Crabby never did use many words, no matter what the situation.

"Are you in serious trouble?" Molly asked softly.

Quinn looked up sharply. He seemed to have snapped out of some sort of trance. He gave her one of his killer smiles.

"Don't you worry about me," Quinn said, reaching across and taking her hand. "I'm never down for long."

Molly decided to change the subject. But she left her hand where it was. Something outside caught the corner of her eye. It was Marni, her ample rear end up in the air as she bent over something on the ground.

"What's going on out there?" Molly asked.

Quinn looked out the window.

"Oh, that's just Marni blowing up the air dancers."

"I missed that. What is she doing?"

"You know those air dancers…giant inflatable balloons with arms and faces," Quinn said, mimicking an inflatable waving his arms. "Car dealerships and new housing developments use them to get attention."

Molly nodded. She knew what he was talking about but couldn't see why Marni was wrestling with one.

"Beamer's always puts a couple up for their anniversary," Quinn continued. "You can see them for miles. They're a real fixture around

Burgoo. The yellow one is called Charlie, the red one is Lucy, and the green one is Seymour."

"How do they work?" Molly asked, the civil engineer in her coming out.

"I don't know exactly," Quinn said. "Some kind of electric fan or generator, I guess."

Marni stood back as the large yellow tube started unrolling skyward.

"I thought it would be noisier," Molly said. "You can't hear it at all. It's really interesting."

"You know what would be interesting?" Quinn said, still looking out the window at Marni. "More coffee."

Marni finally returned to the counter. Quinn's vibes must have reached her, and she rushed over with a pot of coffee. Molly had questions about the air dancers but figured she was a party of one.

"Next month should be fun," Molly said, switching gears again. "Almost time for the first harvest."

"If the deer don't eat all the profits," Quinn said. "They might have been a nuisance during the summer, but as their food supply dries up at this time of year, the trees seem like an open invitation."

Molly let out a sigh. Hard as she tried, she'd found no solution to the deer problem. Manny had given up asking her. He waited for the day Quinn condemned him to spreading the disgusting deer deterrent. Manny had managed to keep Quinn distracted, but now there was no denying the deer were getting more and more bothersome.

Molly stared down at the air dancer when Old Paint lifted into the sky. With its goofy grin and waving arms, it seemed as if it wanted to tell her something.

Molly also loved her late afternoons and evenings at Bale's Tiny Dreams, helping customers visualize what life would be like living tiny. Molly suggested to Bale that she show people the Tower, so they could see a real, lived-in tiny house instead of just a model.

Galileo was always a hit. Even his antisocial remarks were met with cheer. It was just impossible to be in a bad mood around a tiny house.

"You've got salesmanship in your blood," Bale told Molly after they locked up the lot.

"No, I don't. These homes sell themselves."

"Well, they're selling themselves a lot faster since you got here."

Bale was carrying a box from the office to his truck, heading home for the evening. Thor trotted at his heels. Molly had signed for the box earlier in the day. The box was from a company Molly had never heard of, but in the lefthand corner, the name Violet Green jumped out at her. When

Molly took the box from the delivery guy, she could tell it was something refrigerated. The box was cool to the touch. She'd contemplated the box all day.

What was Violet sending?

Champagne?

Filet mignon?

Salmon?

She finally saw Bale carrying the box to the car.

"Thanks for signing for this," Bale said, giving Molly just the opening she needed.

"No worries," Molly said. "I could tell it was some sort of cooled stuff. I almost opened it in case I should have put it in the refrigerator or something."

"It's all good," Bale said. "It has those ice packets that last for days."

"Then I thought…" Molly said, following him to the truck. Her curiosity was killing her. "I thought maybe it was lobster, and if I opened it, they might escape."

"Don't worry about it," Bale said. "It's not lobster. Live lobster is a little rich for my blood."

But was it too rich for Violet Green's blood?

"Is it one of those boxes of food that comes every month?" Molly blurted.

Bale stopped and looked at her.

"Yeah," he said with a sigh. "We Skype all the time and can get to talking for hours about her tiny house design or whatever."

Molly felt a tiny nettle under her skin at the "whatever." Bale was working on Violet's tiny house at his place. He said it was top secret, which drove Molly crazy. She didn't want Bale to have secrets from her. She missed part of what he was saying but returned her focus to him.

"So she bought me one of those healthy foods of the month things. This is the second one I've gotten."

"I've heard of those," Molly said.

Bale put the box in the back of his truck.

"Do you like it?" Molly asked.

Bale turned to her, surprised.

"The food?"

"Yes," Molly said, wishing she could do something as nice, as extravagant for Bale. He might be building Violet the mothership of all tiny houses, but there was no way Violet could owe Bale more than Molly did.

"I feel guilty saying this," Bale said. He looked around as if Violet might hear him. "But it's really not for me. I unload the stuff and then just eat the ingredients instead of cooking the recipes."

Molly smiled.

"Don't tell Violet," Bale said.

"You know," Molly said, touching Bale's arm. "I could cook it for you. We could have dinner together before you went home…or, now that you're working from your place so much, I could come over and cook when I get home from the farm."

Molly saw Bale's face cloud over.

"I don't think you need to come out to my place. It's all the way on the opposite side of the tree farm."

Molly wanted to say she didn't mind. But Bale's expression was not exactly welcoming.

"Now that I'm working out there, it's kind of a disaster area," he said.

"I don't mind."

"I'm not kidding," Bale said. "I'm thinking I might need more room one of these days. I'm not sure working piecemeal, a little work on the lot, a little work at the house, is the best business model."

Molly felt her heart skip a beat.

Bale might leave?

"But you'd stay around here, right?" Molly asked. "You wouldn't leave Cobb."

"I might, I might not." He smiled. "I mean, practice what you preach, right? I can take my tiny houses anywhere."

It struck her that she'd probably be leaving Cobb herself, once she had her degree. Her life had been so crazy she hadn't thought about it recently. But she couldn't visualize a place where she wasn't hanging with Bale.

"Anyway," Bale said. "Right now, everything at my place is in complete chaos."

"That's okay," Molly said. "Violet might not like me cooking for you anyway."

"Oh, she wouldn't care."

Molly was surprised how much that comment stung. What was she—chopped liver?

"But I'll tell you what," Bale said, lifting the box back out of the truck. "If you're serious, let's eat here. There's plenty of food. We could try eating in all the different models. Curry in English Cottage one night, vegetable goulash in the Log Cabin the next. It can be kitchen research."

"Sounds perfect," Molly said. "Why don't we start in the Tower?"

"Good idea," Bale said, walking toward the tiny house with the aviary. "You can decide what we eat. But no cauliflower rice. I don't know what anybody was thinking when they invented that."

Chapter 27

Inspired
Hopeful
Ready

Before she was even fully awake, Molly wrote the words on her hand. The day seemed full of possibilities. The Tower still smelled like edamame stew from the night before. She and Bale had a relaxed evening while she prepared the food, Thor and Galileo blessedly ignoring each other. She hated to admit it: she loved cooking in "her" kitchen, chatting with Bale about what worked design-wise and what could be tweaked. Bale never took offense at any of Molly's suggestions. She had dinner together in less than twenty minutes.

"I'd never even heard of edamame," Bale had said, looking gloomily at the steaming, greenish bowl of food in front of him.

"Do you like it?" Molly asked, as she sat down across from him at the diminutive table.

He took a bite and shrugged.

"I can eat it," he said. "But this stuff is a strange choice if Violet wants me to keep my strength up. I was sort of expecting meat and potatoes, you know?"

Another weird pang of jealously struck her.

What the hell was that about? She should be grateful Bale had a woman who would take care of him.

But I want to take care of him.

She'd never had any romantic or proprietary thoughts about Bale. And she better not start having them now, she admonished herself. She was inching towards a relationship with Quinn, and Bale now had Violet.

"Let's take the bed out," Bale said as Molly stacked the dishes in the sink. Molly almost dropped the bowl she was holding.

"Hello, sailor," Galileo, always one to pick up on Molly's emotions, chirped.

"What did you say?" Molly asked, pretending not to hear.

"Hello, sailor," Galileo repeated.

"Not you," Molly laughed, grateful for the comic relief. She took a deep breath and turned to Bale. "I meant you."

"Let's take the bed out," Bale said, standing up and snapping the hinged dining room table back against the wall. "I'd completely forgot you said the rolling mechanism needed some work. Let's take a look."

Molly felt her cheeks redden.

Get over yourself.

"Oh, I figured out what was wrong and fixed it," Molly said.

"No kidding," Bale said with interest. "Show me."

Molly flushed again but pulled out the bed. She and Bale were both on the floor. She snuck a peek at him.

His interest was clearly in the bed.

"Two of the screws in the springs were loose. It was a simple adjustment," she said.

"That's great," Bale said as he pushed the bed back and forth. "You're amazing."

You're amazing. Why am I just noticing that?

Bale shoved the bed back under the kitchen and stood up.

"I better let you get back to your thesis," Bale said. "I know it's getting down to the wire."

Molly was disappointed, but he was right. She did need to work on the tree house model. They both turned to stare at the miniature tree house, which was by far, notwithstanding Bale, the largest thing in the tiny house.

"It looks like you've finally settled on your design," Bale said, studying it.

"Thanks to you," Molly said as she started to clean up.

"Why thanks to me?"

"You gave me a place to live, took the pressure off. I've been able to concentrate."

"It really is a work of art," he said, before Molly could get sentimental.

Molly hugged herself. She never had to remind Bale about her thesis. His interest in her work was genuine.

"Thanks," Molly finally said. "I hope Professor Cambridge shares your enthusiasm next month."

"Professor Cambridge?"

"Yeah. He's my advisor."

"I know Professor Cambridge," Bale said. "Interesting man."

"You know Professor Cambridge?" Molly squeaked.

"It's a small town, Mols," Bale grinned. "I see him at the gym all the time. He's a really smart guy—and he can kick my ass on the treadmill."

"Now that the season has changed, I'm thinking about taking the model back to the tree fort," Molly said.

"What do you mean?" Bale seems suddenly anxious.

"I told you about the tree fort," Molly said. "It's where that raccoon tried to get in the cage."

"I know the place. I was just wondering why you wanted to go back there. It seems dangerous."

"Oh, not to *live* there. Trust me, I'm very happy here."

Am I too happy here?

"Then why go back?"

"I love being up there. I thought I might take the model up and…I don't know…I might paint it. The fall colors are deepening, and I think they might inspire me with the palette."

"It seems crazy to risk getting the model into the tree," Bale said.

"I've gotten it in and out several times now," Molly said. "I'm a pro."

"That's your decision, of course," Bale said, looking at his watch. "Wow, it's getting late. I better get home. Violet and I are going to Skype tonight and go over some new plans for her tiny house. As soon as we've cemented something, the woman changes her mind."

"You don't have to tell her I made dinner," Molly said. "If you think it might bother her."

"Why would it bother her?"

Ouch.

Molly waved to Bale and Thor as the truck left the lot. Bale had bought an extra secure lock for the front gate and flashed his lights, letting her know she was safe for the night. Molly went to bed, rattled that she seemed to be falling for Bale. She refused to even entertain the words "in love"; those words were reserved for Quinn. But Bale's stock was definitely going up.

"Good night, Galileo," Molly said as she collapsed in bed.

"I love you, Quinn."

Molly put her head under the pillow. Should she teach Galileo to say, "I love you, Bale"?

The morning brought the first cold snap of fall, and Molly felt she had her emotions under control.

"You be good," Molly said to Galileo after giving him his breakfast.

"Bite me," Galileo said before wolfing down a cabbage leaf left over from the edamame stew.

"I hope you appreciate this, Dad," Molly said, looking heavenward. But she knew he did.

Molly went to the small storage unit attached to the back of the Tower and pulled out the box she used to move the tiny tree house. She brought it inside and realized almost immediately that the new, improved model was too big for the box. It was still early. Bale wouldn't be around for a while. She knew he would have no objection to her taking one of the myriad boxes he had on the lot, but Molly didn't want to take even the slightest advantage of him. She still had pangs of guilt for breaking into the tiny house lot. She swore she'd be a better friend.

But she really needed a box.

She measured the tree house model and was startled to find exactly how much it had grown. She threw on a sweater and watched her affirmation words slide in and then pop out of the sleeve. She looked around the lot until she found the perfect box.

She leaned against the tiny log cabin. Should she wait until Bale got to the lot? He didn't keep regular hours, while she had to get to the tree farm within the hour. But she couldn't bring herself to just take it. She wanted to cry every time she recalled Bale's face when he discovered her on the premises that night.

He'd looked...betrayed.

She couldn't ever see that look again. She would work to regain his trust.

His words suddenly came back to her:

"Why didn't you just ask?" he'd said.

It was early. But Molly could shoot him a text, couldn't she? If he answered, fine. If not, she'd wait until tomorrow. She was impatient, but she would keep her vow to herself to be a better friend.

Molly: Hey. Sorry to wake you. I need a box. Can I take one from the lot?

She waited a few minutes, willing the phone to announce a return text. She was just jamming the phone to her jeans pocket when her phone signaled a text. She looked at it and smiled.

Bale: You woke me up for cardboard? Take what you want. Thanks for dinner.

Molly grabbed the box and returned to the Tower. Galileo, busy with his squeaky toy, gave her the side eye, as if to say, "Why are you back?"

"I'll be out of your feathers in ten minutes," Molly said.

Galileo went back to his toy. Molly looked at him, convinced he knew she couldn't concentrate when he crunched into its soft center. She'd tried taking it away from him, but he'd learned to mimic the sound, so he was just as annoying with or without it, so she gave it back.

She carefully packed the tree house model in the box, stuffing clothes around the edges to keep it safe. Even with all the refinements and additional patios, the model was heavier than she'd anticipated. But she managed to get it into the car.

She drove onto the lot before anyone else was there and headed to the big trees. Deer scattered as her car's tires crunched up the gravel road.

Sorry, Manny.

She got out of the car, checked to make sure the pulley system was still sound, then attached the box. With all the physical labor she'd been doing the last few months, she knew she was strong enough to get the box up into the tree. As the box swung over the platform, Molly tied off the pulley, scrambled up the ladder, and hauled the box inside.

She unpacked the box, then flipped it over. It seemed sturdy enough. She carefully settled the tree house model on it. The box was a little low, but it would do for now as a workstation. Molly looked around the lean-to. She'd left some white nylon cording up here. She found it tangled up in a corner, now a rather unattractive shade of dirt. She secured the model with the cording, running the nylon out from the tree house to various nails on the walls. She stood back to admire her work. The tree house, with its whimsically shaped rooms and extensions, which usually looked impressive in its own way, looked ridiculous tied up. The sight made Molly laugh.

"I promise I'll untie you when I'm up here," Molly said. "But I can't risk those damn raccoons knocking you over."

Molly went out on the platform and looked over the treetops. The beautiful evergreens of the farm stood silently in rows by type and height. Molly could see the firs, pines and spruces, all perfectly manicured, waiting quietly for the frantic activity that was now just a few weeks away.

The farm's trees stood in contrast with the deciduous trees, which were starting to lose their leaves. With the lush landscape of green thinning out, Molly could see much more of the vista. She was surprised she could make out Beamer's on the other side of the river. It was just a nondescript building, but Charlie, the bright yellow air dancer, seemed to be waving at her.

She looked down to see two deer heading onto the farm.

She suddenly flashed on an idea.

"I'll be back later today," Molly called to the tree house model before zipping down the ladder.

She drove to the office, hurried inside and wrote a hasty note to Quinn:

Q - Headed over to Beamer's. – M.

Chapter 28

Molly pulled into the parking lot at Beamer's. Marni was already there, letting the air out of the inflatables. Apparently the anniversary was over.

"Hey Marni," Molly said.

"Hey there," Marni said. "I almost didn't recognize you without Quinn. You slumming it this morning?"

"Pardon?" Molly asked. "You usually drop down out of the sky. And now here you are without the pilot or the helicopter."

"Oh, yeah," Molly said.

She understood the idea that Marni might be disappointed in a solo Molly. Quinn was definitely the star attraction.

"Quinn might show up later. I needed to ask you something."

"I'm right here," Marni said, straightening up. "Ask away."

"It's kind of a long, crazy story."

"Come on in then," Marni said. "I'll get you some coffee."

* * * *

Molly was just sipping her second cup of coffee when she heard Marni say, "Hey there, handsome."

Molly looked up. It was Quinn. She didn't hear Old Paint land and looked out into the field where Quinn usually landed. The helicopter wasn't there. Weird that Quinn had taken his truck. She smiled to herself. Quinn was going to be so excited when he heard her news.

Quinn entered, looking grim. Molly felt herself tense slightly. Looked like Quinn had had another bad night—which seemed to be happening more and more lately.

"Hey Quinn," Molly said as he slid into the booth across from her. "Good morning."

"If you say so," Quinn said, signaling Marni for coffee.

"I suppose you're wondering why I took off without you this morning," Molly said, trying to keep the glee out of her voice.

Quinn looked up, startled.

"Uh, no, actually," he said, running his fingers distractedly through his hair. "I didn't really think about it. I've got a lot on my mind."

It occurred to Molly that Bale would have wondered.

Don't compare him to Bale.

Why not compare him to Bale? a little voice inside her said.

Because Bale is with Violet. You took him for granted, and now he's got someone who sees how special he is.

Molly looked back at Quinn. He did look miserably unhappy. She tried to soften her attitude. After all, she wasn't a starry-eyed teenager. She never thought Quinn was perfect.

Yes, you did.

"What's on your mind?" Molly asked at the same time Quinn said, "I'll bite... Why did you take off without me?"

They sat in silence, looking at each other. Quinn took a sip of coffee, leaned back, and closed his eyes.

"Ladies first," he said.

"I have a solution to the deer problem," she said, trying to contain her excitement.

She waited for Quinn to react, but he just sat with his eyes closed.

"Anyway," she continued, "Marni says I can borrow Charlie, Lucy, and Seymour. You know, the air dancers. We can put them up in the rows where the deer are causing the most damage. The dancers have their own batteries and fans, and I was thinking if we used motion sensors, then we could..."

"Don't care," Quinn said through closed eyes.

Molly stopped mid-sentence. Could she have heard him correctly?

"Excuse me?" Molly asked.

"I said I don't care," Quinn said, sitting up and opening his eyes. "Just sold the tree farm. Deer and everything else are no longer my problem."

Quinn reached in his pocket for his wallet. Molly knew this was his signal they were leaving.

"Back up, back up," Molly said.

She put her hand on his arm. He sat back down. The thought crossed her mind that the electricity she always felt when she touched him was less intense. Not gone, but not the high voltage jolt she used to experience.

"What?" Quinn glowered.

"What do you mean, you sold the farm?"

"Just what it sounds like. I sold the farm."

"Why?"

"Why do you think?"

"Gambling?" Molly asked, barely breathing.

"You don't have to whisper." Quinn leaned forward and whispered harshly, "Everybody in this town knows I gamble."

"I had no idea things had gotten so…"

"Shitty?" Quinn finished the sentence for her. "Well, they have. Things have gotten really, really shitty."

"I'm so sorry."

"Don't be. Easy come, easy go, you know. I won the farm and the helicopter in a game. It was never my passion or anything."

"Did you lose Old Paint, too?"

"I didn't *lose* the farm or the helicopter," Quinn said testily. "Give me some credit."

I'm trying. You don't know how hard I'm trying.

"I sold the farm and the helicopter goes with it," Quinn said.

"But you love Old Paint."

"Look, Molly," Quinn said. "Old Paint is just a machine…a thing. You can't love a thing."

"No, but you're a pilot. You can be proud of yourself and your ability when it comes to a *thing*. You worked hard for the achievement. I mean, I've worked hard on my master's and I…"

"Oh, yes, you and your master's."

Molly felt as if she'd been slapped.

"What about me and my master's?"

"You and Manny, with your tree houses and Manny's… What's his deal again? Oh yes, frickin' bagpipes. Some of us have to be realistic. And it's clearly not going to be anybody who works for me at the Christmas tree farm. "

"Used to work for you," Molly said.

She stood up shakily. She saw her words:

Inspired
Hopeful
Ready

She wanted to give them to Quinn. He was so bitter. She wanted to tell him there were dreams to follow, and you were a better person, a stronger person, a happier person if you worked for that dream.

But she knew someone had to learn that for him or herself. Even with all the hard times, Molly never gave up.

She wondered what she could say to Quinn.

"I suppose you're worried about your job," Quinn said.

"Actually, I hadn't gotten that far," Molly said.

"Don't worry, I'm sure the new owner will hire you."

"That's good to hear, but how are you so sure?"

"He's an old friend of yours."

It suddenly hit Molly.

The new owner must be Bale! He was talking about needing more space. There was plenty of room at the farm to expand the tiny house business and still keep the farm going. And she could help him with the tree farm side of things. She knew a lot about evergreens now.

And Bale would be interested in the air dancers.

She knew she'd lost any opportunity to have Bale see her as anything but a slightly flaky, slightly larcenous sidekick, but he deserved her loyalty.

She'd wasted so much time on Quinn.

The familiar roar of Old Paint pierced the deadly quiet of their conversation. Molly looked out the window, but Quinn just contemplated his coffee cup. Marni opened the front door and peered into the sky, then back at Quinn.

"Somebody took off with your helicopter," Marni said.

"That's the new owner, getting the hang of things."

Molly stared at Quinn. She was pretty sure Bale didn't know how to fly a helicopter. But if this morning was any indication, it was that life was full of surprises.

"No way," Marni's face split into a grin. "The old devil is back, is he?"

Quinn shrugged.

"He's back to give me competition again, is he?" Marni asked.

"Not really," Quinn said, a little of his flirtatiousness struggling to break free from the hangover. "I'm your new competition. I might as well give slinging hash a shot—I've tried everything else."

"I've got all Crabby's customers now," Marni said. "I'll bury you in a month."

"You won't be the first," Quinn said miserably.

"Are you changing the name to Quinn's—or still gonna keep it 'Crabby's?'" Marni asked.

"Marni, give me a break," Quinn said, squeezing his temples. "I haven't gotten that far."

What was going on? Quinn bought Crabby's? Bale could fly a helicopter? Marni had a competitive streak?

Was Molly still asleep and this was all a dream?

"Wait, wait, wait," Molly said. "You bought Crabby's?"

"Yeah," Quinn said. "With the profits from the sale of the farm."

Molly listened to the droning sounds of Old Paint in the sky.

Crabby!

Crabby could fly a helicopter.

"Is Crabby the new owner of the farm?" Molly asked in a whisper.

"Of course," Quinn said as if it were the most obvious thing in the world. "Who else would take on such a losing proposition?"

Molly thought "Anybody with vision"—but she didn't say it. It occurred to her with some irony that Quinn now was the new owner of her "storage unit" in the back of the restaurant.

She better not piss him off. She suspected he wasn't going to be as nice as Bale was about the tiny house lot break-in.

"So, he's just up there, getting the hang of Old Paint?" Marni said, squinting into the sky.

"No," Quinn said. "When we were walking the farm, he said the big trees were getting tangled in the power lines. He's up there topping the largest trees."

Molly's heart beat wildly in her chest.

"I've got to go," Molly called as she jumped out of her seat.

Her hands shook violently as she tried to jam the key into the ignition. She needed to get back to the tree fort, which was in the largest of the big trees. She tried to keep Old Paint in sight from the road, trying to see if Crabby had the tree topping mechanism attached to the helicopter's undercarriage. But the helicopter was still too far away.

As she sped toward the farm, she tried to remember all she knew about tree topping. It was a very controversial procedure. It could stunt the growth of trees and leave them open to disease but was also a quick way to clear power lines tangled in branches, which caused a fire hazard. Molly wished she knew more. All she did know for sure was if she could see a chain hanging from the undercarriage of Old Paint with a large saw in the middle, then Crabby meant business.

The procedure shook the trees violently. Molly was pretty sure the rickety lean-to and platform would not be able to withstand the impact. It would be the end of her thesis.

She was close enough now to see the helicopter and the chain swinging menacingly in the wind.

She had to get to her tree before Crabby did.

She drove as if her life—and her dreams—depended on it.

Molly almost lost control of the car as she drove frantically toward the big trees. Crabby was directly overhead. She parked right below the tree fort. If Crabby hadn't noticed the car as she drove up, she was now safely out of view. She got out of the car and raced to the tree. She stopped dead in her tracks. Bale was coming down the ladder.

At first she thought he'd somehow known to save her tree-house model. But he was empty handed. He almost ran into her as he turned around.

"Molly!" he yelled, trying to be heard over the roar of the helicopter. "What are you doing here? Something's going on—and it looks dangerous."

"I can't explain now," Molly said, pushing past him.

She didn't have time to ask what he was doing here or to explain the finer points of tree topping. She needed to get up to the platform. She started up the ladder, but suddenly found herself stuck. Her foot wouldn't move. She looked down. Bale had her by the ankle.

"Get down," Bale said, as the tree shook. "It's too dangerous."

"Let go of me," Molly said, trying to kick him away.

He held tight. "You can't go up there," Bale said again.

The tree shook. Violently.

Molly heard the sounds of splintering wood. Bale swung onto the ladder step with her and tried to shield her from the falling debris. She held on to the ladder with one hand and pushed at Bale with the other.

Then she saw it. Her magnificent thesis, her years of hard work, her labor of love and hate, falling tree-limbs-first, through the air, toward the ground.

She pushed past Bale and took a leap of faith into the air.

Chapter 29

Molly wondered if she were dreaming. She could feel her mother's hand stroking her forehead. As she drifted in and out of consciousness, she heard her father crooning *Tura Lura Lura*.

Maybe I'm not dreaming. Maybe I'm dead.

She heard Bale but couldn't make out what he was saying.

She slept.

Chapter 30

"She's waking up," Molly heard someone say.

She wondered who was waking up.

"Molly?" Bale's voice penetrated the fog. "Molly? Can you hear me?"

Of course she could hear him. He was talking to her. What kind of question was that?

But she couldn't make her mouth say the words. She tried to go back to sleep.

"Molly?" Bale persisted. "Molly?"

Molly willed herself to open her eyes, if only to shut him up. It took her a moment to focus. Bale was standing over her. She remembered now. She had fallen out of the tree, chasing…chasing…

The pain was searing as she remembered her model crashing to the ground. The next thing she remembered was Bale on the ground beside her. She tried to capture the details. She'd jumped. Had he jumped after her? She closed her eyes again, but the memories were piecing themselves together against her will. Bale was on his knees, gently stroking her cheek, while she lay like a ragdoll on the ground. Quinn was there, and so was Manny. At some point, Crabby had joined them. Everything was quiet. The tree wasn't shaking anymore. But she hadn't gotten to the tree fort in time. Pieces of Molly's tree house model and remnants of her tree fort lay scattered around her.

She could hear herself whimper.

"Stay with me, Molly," Bale's voice was strong.

She opened her eyes again.

She looked around. She wasn't at the tree farm. She was in the hospital.

"What?" Molly croaked.

"Don't talk now," Bale said. "Just get better. Please. Just. Get. Better."

"Well," Molly whispered, "when you put it like that…"

Bale leaned over her and kissed her forehead. His right arm was in a sling.

"What happened to you?" she asked. She remembered him on the ground beside her. "Did I do that?"

"Don't flatter yourself," Bale said. "I take full responsibility for my part in this fiasco."

"My thesis," Molly said.

"Don't worry about that," Bale said. "Everything is going to be fine. Just rest."

* * * *

Molly hadn't been dreaming. Her mother was there. So was her brother. She felt a stab when she realized they were supposed to be coming for her graduation but had used their tickets to come visit her in the hospital instead.

"You scared us all to death," her mother said.

"Totally," Curly said.

"Amen, brother," came a muffled voice inside Curly's jacket.

Molly's eyes widened as Curly retrieved Galileo from his pocket.

"Horse's ass," Galileo said as he gave Curly the side-eye.

"I tried to get him in here as an emotional-support parrot, but his bedside manner left something to be desired."

"I can imagine," Molly said.

"Everyone has been so nice," Molly's relentlessly cheerful mother said. "Bale has put us up in one of the tiny houses. He said you'd want to know which one. It's the Victorian. It's just adorable. I can see why you find them so interesting."

Molly knew nobody was going to mention her thesis. It was bad enough she'd failed. It was bad enough her model was in ruins. But the worst of it was, she'd let everyone down.

"I'm sorry for everything," Molly said, tears springing suddenly to her eyes. "You must be so disappointed in me—again."

"Bite me," Galileo squawked, reacting to Molly's tone.

"What are you talking about?" her mother said. "You've never let us down."

"Although jumping out of that tree with a buzz saw over your head was not your smartest move," Curly said.

"Horse's ass," Galileo said, responding to Molly's reaction to Curly's statement.

"Footsteps," Molly's mother whispered as a rustling could be heard in the hall.

Curly shoved Galileo back in his jacket.

"And be quiet," Curly said to his pocket. "Or we'll all get thrown out of here."

Bale appeared in the doorway. Seeing his arm in a sling hurt every time she saw him.

"I love you…" came the muffled voice in Curly's jacket.

Molly looked horrified.

Bale was too far away to hear, thank God. Curly walked quickly to the door to intercept Bale.

But the muffled voice continued.

"I love you, Bale."

I love you, *Bale*?

Molly shot a look at her mother.

"I've been working with him," she said with a wink. "After hearing everything that's been going on, I figured you'd want to nip that 'I love you, Quinn' thing in the bud. Although Quinn does say he'll give you your property back, which was stowed illegally on his property. I swear, Molly, who raised you to do something like that?"

"Thank you," Molly said.

"You've always had terrible taste in men," her mother said. Glancing over at Bale, she added, "Until now, I hope."

"I hope so, too," Molly said.

Her mother kissed her and headed to the door to say hello to Bale. Molly felt sorry for her mother, who she could tell was going to try her damnedest to will Bale into seeing all the fabulous attributes of her daughter.

She watched her family chat easily with Bale. They'd become friends while she was lying in a hospital bed. Molly knew her family only saw that Bale had tried to save her. But, *she* knew that didn't mean he was in love with her.

He would have saved anybody.

Violet was a very lucky woman.

Molly's mother gave her one last look, which said, "Don't blow this," as she and Curly left the room.

"You're looking good," Bale said.

"Everybody says that," Molly said. "But I know I look terrible!"

"Yeah, you do," Bale agreed. "But you look better than you did yesterday and the day before. So, pretty soon, we'll all be able to say that, and it will be true."

"Something to look forward to, I guess."

"You scared the crap out of all of us, you know."

"I do know," Molly said. "And believe me, my mother is never going to let me forget it."

Molly was feeling stronger. She needed to fit the last remaining puzzle pieces into place. Everyone was acting unnervingly cheerful on their visits, but it was time to hear the rest.

"So, let's start with your arm," Molly said, as if in mid-conversation with her thoughts.

"It's broken, but it'll heal," Bale said, looking down at his sling.

"I thought you'd bought the tree farm," Molly said.

"What would I do with a tree farm?" Bale asked. "Don't I have enough problems?"

"Why were you there?"

"I...this is going to sound nuts...but I wanted to check out the tree house model. To see what you'd done since you started painting it."

That did seem nuts, but it was as reasonable an explanation as any.

"Can you work with it like that?" Molly said, indicating his arm.

"Hell, no. But that's okay. I've hired a few of the guys who drive the tinies to the conventions. They know assembly. Some of them are going to stay on."

"I feel like I ruined everything," Molly said, her eyes welling up.

"That's not like you. You always look on the bright side," Bale said, as he took her hand. "Just think of it as my expansion taking place ahead of schedule."

As much as she needed to know, Molly couldn't quite bring herself to ask about the tree house model's remains, so she skirted around it.

"So did Quinn move over to Crabby's?" she asked.

"Yep," Bale said. "And he found your stuff."

"I know, my mom told me."

"I did some fast-talking and promised I'd give everything to you when you got out of here."

"Was he angry?"

"Not really," Bale said. "We bonded over your amazing talent for breaking and entering."

Molly blushed.

"Quinn isn't a bad guy," Bale said. "He just...I don't know...keeps looking for something that isn't there."

"Like what?"

"How should I know? It isn't there."

"Very philosophical."

Molly looked at Bale. She was looking for something that *was* there—something that was in front of her this whole time—and she never saw it. Was she any better off than Quinn?

"The air dancers have been a big hit," Bale said.

"Do they keep the deer away?"

"For a while," Bale said. "But between the air dancers and Crabby dive-bombing them to scare them off, the trees are doing pretty well."

"It's impossible to think about Crabby being even more reckless than Quinn up there," Molly said.

"It'll be interesting to see what they do now that they've changed jobs," Bale said.

"I wonder if either one of them will hire me when I get out of here," Molly said.

"Don't worry about that," Bale said. "You have enough on your plate. You need to focus on getting well."

"I guess," Molly said, her eyes brimming with tears as she thought about not graduating. "Since I don't have anything else to focus on."

Chapter 31

Molly's mother helped her dress on the morning she was going to be released from the hospital.

"Ouch," Molly said, as her mother pulled her hair into a ponytail.

"You always used to say that when you were a little girl. I'd think you'd have toughened up by now."

"I'd think you'd have learned how to put in a ponytail without scalping me by now."

"You have to look nice."

"Why?"

"You used to always ask that when you were a little girl, too."

"Seriously, Mom, why do I have to look nice?"

"Because Bale asked if he could pick you up."

"Why?"

"Molly!"

"Sorry."

"You know he's a wonderful man, don't you?"

"Yes, Mom."

"Well, then. If he wants to pick you up, we'll let him."

"But you're already here."

"Honestly, honey. Have I taught you nothing?"

An orderly arrived with a wheelchair.

"Ready to get out of here?" he asked.

"And how!" Molly's mother said with enthusiasm.

She looked sheepishly at Molly, who had raised an eyebrow in annoyance.

"I guess you can speak for yourself," Molly's mom continued.

"That's okay, Mom," Molly said as she settled into the wheelchair. "Thanks for coming here. Thanks for..."

Molly wiped a tear from her eye.

"Now don't get all sentimental," Molly's mom said, wiping away her own tear. "You can't have swollen eyes when Bale sees you."

The orderly swung Molly around and headed down the hall.

"I'll see you later tonight," Molly's mom called after them.

"Aren't you coming?" Molly leaned sideways in the wheelchair and looked back at her mother.

"Good heavens, no! You could still learn a lot from me, you know."

Molly found herself getting nervous as they approached the hospital entrance. She could see Bale's truck outside the two massive sliding doors. She looked behind her, hoping her mother had changed her mind, but the corridor was empty.

Molly was on her own.

"Hey," Bale said.

"Hey," Molly said, looking up from the wheelchair. "This is so nice of you."

Bale signaled the orderly that he could take it from there.

"No problem at all," Bale said, helping her out of the wheelchair and into the truck.

"Can you drive with your arm in a sling?"

"Nope. Is that a problem?"

Had everyone gone crazy since she'd been in the hospital?

"Sorry, just joking," Bale said. "I can drive with the cast, just not the sling. Besides, we're not going far."

As they pulled out of the parking lot, Bale turned left.

The tiny house lot, the Tower, and Galileo were all to the right.

"Where are we going?" Molly asked.

"To my house."

"Does my mother know?" Molly asked. Aghast at how childish she sounded, she added. "It's just that she might be expecting me."

"She knows where we're going," Bale said. "But, to be honest, she doesn't know why."

Molly turned to look out the window. She really wasn't sure what to say. "Does Violet know" came to mind, but she rejected it. She'd just have to wait and see where this day would take her.

They pulled into Bale's long gravel private road and crunched up the driveway. Bale's house was an old farmhouse with a front porch. Molly smiled. One of his first tiny houses was based on his own home.

Bale drove past the house, driving along the river. He stopped in front of a new tiny house. It was stunning. It was steampunk with added flair—an industrial, Victorian, gypsy wagon. Molly knew immediately what it was.

"This is the house I built for Violet," Bale said proudly. "I incorporated a lot of the design ideas you and I talked about. I thought you might want to see it."

"I do," Molly said, trying to hold back the tears.

He brought me here to show me the masterpiece he built for another woman.

"Let's go inside," Bale said.

Molly's brain could barely register the interior as Bale showed her the two lofts, the full kitchen, and the colorful bathroom.

"I hope you like it," Bale said as he helped her down the stairs. "You really were my inspiration."

For all the good that does me.

"I should be getting back," Molly said. "I don't want to keep Mom and Curly waiting."

"I just have one other thing I want to show you," Bale said. "It's walking distance, if you're not too tired."

Molly *was* tired—and heartbroken—but Bale had done so much for her. What could she say?

"I'm fine," she said with false cheer. "Let's go!"

They walked along the river's edge on a path with yellowing leaves underfoot. Bale kept up a steady stream of conversation, but Molly really didn't hear anything.

"Okay," he said. "I need you to close your eyes."

Molly was about to ask why but decided against it. She just closed her eyes.

"Okay, I'm going to guide you," Bale said. "It's only a couple steps around the bend. Do you trust me?"

"I trust you."

Molly could hear the leaves underfoot. She could hear the river rushing along her left side. Suddenly, they stopped walking.

"Okay," Bale said, holding her shoulders. "Open your eyes."

Molly opened her eyes. She was staring into Bale's. He stepped to one side. Molly staggered, but Bale caught her.

She walked past him and stared up and up and up.

The tree, which Bale had described to her as the perfect setting for her model, stood before her, its branches arching out in just the way he'd said they did. The trunk curved faithfully to his description. But that wasn't all.

Her tree house model stood before her, life-sized, more beautiful than she could have ever imagined.

"How did this happen?" Molly asked.

"You're the civil engineer," Bale said. "You should be able to figure that out."

"I know...I mean... Why did you do this?"

The question hung in the air. The silence stretched on and on. Finally Bale spoke.

"Don't you know why?" he asked gently.

"What about..." Molly pointed back to the steampunk tiny house back in the front yard. "What about Violet?"

"What about Violet?"

"Aren't you guys...you know..."

"We were almost...you know," Bale said, making one-handed quote marks with his good arm. "I thought it might work out with her. When I went to see her, we had a romantic dinner. Then we went back to her place."

"I'm not sure I need to hear the gory details."

"That's okay," Bales said. "Because there are no gory details. We kissed, and she said to me, 'I don't know who she is, but you need to go after her.'"

"And did you?' Molly asked. "Did you go after her?"

"I built her a tree house," Bale said in exasperation, pointing to the tree behind him.

Molly threw her arms around Bale. He lifted her up in his one good arm.

"I didn't know you felt the same way I did," Molly said. "I was so afraid to say anything."

"Me too," Bale said, as he nestled his face into her neck. "But we're good now, right?"

"We've very good," Molly said as Bale put her back on the ground.

"Molly, listen." Bale got very serious. "We've wasted so much time. I want..."

Someone cleared his throat behind them. Molly and Bale both whirled.

"Professor Cambridge?" Molly asked, stunned.

"Hello, Bale. Hello, Ms. McGinnis," Professor Cambridge said in his disapproving way. "What's going on here, Bale? I got your note and your directions to meet you here."

"Yes, sir," Bale said. "Thank you for coming."

"And exactly *why* am I here?" Professor Cambridge asked.

Bale and Molly looked at each other. A giant tree house stood in front of him. Wasn't that a clue?

"Well, sir," Bale said. "I know you heard about Molly's accident."

"Yes, most unfortunate." Professor Cambridge nodded to Molly.

"I thought maybe if you saw what she'd designed," Bale said, sweeping his arm to point out the tree. "You might…"

"I might what?"

"You might approve her thesis," Bale said.

Molly gasped. She looked at Professor Cambridge, and any hope died. He looked as sour as ever.

"If memory serves, Ms. McGinnis was supposed to build a model, not an edifice."

"But this tree house is built faithfully on her design," Bale said.

He really was at the tree fort checking the design for changes, Molly realized. Now it made sense.

"All right," Professor Cambridge said. "I've come all this way. Let's take a look."

Molly was shaking. In her wildest dreams, she never could have imagined seeing her tree house realized. Now here it was, built by the man she loved, who loved her—and they were about to tour her dream with Professor Cambridge.

Two out of three ain't bad.

"Lead the way," Bale said to Molly.

She was about to say she'd never seen the place, but of course she knew every inch of it. She smiled.

"Right this way, Professor Cambridge," she said proudly.

She showed him the bathroom on the ground floor, answering questions about gravity and hydraulics. They climbed the stairs to the living room and kitchen, looking out over the river and the town from the large windows. Most of the furniture was built in, but Bale had accessorized the place perfectly, incorporating Molly's own possessions from Crabby's back room. They stepped onto the balconies that appeared in every nook of the branches. As they approached the almost vertical stairs to the bedroom, Professor Cambridge stopped.

"I've seen enough," Professor Cambridge said. "I've already done my stairs at the gym today."

Molly was grateful. She didn't really want to share her first glance of the bedroom with Professor Cambridge.

"What do you think?" Bale asked, because Molly couldn't.

"It's not what we agreed upon," Professor Cambridge said.

Molly tried to breathe. She reached for Bale's hand.

"But it's a hell of a tree house," Professor Cambridge said, looking around disapprovingly. "I used to have a tree house when I was a boy. I think it's what made me want to be an engineer. I'd completely forgotten that."

"So, it's approved?" Molly asked, her voice in a whisper.

"Yes, yes," Professor Cambridge said irritably. "It's approved. Now how do I get down from here?"

Molly and Bale watched Professor Cambridge round the corner. When he was out of sight, Bale guided Molly to the balcony that looked over the river.

"Where were we?" Bale asked.

"Something about we've wasted so much time," Molly said.

"It took me a lot longer to finish the tree house than I'd hoped," Bale said. "You know, the one-arm thing really slowed me down."

"It looks perfect to me."

"It is perfect!" Bale laughed. "That's not what I meant."

"What did you mean?"

Bale took her hand and dropped down on one knee. Molly dropped to her knees and threw her arms around him and sobbed.

"I don't think you're supposed to be down here, too," Bale said into Molly's heaving shoulder.

"You're such a wonderful man," Molly said. "I don't deserve you."

"Hey, wait," Bale said. "Are you saying no? I mean, I built you a tree house and got your thesis approved. I'm not taking no for an answer."

"The answer isn't no. The answer is yes…forever and ever…yes."

Bale and Molly stood back up, embracing as they looked out over the river. Bale picked up Molly's hand to kiss it.

"You don't have any words written on your hand."

"I gave that up," Molly said. "After everything that happened, I thought it was stupid."

"It wasn't stupid," Bale said. "But you only need one word."

He pulled a pen out of his shirt pocket. He took her hand and wrote: "Love."

If you enjoyed *Tiny House in the Trees*, be sure not to miss all of Celia Bonaduce's Tiny House series, including

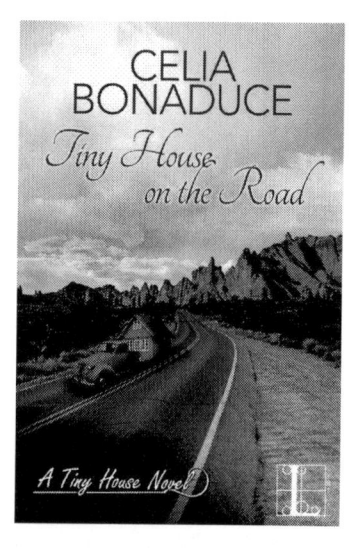

CELIA BONADUCE
Tiny House on the Road
A Tiny House Novel

At twenty-two, Vivien is already a homeowner—albeit of the tiniest of tiny houses, a whopping 64 square footer called "Shrimpfork." It's the perfectly portable home from which to run Organization Oracle, Vivien's new business as a personal organizer. In fact, she'll be toting Shrimpfork to her upcoming client's home near Taos, New Mexico.

Seventy-year-old Priscilla has a colorful past, a rambunctious boxer named Clay—and a home crammed with treasures.... Priscilla also has a love for the TV program "This Old Thing?" Her twenty-five-year-old neighbor, Marco, is happy to watch it with her—while watching over her. When Vivien arrives, it's clear she and Marco are suspicious of each other's intentions. But Priscilla's determination to get her most cherished possession appraised on "This Old Thing?" soon has all of them grudgingly working together. Vivien and Marco find themselves in cahoots, Priscilla discovers the wider world, Clay digs up trouble—and everyone learns that sometimes the greatest treasures are valued for their flaws...

Keep reading for a special look!

A Lyrical e-book on sale now.

Chapter 1

All Vivien wanted was some coffee—and maybe a ladies' room. Vivien Orlando had planned her route meticulously. She had checked Google Maps. She had studied MapQuest. She followed Waze's advice when traffic even hinted at slowing. For the drive from Jacksonville, FL, in her hand-me-down battered orange truck stuffed with all her worldly goods, she had plotted a course to Cobb, Kentucky that would take twelve and a half hours with stops for food and gas. Following her strict calculations and driving through the night, Vivien was confident she would pull into her final destination when the place opened at exactly eight in the morning.

Instead, she sat shivering in the truck in the predawn light in front of a locked gate, wondering when she'd learn to give up on the "precise plan" idea.

Vivien yawned. She had another two hours until the place opened for business. Maybe she could find a cup of coffee in Cobb's downtown area. Cobb seemed like a sleepy little town, even by Kentucky standards. But after a ten—not twelve and a half—hour drive, it was not as sleepy as Vivien. Main Street offered nothing until seven o'clock. Vivien was relentlessly optimistic, but even her good nature started to flag. She remembered passing a place on her way into Cobb that at least had its lights on.

Maybe *they* were open?

Trying not to see it as a bad omen, she turned the truck around and headed back the way she came, pulling into the parking lot of a place called Crabby's. Perched on the Kentucky River, the restaurant must have been picturesque during the day, but now it just looked cold and inhospitable—even with the giant neon crab sign blinking its deranged invitation to come on in. Vivien's was the only vehicle in the parking lot. Through the window she could see a woman with bright red lipstick and a black ponytail, setting up the restaurant for the morning. Vivien sat, huddled in her truck, waiting for the Closed sign in the restaurant's window to be turned around.

Vivien got out of the truck and set her car alarm. It sounded unnaturally shrill in the eerie silence of the parking lot. The chirp attracted the attention of the woman inside. The woman looked up from behind the counter and smiled at Vivien. She came to the front door and flipped the Closed sign to Open before returning to the coffeemaker behind the counter.

Maybe things are looking up.

Vivien slung her messenger bag over her shoulder, before remembering she hadn't zipped up the front pocket after grabbing her toothbrush and deodorant at the last rest stop. Toiletries scattered in every direction. She stooped in the dark, feeling around the gravel for errant products. Stuffing things unceremoniously back into the bag and blinking back tears, Vivien pulled open the restaurant's door.

"Welcome to Crabby's! I'm Molly." She waved a pot of coffee across the counter. "First brew of the morning. Want a cup?"

Vivien tried to say yes, but instead burst into tears.

"I'm so sorry," Vivien said as she plunked herself down at a table and grabbed a paper napkin. "It's just been a bad day."

"It's only six in the morning," Molly said, rushing over. "How bad can it be?"

"You must think I'm a crazy person." Vivien continued to sob.

"Hey, don't worry about it. I work at the only place open for breakfast for twenty miles. I know crazy when I see it. You're okay. Here...." Molly extended a linen napkin. "Have one. We switch to cloth napkins at five. On the house."

Vivien nodded gratefully and blew her nose, honking extravagantly. Molly was young—probably just a few years older than Vivien herself, but seemed to have a much better handle on things.

"It's just that..." Vivien said, starting to cry again. "This was going to be the first day of the rest of my life. I had everything planned."

"Your whole life?" Molly asked, pouring coffee into a large porcelain mug. "That's some plan. I hope you left some room for a few surprises."

Vivien smiled at Molly and ordered the World Famous American Sunrise Breakfast. Vivien wasn't exactly sure what that was, but maybe Molly was right. Maybe she should leave herself open for a few surprises—especially with the new life she had planned.

"We're pretty slow at this hour," Molly said, looking around the restaurant to indicate the lack of action. "So I'm the cook too."

Before Vivien could ask, Molly pointed down a hallway on the left. "Ladies' room is that way."

Molly was still busy in the kitchen when Vivien returned from the restroom, face washed and hair brushed. If she didn't feel less like a crazy person, she at least looked less like one. While the soothing smell of bacon and eggs floated in from the kitchen, Vivien closed her eyes and took a few deep breaths.

* * * *

The clatter of plates on the table startled her. When she opened her eyes, she was staring into a happy face of food. The bright yolks of two sunny-side-up eggs looked up at her, while a strip of curling bacon formed a smile. A tiny salt and pepper shaker set sat in the middle, filling in as the nose. Vivien glanced up at Molly, who was beaming lovingly at the plate.

"The salt and pepper shaker nose was my idea," Molly said. "More coffee?"

Vivien assumed she wouldn't be able to eat a bite, but she surprised herself. She wasn't sure if it was the comfort food or the sight of the sun rising over the river that lifted her mood, but she was thankful. As she buttered the last biscuit, her optimism and the possibilities of her new life seeped back into her spirit. Keeping the doubts at bay was as daunting as driving for hours.

Several people had entered the restaurant in the last hour. Molly was too busy to continue their conversation, for which Vivien was grateful. Vivien was a little embarrassed by her tears and really didn't want to go into any more detail about her future plans. She'd exhausted herself explaining it to family and coworkers over the last few months.

Her iPhone made a soft purring noise. It was her alarm, letting her know it was time to head back; the gates would be opening in ten minutes.

She caught Molly's eye. In the sign language of the road, Vivien signaled for the check and Molly signed back that Vivien should meet her at the cash register.

"You have good day," Molly said, handing Vivien her change. "So, I'm guessing you're headed over to Bale's to check out the tiny houses?"

Vivien almost dropped her palmful of change.

"How did you know that?" Vivien asked.

Molly's eyes shot to the parking lot, where Vivien's overstuffed orange truck stuck out among the more sedate sedans.

"I've gotten used to spotting Bale's customers," Molly said.

What does that mean?

Vivien couldn't get Molly's words out of her mind. As she threaded her way back to Bale's Tiny Dreams, she wondered if everyone who pulled into the tiny house lot was a woman in her twenties with a restless desire to forge her own path. Vivien suddenly smiled. There were worse accusations, she supposed. And there was no denying the truth of it—at least in her case.

She pulled up to the now open gate. It was amazing what sunlight could do. In the predawn gloom, the tangle of tiny pitched, flat, and gabled roofs had looked like a haunted miniature golf course—she had half expected a goat dressed in country club gear shaking a nine iron to come rushing out to the fence, threatening her. Now, as she slowly pulled in among the confection of diminutive homes, the place looked more like a village for peaceable gnomes.

When she heard a rasping barking coming up behind her, she looked around for the goat.

Vivien had lived her entire life in the city, so she was no expert. But she was pretty sure the animal now yapping at her heels was no goat.

"Thor!" rumbled an authoritative voice. "Crank it down a notch."

Vivien knew the voice. It belonged to Bale Barrett, the proprietor of Bale's Tiny Dreams. She'd spoken to him on the phone so many times over the last few months designing her tiny house that she would have known it anywhere.

The creature immediately sat down quietly and thumped its tail. In repose, the animal looked even more unusual. Vivien assumed it was a male—after all, its name was Thor. Thor was mostly white with a black mask, making him look like a cartoon bandit. He had the build and blank expression of a bull terrier—broad-chested with turned-out, short legs. She would have settled on assigning Thor to the family of "dog," except for the shock of reddish fur sprouting wildly between its ears, like a Mohawk. He looked like a cross between a dog and a woodpecker.

"He won't bite," Bale's voice rang out again. "I'll be right with you."

Vivien looked around, but couldn't tell where the voice was coming from.

"Okay," Vivien called back.

Vivien regarded Thor. She wasn't much of an animal person. She had nothing against cats and dogs in theory. She'd just never had pets growing up and, at twenty-two years old, had not acquired an affinity for them in her few short years as an adult.

Thor stared up at her. Even with his disconcertingly blank expression, he seemed to want something.

"Good doggy," she said.

Thor needed no further encouragement. He leaped up, seemingly propelled by the wagging tail. Vivien let out a little squeak and closed her eyes. She staggered backward, pressing up against her truck for safety. She could feel the dog's paws on her midsection.

"Thor!" came the voice again. "Get down!"

The pressure on her stomach suddenly ceased. Vivien opened her eyes. She found herself looking into the gentle eyes of a man. She knew it was Bale—she'd watched his tiny house videos online and followed him on Instagram. They had also used FaceTime when discussing design ideas.

He had a ruggedness she found attractive, although he had a few lines around his eyes and some gray in his hair. This man was much too old for her—he had to be forty. She found herself weirded-out that she found him appealing; she was new to the idea that someone close to her father's age could be attractive.

"Sorry about the dog, Vivien," Bale said, holding Thor by the collar. So he recognized her too! "Thor showed up here a few weeks ago and I'm still working on his manners."

Vivien tried to think of something to say. She settled on, "Thor is an interesting name."

"He's an interesting dog."

"What kind of dog is he?" Vivien asked.

"Beats me," Bale said, looking down at Thor. "I named him Thor because he's got that weird red hair between his ears. I figured he must have Viking blood."

Vivien looked up sharply, wondering if this was a joke. The twinkle in Bale's eyes said it was. She relaxed.

"Speaking of no manners," Bale said, putting out his right hand, while keeping a firm grip on Thor with the left. "I'm Bale, in case you haven't guessed."

"Yes, I figured that out," Vivien said, shaking his hand and trying to regain her composure. "Nice to meet you finally. I'm Vivien—in case *you* haven't guessed."

"Come on back to the office," he said, letting go of Thor, who walked politely beside Bale, having lost all interest in Vivien. "Coffee?"

"No thanks," she said, as she tried to guess which of the tiny houses was hers. "I stopped at—"

"Crabby's," Bale said. "Yeah, I saw the loaded down truck in their parking lot on my way in this morning and thought that might be you."

"Does every truck that comes through Cobb stop for a tiny house?" Vivien asked, trying not to seem defensive.

"Pretty much," Bale said, holding the door to the office open for her.

"Really?" Vivien asked in amazement.

"No," Bale said, smiling. "But we get our fair share. Let's face it, anyone who's committed to trying out this lifestyle has pretty much done the emotional heavy lifting and arrives with no more than a truck full of stuff. My customers are usually pretty impatient to hit the road."

Thor squeezed ahead of Vivien and shot into a dog bed in the corner of the office. Bale indicated a chair across from his well-worn desk. As they settled into their seats, Vivien thought about what Bale had said. He was certainly right as far as her own story went. She had been ruthlessly tossing out everything that wouldn't fit in her truck, let alone her soon-to-be home, and she was more than impatient to start this new adventure she hoped would be her life.

"So, Vivien," Bale said as he rummaged around the mountains of paper on his desk. "I know I have all your paperwork here somewhere... Tell me about your plans."

"My...plans?" Vivien faltered.

"Yes," Bale said, continuing to flip through papers. He seemed to be talking to himself more than her. If I recall correctly, you're a barista at Starbeams, right?"

Vivien held her breath. She had paid for the tiny house in full, so Bale shouldn't really care that she quit her job. But still... This was the first time she'd let anyone in on her new plans.

"I'm not there anymore," she said.

"Well, there are Starbeams everywhere," Bale said, giving her a quick smile. "I'm sure you can pick up work anywhere."

"Actually," Vivien said, taking in a deep breath. "I've moved on. I've gone into a completely new line of work."

"Oh? What do you do?" Bale asked as he slipped a pair of reading glasses onto his nose.

Vivien thought the glasses made him look older. He moved quietly into the "dad" role. Vivien didn't mind. She was about to become a vagabond and romance was the farthest thing from her mind.

"I'm an oracle."

Bale stopped shuffling his paperwork and looked at her.

"An oracle?" Bale asked, his eyebrows arching over the reading glasses. "Like a prophet?"

"Sort of," Vivien said. She was new at describing her self-created job and still wasn't comfortable explaining it. She knew it sounded weird.

"I didn't know there was much of a job market in that," Bale asked. "Since Ancient Greece, I mean."

"I'm freelance."

"How's that working out for you?"

Vivien wondered if Bale was being sarcastic, but he looked genuinely concerned.

"I don't really know yet," Vivien said. "I just started my own business. I'm a professional organizer."

"And oracle."

"They go together," Vivien said, warming to her subject. "After Starbeams, I worked for the Kloset Kompany. Two Ks. We organized stuff."

"What kind of stuff?" he asked.

"Oh, you know, the usual—closets, attics, basements, paperwork, wine."

"Wine?"

"Yes," Vivien said. "I organized a man's wine collection right before I came here."

"That sounds pretty interesting."

"It was, but most of the time it was the same old, same old. You can't just keep your fingers crossed that a wine collection is going to come along every now and then."

"I guess not."

"So, I decided it would be cool to travel around, instead of staying in one city," Vivien said. "I put a new spin on the whole business model. I'm going to provide personalized service. I'll take on a client, they'll explain their problem and I'll *see* what they need right away. That's why I call myself the Organization Oracle."

From the look on Bale's face, Vivien could tell he wasn't a fan of her new name.

"I was also thinking of calling it 'Vivien Orlando! I put the O in Organization.'"

"I think the Organization Oracle is a great name," Bale said.

He smiled at her. Which was very different from laughing at her. She smiled back.

"I can't find your paperwork," Bale said, throwing up his hands. The stacks of binder-clipped papers settled into place after being disturbed by his quest.

"It's five contracts down in the left-hand pile...well, the right-hand pile for you," Vivien said.

Bale stared at her for a second, then thumbed through the stack. Five contracts down and there it was. The final contract for Vivien Orlando.

"That's a miracle," Bale said, holding up the contract and staring at it. He smiled at Vivien. "You really are an oracle."

Vivien shrugged shyly.

Should she tell him she'd seen her name, recognizable even upside down while he was frantically flipping through his untidy stacks?

"Maybe I can hire you," Bale said, looking around his cluttered office. "I could use the help."

"Thanks," Vivien said sincerely. "But I'm headed to New Mexico to my first client as soon as I pick up the house."

"New Mexico?" Bale said, sounding impressed. "Sounds exciting."

"The lady who is hiring me lives in a place called *Casa de Promesas*," Vivien said, knowing she shouldn't be giving away anything so confidential, but wanting to up the "exciting" ante.

"House of Promises," Bale said, now looking for a pen among the rubble of his desk. "Sounds like a good omen."

She knew she shouldn't give away any of her organizing secrets. But she liked Bale and wanted to make up for her little subterfuge about spotting her name. She offered Bale a little advice.

"You should use color-coded binder clips," she said. "I mean, you use paper clips anyway, so why not sort them with various colors? One color for advertisement, one for bills—that sort of thing."

"That's a great idea," Bale said. "I bought a label maker to use on black binder clips, but…"

"But," Vivien said, "you never get around to actually making the labels."

"Exactly!" Bale said.

"If you want to take it one step farther," Vivien said, eyeing the wall behind his desk. "You could paint that wall with magnetic paint. They have magnetic binder clips, you know. So everything would be off your desk, but easy to reach and—"

"And not put away in a filing cabinet," Bale said, staring at the wall as if he'd never seen it before. "Because as you've probably guessed…filing is never going to happen."

"One thing about getting organized," Vivien said. "It's not one size fits all. You've got to know what you'll stick with. You know what I mean? You have to know who you are."

"Funny you should say that," Bale said, finally locating a pen. "I say the same thing about living in a tiny house. You really have to know who you are before you take it on."

Remembering what she'd learned in her college course on Start Your Own Business and Soar!, Vivien quickly added, "I can call you when I'm finished in New Mexico. Maybe we can work something out."

"Sounds good," Bale said. "Want to go see your house?"

Vivien nodded, too overcome to speak. She was giddy with possibilities. Maybe she *was* going to soar!

Meet the Author

Credit © William Christoff Photography

Celia Bonaduce, also the author of The Venice Beach Romances and the Welcome to Fat Chance, Texas series, has always had a love affair with houses. Her credits as a television field producer include such house-heavy hits as *Extreme Makeover: Home Edition*; HGTV's *House Hunters*; and *Tiny House Hunters.* She lives in Santa Monica, CA, with her husband and dreams of one day traveling with him in their own tiny house. You can contact Celia at www.celiabonaduce.com.

Website: www.celiabonaduce.com/
Facebook: www.facebook.com/pages/Celia-Bonaduce/352890508156101
Twitter: @celiabonaduce
Instagram: Yocelia
Media: www.celiab.name

Summer Murray is ready to shake things up. She doesn't want to work in risk management. She doesn't want to live in Hartford, Connecticut. So she plans a grand adventure: she's going to throw out all the stuff she doesn't want and travel the country in her very own tiny house shaped like a train caboose. Just Summer, her chihuahua-dachshund, Shortie, and 220 square feet of freedom.

Then her take-no-prisoners grandmother calls to demand Summer head home to the Pacific Northwest to save the family bakery. Summer has her reasons for not wanting to return home, but she'll just park her caboose, fix things, and then be on her way. But when she gets to Cat's Paw, Washington, she's shocked by her grandmother's strange behavior and reunited with a few people she'd hoped to avoid. If Summer is going to make a fresh start, she'll have to face the past she's been running from all along…

Livin' Large In Fat Chance, Texas

CELIA BONADUCE

From ghost town to growing community, it's been a few years since a group of strangers inherited property in tiny, deserted Fat Chance, Texas. And besides creating businesses, they've developed friendships and romances too. But plans to pave the town may put Dymphna Pearl and her beau, Professor Johnson, on opposite sides of Main Street. In his zeal for the project, he's making great decisions for Fat Chance, but not for them as a couple. Disgruntled, Dymphna heads back to Los Angeles to collect the rabbits she's created a special place for in the hot Texas climate. But the professor is in for another surprise…

Professor Johnson didn't even know about Dympha's sister, Maggie, and when he meets her in a most unexpected way, he begins to understand why. In the meantime, Dymphna is off pursuing an exciting venture to let the world know about Fat Chance—one that will bring a talented new crew to the eclectic group. The kitschy little place they call home is clearly destined for bigger, better things—but with so many changes a-coming will the same be true for everyone in Fat Chance, including the professor and Dymphna?

It's been a year since an eccentric billionaire summoned seven strangers to the dilapidated, postage stamp-sized town of Fat Chance, Texas. To win a cash bequest, each was required to spend six months in the ghost town to see if they could transform it—and themselves—into something extraordinary. But by the time pastry chef Fernando Cruz arrives, several members of the original gang have already skedaddled...

Fernando's hopes of starting a new life in Fat Chance are dashed when the town's handful of ragtag residents—and a mysterious low-flying plane—show him just how weird the place actually is. His hopes of making over the town's sole café into a BBQ restaurant for nearby ranchers threaten to turn to dust as a string of bizarre secrets are revealed. But just when the pickins' couldn't get any slimmer, the citizens of Fat Chance realize they might be able to build exactly the kind of hometown they all need—but never knew they wanted...

"A fresh, heartwarming voice."
—Jodi Thomas, *New York Times* bestselling author

Home is where your heart is...

Welcome to Fat Chance, Texas

CELIA BONADUCE

For champion professional knitter Dymphna Pearl, inheriting part of a sun-blasted ghost town in the Texas hill country isn't just unexpected, it's a little daunting. To earn a cash bequest that could change her life, she'll have to leave California to live in tiny, run-down Fat Chance for six months—with seven strangers. Impossible! Or is it?

Trading her sandals for cowboy boots, Dymphna dives into her new life with equal parts anxiety and excitement. After all, she's never felt quite at home in Santa Monica anyway. Maybe Fat Chance will be her second chance. But making it habitable is going take more than a lasso and Wild West spirit. With an opinionated buzzard overlooking the proceedings and mismatched strangers learning to become friends, Dymphna wonders if unlocking the secrets of her own heart is the way to strike real gold...

The Rollicking Bun—Home of the Epic Scone—is the center of Suzanna Wolf's life. Part tea shop, part bookstore, part home, it's everything she's ever wanted right on the Venice Beach boardwalk, including partnership with her two best friends from high school, Eric and Fernando. But with thirty-three just around the corner, suddenly Suzanna wants something more—something strictly her own. Salsa lessons, especially with a gorgeous instructor, seem like a good start—a harmless secret, and just maybe the start of a fling. But before she knows it, Suzanna is learning steps she never imagined—and dancing her way into confusion.

Erinn Wolf needs to reinvent herself. A once celebrated playwright turned photographer, she's almost broke, a little lonely, and tired of her sister's constant worry. When a job on a reality TV show falls into her lap, she's thrilled to be making a paycheck—and when a hot Italian actor named Massimo rents her guesthouse, she's certain her life is getting a romantic subplot. But with the director, brash, gorgeous young Jude, dogging her every step, she can't help but look at herself through his lens—and wonder if she's been reading the wrong script all along…

Look out, Venice Beach—the Wolf women are all together again. But when 70-year-old Virginia arrives with her teacup Chihuahua and unshakeable confidence, she senses trouble. Erinn is keeping secrets—like being broke and out of work—and Suzanna is paying too much attention to the wrong man—a Latino dance instructor who nearly broke her heart once before. Virginia's ready for the third act of her life, and she intends to make it rousing and romantic. Now she just has to convince her daughters to throw out their old scripts. If life has taught Virginia anything, it's this: there's more than one way to a "happily ever after"…

Made in the USA
Middletown, DE
24 September 2019